Praise for *The Smithsonian Institution*

"Vidal goes where many mainstream authors fear to tread when they use elements of the fantastic. . . . Vidal is in fine form here. *The Smithsonian Institution*, perhaps because it frees him from having to write realistically, is a masterpiece of frenzied invention. It manages to be playfully sexy, thought-provoking and immensely entertaining, all at once."
—*Chicago Tribune*

"Another merry riff on Washington power politics, struggles, and failures from the venerable curmudgeon and sage: an appealingly unholy marriage of *Burr, Duluth,* and a suavely Vidalian amalgam of Tom Sawyer and Tom Swift . . . This may be the wisest book that Vidal—this incomparably urbane observer of our revered past, debased present, and unpromising future—has ever written. It is, as well, entertainment of the highest order. Even Norman Mailer will like this novel."
—*Kirkus Reviews* (starred)

"This science fiction tale is a high-spirited tour of American history, romance and Washington politics interpreted by Vidal's unique brand of social commentary. *The Smithsonian Institution* wins the literary lion a small victory in his running battle with Washington's pomposity by proving that humor is mightier that the sword."
—*Sunday Denver Post*

"*The Smithsonian Institution* is a wild and wise celebration of the absurdities of American history."
—*The Baltimore Sun*

"Fans of Vidal's comic novels can expect the usual mixture of earthiness and erudition, though on a more restrained level; the novel provides the author with the chance to put words in the mouths of a dozen presidents, noted scientists, and pop culture heroes. Good fun, and sure to garner attention."
—*Library Journal*

"*The Smithsonian Institution* is, at once, a meditation on the course of American history, a look at the bizarre multiverse opened to us by quantum physics, and a playful romp ranging from dry wit to broad comedy. A lively read by a virtuoso."

—*Minneapolis Star Tribune*

"We can delight that, once again, Gore Vidal has turned his literary lights back upon not only the city of his youth, but also, fancifully, the corridors of the past. . . . An entertaining romp through time and space, and a thoughtful history lesson from a modern master." —*Sunday Oregonian*

"This book is, for all its delightfully scathing wit and expert comic effects, a serious plea against the madness of war, a poignant elegy to a lost soldier, and a payment of heed to time lost and to all future time—future time that is perhaps as precarious a concept as any fictional device in the brilliantly imagined pages of *The Smithsonian Institution*."

—*Milwaukee Journal Sentinel*

"Phantasmagoric . . . At the heart of *The Smithsonian Institution* is a dramatization of Aristophanes's conceit. For all the novel's witty arabesques of plot, T.'s passion to make himself whole is what finally lends the story its substance."

—*The New York Times*

"Vidal's gift for storytelling and mimicry remain in peak form." —*Chicago Sun Times*

THE SMITHSONIAN INSTITUTION

GORE VIDAL

The Smithsonian Institution

A Novel

A HARVEST BOOK
HARCOURT BRACE & COMPANY
San Diego   *New York*   *London*

First published by Random House in 1998

Library of Congress Cataloging-in-Publication Data
Vidal, Gore, 1925–
The Smithsonian Institution/Gore Vidal. — 1st Harvest ed.
p.   cm. — (A Harvest book)
ISBN 0-15-600648-0
1. Smithsonian Institution Fiction.   2. Gifted teenagers Fiction.
3. Time travel Fiction.   I. Title.
PS3543.I26S65   1999
813'.54—dc21   99-15151

Printed in the United States of America

First Harvest Edition 1999
A C E D B

THE SMITHSONIAN INSTITUTION

1

WAR CLOUDS were gathering over Europe as T. came out of the lower school dormitory of St. Albans and hailed a taxi. Since St. Albans was an Episcopal school, cabs—not Mary—got hailed along that part of Wisconsin Avenue.

"Take me to the Smithsonian Institution." T. enjoyed the driver's confusion: on Good Friday, 1939, the Smithsonian would be shut in the morning.

T. was a decisive, tall lad of thirteen, not one to be brooked, as his history teacher, a Canadian, liked to say. "There are many entrances to the Smithsonian," T. said, tossing a lock of blond hair out of grass-green hunter's eyes. "Drive on," he commanded, holding his overnight bag on his knees like the potential skull breaker it was. He wore the school blazer with its coat of arms over the breast pocket while, in an inside pocket, he carried a brand-new checkbook from the Briggs National Bank. Due to a bookkeeping error of the sort that had kept President Roosevelt's New Deal in clover, T. could now, until discovered, draw on $100,001 with a simple squiggle of his pen.

Pennsylvania Avenue was nearly empty at this hour. Presumably, the frightened citizenry were all at home listening to their president on the radio as he spoke from his fireside to them at their firesides. Rifest rumors as of that Friday: Hitler was already encamped on Staten Island, threatening the Trylon and Perisphere of the World's Fair, while Mussolini had been spotted in the Englewood, New Jersey, area, where every day is Columbus Day. Farther afield, the Japanese emperor had been sighted, riding his white horse through San Francisco's Chinatown, enigmatic lips set in secret smile. Yes. There would soon be war, a war to end *all* speculations about the possibility of war if these wild mass hallucinations should prove to be, as the *New York Times* pundit Arthur Krock hinted, premonitions.

The taxi driver turned off Pennsylvania Avenue at the old post office, a dark rosy Romanesque tower that had become the world's largest repository of postal secrets after James A. Farley was made postmaster general and refused, so it was rumored in the city of rumors, to allow a single letter that entered the building to go unread either by him or by his closest confidante, Mrs. Farley.

"All my wife's love letters are in that building." The driver unwisely invited confidences of a sort that T. never dealt in.

They were now at the main building of the Smithsonian: the Castle—with its dark dried-blood red brick crenellated towers and wide moat in which swam not swans—this was Washington after all—but chilly soldiers on leave from nearby Fort Myer. Since the drawbridge was down, the cab was able to penetrate the first of no one knew how many courtyards. "He who comprehends the Smithsonian Castle comprehends the universe" was an old Washington proverb, attributed, depending on your informant, either to Anonymous or to Joseph Alsop, the war correspondent with the portable typewriter and weight problem.

The first courtyard was empty. A sign reading CLOSED hung beside the massive elm doors.

"It's closed," said the driver, pleased to be the bearer of bad news.

"Shut up," said T., as he got out of the taxi. "I'll write you a check on Briggs Bank for the fare."

The feral face cracked wide with unpleasant laughter. "Cash or else, buddy boy."

But by the time the driver had got to the word "boy," long drawn out to show contempt, T. had slipped through the great doors, conveniently ajar, as Papa Chasseau, the French teacher at St. Albans, had told him they would be; then before the odious driver could get to him, T. had shut the doors with a crash and slid the iron bolt that locked them. The faint sound of tiny fists beating on elm wood could barely be heard in the huge entrance hall with its high mullioned windows and the banners of the forty-eight states hanging from carved wooden beams. At last T. was at the heart of the American world, or, if his French teacher was to be believed, the universe itself, not that T. thought that there could be such a thing as a center. He had always known that New York's planetarium with its starry skies and unconvincing planets was simply a diversion calculated to confuse anyone who might actually—like T.—be in a position to work out what, if not where, the universe was.

"Anyway, I'll find it—you'll see—because if it's anywhere it's right here." T. addressed the only person in the vicinity, a uniformed man seated beneath a "Lost and Found" sign.

"My name is T." T. was unexpectedly nervous. "You see, sir, I am an orphan. My parents were killed aboard that zeppelin. Remember the one? The *Hindenburg*? They were burned to a crisp in the sky over New Jersey, two years ago. Since then I've been the ward of Bishop Freeman. He's the bishop of Washington. The one who works out of the cathedral that's never going to be finished up on Wisconsin Avenue."

"Very interesting," said a woman's voice behind him. "But your curriculum vitae is wasted upon 'Lost and Found.' He is wax."

"Wax?" T. turned to find a tall, stout, handsome lady in the garb of yesteryear, though which of a multitude of yesteryears he could not place.

"Wax," she repeated helpfully. She had a pretty smile, thanks to a number of regular black teeth, and a large bust.

T. looked at the man at the desk and saw that he was indeed made, rather crudely on close inspection, of wax.

"On holidays we use only wax personnel." She pointed to a half dozen uniformed guards at the far end of the great hall. "So much less of a bother than flesh and blood and not so heavy as plaster of Paris."

"Well, *you're* not wax." T. knew how to flatter women of any age including the certain age. He had three aunts who lived in a house in K Street and he stayed with them on holidays.

The lady giggled and flushed pinkly. "Allow me to introduce myself. I am Mrs. Benjamin Harrison. We presidential wives take turns on duty when these boring holidays come around."

"I guess I've seen you," said T., impressed against his better judgment, "in the hall where they keep the inaugural gowns."

"Yes, we're far and away the most popular exhibit here."

"Only you don't have heads in there. You're just a lot of dresses on dummies."

Mrs. Harrison frowned. "True. But after hours, we are ourselves again, out of sight of the public, of course. Also, on holidays or—private missions, like Mrs. . . ." Mrs. Harrison frowned. "Well, speak no evil, as they say. Anyway, you are quite right. They are always trying to save money round here, and on *us* of all exhibits! So we're preparing a petition. Martha—she's our chair. Or Lady Washington, I should say. She insists on the title. Of course, she *was* English most of her life. Anyway, Martha has given up on getting us all heads and proper shoulders through channels, and so she has gone straight to Eleanor—Roosevelt, that is—as the poor thing is still alive and still first lady and she swears that she—the live Eleanor of 1939 swears—she will go to her husband and insist that we have full-time heads. But I'm not holding my breath." Mrs. Harrison indicated T.'s bag. "You will be moving in, I see."

"Oh. Yes." T. was becoming oddly excited by the glamour of waxness versus flesh.

"Naturally, you'll want to penetrate the inner mysteries of the Smithsonian while you're here. So follow me." Mrs. Harrison opened a small door beneath a frayed, cannon-torn Confederate flag; then she led him down a long corridor with a painted ceiling and doors to the left of them and doors to the right, like a hotel.

"The housekeeper is putting you in one of the rooms on the left, with a view of"—Mrs. Harrison threw open the door to a spacious bedroom with a large window overlooking Pennsylvania Avenue—"the avenue where all of us girls, except Lady Washington of course, there being no avenue then, had our proudest moment, riding to the Capitol to watch our beloved, the first magistrate, be inaugurated."

T. liked the room, which reminded him of the guest room in his aunts' K Street house. There was the same four-poster and chintz all over everything. He put his suitcase down on the bed. "I suppose I'll be here for some time. Won't I?" T. was probing.

Probed, Mrs. Harrison nodded. "Naturally, you can leave whenever you like. But if you mean to penetrate the mystery of the Smithsonian, which is the mystery of life itself . . ." Mrs. Harrison was now redoing her hair in the cloudy mirror of the Empire armoire; she was also, T. could tell, speaking tonelessly, as if she had no idea what she was saying. "Rest assured that here, somewhere in the bowels of this ancient structure, past all the monsters both living and dead, past blockades and safe places, doublets, penalties . . ."

"Monsters?" T. perked up considerably. He liked monsters and whenever he could get time off from his busy classroom schedule, he would play hooky from school and go up to the Capitol and look at the Senate.

"Oh, yes. Monsters. Or so they say. We first ladies are sheltered from the worst of the horrors in the basement. In fact, the management insists we keep pretty much to our own quarters except for . . . Well, there's always one rotten apple in every barrel. And wonderful Eleanor—so intrepid—going wherever she likes, doing good. But . . ." Mrs. Harrison chuckled. "Lady Washington constantly complains that the management never lets *her* see any of the real monsters, much less mysteries, only the Potemkin ones."

"The what ones?"

"I only repeat what the management requires me to say." Mrs. Harrison was at the window, looking down on the streetcars as they rattled past, and the pedestrians—mostly men—in white straw hats. Spring was at hand. Cherry blossoms. Dogwood. "Come here and I'll show you how the thermostat works. It's fun."

T. joined her. "What's a thermostat?"

At the window she showed him a small enamel box with a dial on it. "The Mechanics' Room thinks up all these new inventions, like this one which controls the temperature of the room. Only it's not on the market yet. Then one evening when the Chief Mechanic was working late in his own private laboratory up in the tower, he, somehow, don't ask *me* how, attached the thermostat to a clock—or was it an hourglass? And then to a carbon-dating calendar, whatever that is, something like the ones the mortuaries used to send you at Halloween in my day, and now—well, look!" Mrs. Harrison twirled the dial to the left. "This is rerun."

T. looked down and saw the avenue blurring and changing. Streetcars were replaced by horsecars, and everyone's clothes changed. "It goes back in time!" T. shivered with excitement. Mrs. Harrison stopped the dial. There was now a bright clear view of the avenue, as a great hearse, drawn by huge black horses, moved to the dirgelike music of a military band. The men standing on the sidewalk uncovered as the beflagged coffin passed. Women wept.

"Lincoln's funeral," said T., with the authority of one who had spent many hours in the Palace Theater on Fourteenth Street. "Is it an old movie?"

"Oh, no. There weren't any movies back then. . . ."

"We've had an awful lot since. In the one with Raymond Massey—"

"This, buster," said Mrs. Harrison with the quiet majesty of a true first lady, "is the real McCoy." T. pressed his nose against the glass and looked up the street toward the Capitol and then down the street in the direction of the White House. The lady was right. Whatever it was that he was watching was not a movie. The crowds were endless as far as he could see under a real sky, not Technicolor as in *Gone With the Wind*, which he had only just seen at the Capitol Theater.

T. put his hand on the thermostat. "What happens if I turn this even further back?"

"You'll be able to look further back in time, as we did just now with Lincoln's funeral."

"How far?"

"No one knows. It would take somebody centuries, they say, to get back to the beginning of the world, and your hand would probably fall off long before. The Chief Mechanic claims to have seen a dinosaur swimming out there when all this was underwater." Mrs. Harrison returned the dial to the present day.

"What happens if you turn it forward, to the future?"

"The Chief would rather we *not* do that. Too depressing, I suppose, what with war clouds over Europe and you-know-who on Staten Island."

T. made a mental note to see as much of the future as possible. Perhaps this was the Secret of the Smithsonian. The ability to see what will be as well as what was.

Mrs. Harrison indicated a placard on the door. "These are the times your meals will be delivered. When you're finished, leave the tray outside in the hall. Now I must get back to the Assembly." She gave a radiant if overplump smile. "We seldom get visitors, you know. I mean, *overnight* ones, like you. The Chief Mechanic thinks *you* may be important now that storm clouds are, once again . . ."

Suddenly the entire room—building? T. could not tell— gave a shudder. T. felt mildly sick to his stomach as he rushed to the window where 1939 was doing its usual dull Good Friday thing.

"Is the Smithsonian on a seismic fault?" he asked, turning to Mrs. Harrison. But she had disappeared.

As T. started to the door, an African-American native of D.C., the District of Columbia, appeared with a great smile and a small tray. He wore a Pullman car waiter's white uniform.

"Lunch," he announced, putting the tray down on the desk in front of the window. With a flourish he removed the battered pewter cover to reveal chicken à la king.

"That's always Friday's lunch since the local Catholics stopped being so kosher about the fish. And tapioca pudding for dessert as well as the Smithsonian special salad with— you'll find it under the napkin—the *recipe* for the special dressing which you can make right here in bed . . ."

"Thanks," said T., who was very partial to chicken à la king.

The waiter removed a miniature xylophone from his pocket and struck three melodic chords, just the way they do on the trains. Then he, too, was gone.

T. wolfed down lunch. The Smithsonian's mysteries had given him an appetite. Then he put the tray, as requested, outside his door. Next he got his notebook from his suitcase as well as a brochure giving the history of the Smithsonian and a description of its contents. He was particularly eager to see the Hall of Aviation, where old airplanes were kept. The

Assembly of First Ladies Exhibit—nice as Mrs. Harrison had been—didn't really attract him. They were all so old and probably spent their free time playing bridge like his three aunts in K Street.

For a moment he studied the administrative chart of the Institution. Under the heading "More Chiefs than Indians," numerous department heads were listed. Mrs. Harrison had mentioned the Chief Mechanic, but which one? Five were listed. Which one had sent for him?

Yesterday, the telephone had rung in the dormitory of the lower school. The Canadian dorm master and history teacher, Mr. Pratt, T.'s sworn enemy, had answered it. Grudgingly, he passed the telephone to T., who heard a man's voice say, "The secret of the universe is here at the Smithsonian Institution. Check in at the Castle on Friday morning. Papa Chasseau will leave the door open. Tell no one. War clouds are gathering . . ." The usual. Then the sign-off: "This is the Chief."

Now here he was, as requested, ready for anything. Well, almost anything. Certainly, he was not ready for the contents of an envelope that someone had pushed under his door. He assumed that it was from Mrs. Harrison since it smelled of her frangipani.

There was no salutation and no signature. Only the bleak message. "Shun Mrs. Grover Cleveland as she is a voracious chicken hawk." That was all. But what did it mean? Something to do with the delicious chicken à la king he had had for lunch? In any case, how could an old, not to mention dead, first lady be a hawk of any kind? Truly the Smithsonian was proving to be full of mysteries. Now it was time for him to meet the chief who had rung him in the dormitory.

On the map of the building's interior in the brochure, T. marked with an X his room on the Pennsylvania Avenue side, noting that at the end of the corridor where his bedroom was, another corridor branched off to the right, ending in a room marked "Chief Director of Historical Evolution and Ceramics Evaluation." This could be the chief he was looking for.

T. walked slowly down the hall, opening doors as he passed, revealing bedrooms that were a duplicate of his own. But, alarmingly, in each of these rooms there was a tall, lanky, golden-haired youth whom he recognized as a duplicate of himself. This was dismaying. Worse. With so many copies, which T. was *he*? As usual, when puzzled, he began to mathematize the problem. Should one T. be raised to the *n*th power . . . But mathematics failed him. He had been, somehow, for no apparent reason, copied—six times, always assuming that the T. in the corridor was himself the original, the prototype. First Mystery of the Smithsonian.

At the end of the corridor with its half dozen bedrooms containing other T.'s, he turned right.

The new corridor was wider, higher, longer than the one that housed the multiple T.'s. Between large stained-glass windows depicting the westward expansion of the original American settlers, he could make out the dome of the Capitol in the distance.

Suddenly, a sound of drumming, not unlike Gene Krupa's recent gig at the Capitol Theater. The sound seemed to be coming from behind a massive mahogany door flanked by two wax guards.

T. tried the door handle; it turned; he pushed the door open just wide enough for him to poke his head into— another world!

A sign identified this world as the Early Indian Exhibit room, a favorite exhibit of T.'s childhood. A couple of dozen Indian braves and their squaws and papooses—papeese?— were going about their business in and out of wigwams on a sunny day, while a realistic painted backdrop, called a diorama, showed their native environment: trees, a distant plain with buffalo roaming, blue mountains.

But something had radically changed since his earlier visits. The Indians were no longer artfully molded and tastefully painted figures of plaster; instead, they were now real men and women and children in colorful native garb, while the mock fire—over which a cauldron of stew had been placed—was very much a real fire, with eye-stinging black smoke, and the pot had a section of what looked to be a real moose floating in it. The background was no longer painted but real: tall aboriginal trees, endless grassy plains where buffalo ambled in the middle distance and a hawk suddenly soared across the intense blue sky of yesteryear.

T. was about to slip out of the exhibit before its occupants became aware of him, but, as he was backing toward the door, suddenly it slammed shut and the sinewy arm of a sweaty young brave encircled his neck.

"Got ya!" said the brave in flawless American-Indian reservation English.

T. struggled to get free, but the brave was as strong as an ox. Also, get free for what? Where the door to the exhibit had been, there was now just another wigwam, with a running stream back of it in which naked papeese splashed about.

"I'm a guest of the Chief." T. gagged out the words as the pressure on his Adam's apple kept increasing. He could not utter the presumably magic word "Mechanic."

"I take you to Chief Yellow Sky Bird. He big chief here, Puritan white boy."

Then the redskin dragged T. to the largest of the wigwams, where, on a log, the chief sat, knitting himself a warbonnet of eagle feathers.

"How," said T. A greeting he had gleaned from a recent film about the taming of the West.

"How yourself." The chief looked down at T. who now lay on his back, staring at the chief's moccasins, a supine position that the young brave had arranged for him.

"What brings you to our neck of the woods, Puritan white boy?"

Behind the chief, two squaws were beating a blanket. One, to T.'s amazement, was as white as he, with long chestnut-colored hair, a truly saucy minx of a colleen.

"Miscegenation," blurted T., his conscious mind inadvertently overthrown by his racially sensitive District of Columbia unconscious.

"You've been reading too much Parkman. Racially, we are pure and intend to remain so until the cows come home. Where you from, boy?"

"Up on Wisconsin Avenue." T. was evasive. No use involving the school in his caper.

The chief sighed and put down his eagle-feather knitting. "At least you're not using the old 'I just happened to be visiting the Smithsonian,' like so many of the strays do. It's got to be some sort of mass hypnotism or, maybe, hysteria out there. We often debate around the campfire whether or not there *is* such a thing as the Smithsonian Institution. A place where we exist in a negative—even entropic—state, on permanent exhibit, as so many of our visitors like to tell us before we cut their tongues out."

T. did not like the sound of any of this. But he was also not about to be cowed. "You are—like it or not—a permanent exhibit. I know. I've been looking at you ever since I was a kid. Fact, thousands of people come here to see all of you in your colorful native clothes, doing colorful native things, except, of course, you're really all just a bunch of painted dummies . . ."

"We're what?" The chief's scowl betrayed a suspiciously broad knowledge of D.C. slang.

T. had by now worked himself to a sitting position on the ground. The fire's smoke was making his eyes water. "I mean you're just plaster or plastic, or something, you know, models."

"Does this look like plaster?" The chief revealed a bare arm with a powerful biceps.

"I guess you've been working out quite a lot, at the gym."

"I have no quarrel," said the chief, "with the *metaphysics* of your argument. I accept the proposition that there are numerous simultaneous worlds of us Iroquois. So your Smithsonian concept is a sort of metaphor—yet another world imposed on ours and invisible to us. Except for the odd stray, like you, from the British or French colonies." The chief turned to the brave who had captured T. The bronze youth lifted him by his hair from a seated position to a standing one. T. thought he was going to be scalped.

"Fanny Farmer time," said the chief comfortably. The brave removed T.'s jacket, unbuttoned his shirt.

"Hey, what are you doing?"

"Preparing you for the Great Spirit's pleasure." A second brave was now removing T.'s shoes and socks.

"You aren't going to take all my clothes off?" T. was aware of the morbid interest of the women all around him, particularly the white girl. T.'s question proved to be rhetorical. Trousers were yanked off. Now he stood naked except for his so-called Jockey shorts, a recent invention that the boys at school were addicted to.

T. wondered if he made enough noise one of the many chiefs of the Institution might hear. But then if they couldn't hear the racket that the Indians were making, it was unlikely that they would hear him. Besides, it was Good Friday, a day of special celebration in the District of Columbia, when the Daughters of the American Revolution, clad in tasteful black and shocking beige, made their way, lamenting, from Constitution Hall to the Great Lingam itself, the obelisk monument to Washington, where the current president, in his wheelchair, would receive them in the phallic shade, chewing on his cigarette holder, little dog, Falla, at his side.

T. was well and truly trapped by demented Red Indians. Just back of the chief, one of the braves was sharpening a knife, with many a flashing smile in T.'s direction.

Fortunately for T.'s modesty, the Jockey shorts were not removed. Unfortunately for T.'s life, his arms were being bound behind his back; then his ankles were bound, leaving just enough space between them so that he could shuffle but not run.

The chief was now on his feet. He came so close that T. could smell the buffalo fat and who knows what else on that massive body. A huge rough hand sandpapered T.'s smooth chest, erecting a nipple in the process.

The chief beamed. "Prime veal," he said, and the braves at the fire all sycophantishly repeated the sinister phrase. T. himself hated veal, and, for a moment, wondered if dinner was about to be served. If so, he would explain, tactfully, that he was a vegetarian and a single new-world potato would suit him just fine.

The chief tugged at the solitary tuft of golden hair under T.'s arm, outward and visible sign of a formidable if precocious sexual maturity; for sheer copiousness, his wet dreams were the talk of the dormitory. "Ow," said T., thoughtfully— he *was* thoughtful as he pondered just what the chief had in mind for dinner. Could prime veal be . . . ?

The chief turned to a brave whose face was painted in red, white, and blue stripes. "Brave, bring me preprandial Scotch on the rocks."

"You drink firewater?" T. was intrigued because, if he did, the white man had already begun his corruption of the noble red man.

"Only the best," said the chief. "Joe Kennedy is our bootlegger. We call him Great Hyannis Hyena."

"Gosh." T. could think of nothing else to say. The present Ambassador to the Court of St. James's in England was supplying, probably illegally, bonded firewater to the Smithsonian Early Indian Exhibit.

In the middle distance T. could see the lovely white girl as she and two comely squaws presided over a huge cauldron atop a blazing fire. As the water bubbled, they threw in ears of corn and Birds Eye frozen lima beans—a sensation that season which had even found favor in K Street, where the aunts agreed that, for once, you couldn't tell the frozen lima from the real thing. Plainly, the Indians' cuisine was being kept up-to-date by the Smithsonian even though none of these exhibits seemed to have any idea where they were situated or who was looking after them—except for the chief's curious remark about the Great Hyannis Hyena. Otherwise, they appeared to believe that they were living in the primordial wilderness and preparing for a dinner of prime veal.

Sweat trickled down T.'s side, tickling him. Tumbler of whisky in hand, the chief said, "Well, here's looking at you, Veal."

T. felt dizzy; legs began, inadvertently, to shudder. "You're not cannibals, are you?"

"Let's say that like our Aztec cousins down Mexico way, we crave protein of the sort that can only be got by eating flesh. Indian cannot live by succotash alone." In unison, several braves in the vicinity chanted this line, apparently the chorus to a hymn to meat.

With his head, T. indicated the herd of buffalo roaming in the distance. "There's a lot of prime beef out yonder on the range."

"True," said the chief, accepting yet another tumbler of Joe Kennedy's best. "But have you ever tried to spear a buffalo after a hard night at the old wassail bowl? Then there's the sheer drudgery of dragging it back to the campfire and the awful mess of skinning it . . ." The chief gave T.'s crotch a playful tweak. "Which reminds me, since you're being boiled, we skin you first. Alive. This means that every one of our squaws is going to find a lovely pair of white kid gloves in her Christmas stocking. Meanwhile, I'm about to have me a pair of mountain oysters."

T. never knew whether it was the white kid gloves, or the thought of his mountain oysters, but terror seized him and he pissed into his Jockey shorts as the braves roared with more than a hint of homoerotic delight. "Take Veal to the skinning wigwam," said the chief. "And bring me some of them smoked mountain oyster canapés, to whet my appetite for the fresh ones coming up." A second squeeze of his crotch and T. swooned dead away. When he came to, he was still trussed like a veal and the soaked Jockey shorts were gone. Naked as he was born, he lay in front of the pale-eyed chestnut-haired squaw who held in one hand an early Bronze Age knife with a carbon-14H dating tag on it—plainly lifted from another exhibit. In her other hand, she was playfully juggling T.'s mountain oysters.

"No!" he bellowed.

"These are going to make a tasty dish for our chief. How old are you, Veal?"

"Thirteen," he stammered. She looked at him, appraisal in her eyes.

"On a clear day," she observed thoughtfully, "you could pass for fourteen."

"How about getting me out of here? I mean we're both white."

"Oh, but I'm a captive squaw." She let go his mountain oysters. "A slave to the lust of my brave. He's the one with the double braids that I got him to work red ribbons into, using bear grease, of course, and practically over his dead body as, he kept saying, 'me no Nancy boy' . . ." During this the beautiful white squaw was using her razor-sharp anachronistic carbon-14H bronze knife to cut not T.'s smooth white skin, but his bonds. Freed at last, T. sat up; hands and feet tingled as blood recirculated.

The white squaw was now looking out the wigwam to see if the coast was clear. Then: "Wrap yourself in that blanket over by the chest. The one that says 'Pullman.' And cover your head. The sight of our golden hair and eyes and skin turns your average brave into a beast. Thank the Lord," she added contentedly to herself. Quickly, T. shrouded his blond hair and veal-white body in the Pullman blanket. Plainly, wherever—whenever—those Indians were supposed to be living, the plow had already broken the plain, and the great iron horse—a train—could be seen crossing the tawny plains of older times in the distance.

"Follow me." Like some great cat or a small pony, she led him out of the wigwam, which was at the edge of the settlement hard by a stand of cottonwood trees.

"We go *through* the stand," she whispered, urgently. At the other end of the settlement the braves could be seen, sitting cross-legged around their chief, quaffing cocktails prior to a succulent dish of prime veal from the pot where the squaws, salivating at the thought of what was to come, were now adding okra and kiwis to their aromatic bubbling stew.

T. dashed through the woods, barely able to catch up with the fleet-footed white squaw while holding on to his Pullman car blanket at the same time; the fact that he was barefoot slowed him down considerably as she led him through a cactus rock garden, then across a shallow pebbly stream toward a thickly wooded hill.

T. was breathing heavily by the time they had made it to the "safety," her optimistic word, of the forested hill whose view of the wide dusty plains ended in a vista of snowcapped purple mountains, originally painted in as background for visitors to the exhibit but now very much, if not the real thing, rendered in astonishing 3-D. A herd of buffalo munched their way toward them, like so many slow-moving burlap sacks.

"I've saved you, Veal darling." The white squaw threw her arms around him. Pullman blanket fell to mossy bank. She held his sweaty body to hers, tickling and tweaking and otherwise arousing him—a waking wet dream in dizzying 3-D, he thought, tugging at her maidenly wraparound of deerskin which, in less than a trice, she wriggled out of.

They were the same height. Green eyes gazed into hazel eyes. Warm loins pressed against even warmer loins. Did he fling her, or did she fling him onto the mossy sward? No matter. There was no sequence of consequence, only confluence.

"Fuck me, Veal," she whispered.

"I'm a virgin," he gasped, "but I'm ready." With a powerful thrust, he manfully entered, of two possible holes, the wrong one.

"Not there, *there!*" Woman's prehistoric, nay, primeval, cry sounded yet again and not, alas, as woman knows, for the last time in the tragic human story. Dutifully, Veal withdrew and again aimed blindly through moist thickets to full blissful bullhood in the absolute right place at the absolute right time. Bull's-eye is no idle Wittgensteinian concept, he realized, in the field, as it were. For T., it was a miracle to become himself a bull in the Indian exhibit at the Smithsonian Institution on Good Friday, 1939, as storm clouds gathered over Europe, and T. and his squaw were as one in total diluvian ecstasy.

Like most teenage mathematical geniuses, T. had read the dirty parts of a lot of forbidden books and now he understood the cataclysmic nature of what he had done with the white squaw; and realized, gratefully, that all those messy wet dreams had been simply so many run-ups for the main event.

As sated as Adam and Eve, they walked, hand in hand, to a nearby crystal spring and tidied up. T. knew the squaw was an old woman of twenty-two or maybe, worse, -three, but she *had* saved his life and shown him a good time, too. He helped her tidy both orifices and she bathed his mountain oysters with feather touch, exciting him yet again. But this time she only smiled and shook her head. "Not now, Veal. They are looking for their dinner and sooner or later they'll catch our spoor."

T. started to shake and his pale white skin was suddenly studded with goose bumps. "What happens then?"

Squaw looked up at the sun in the sky; then smiled. "Don't worry. Good Friday's a half day. The exhibit is about to open. You're safe. We can go back."

T. did not think this the best idea that he'd heard in too many a moon but, modestly covered by the Pullman blanket, he allowed the fully clothed Squaw—his name for her—to lead him down through the cottonwood stand to the encampment.

The braves and their squaws were glumly eating Heinz's baked beans out of tins. The boiling cauldron, vealless, boiled no longer.

The chief stood beside the smoking fire and shook his fist at them. "How!" he declaimed.

Squaw and T. "howed" him right back. Then she said, with a straight face, "Just as I started to skin him, he got loose and I had to chase him as far as the Crystal Spring 'Neath the Big Dipper . . ."

"So once you caught him, why didn't you prepare him for the feast?"

"He's very large for your average veal, O Chief. I couldn't do it all alone, could I? With no one to help me sit on the darling."

The double-braided brave whose squaw Squaw was raised his tomahawk. He was in a fettle less than fine. "Don't worry, Chief. She'll be punished for tampering with a minor. Do not the gods of us Iroquois punish pedophilia—not to mention veal snatching—with the death of the thousand and one for good measure cuts?"

Braves and squaws all began to smack their lips. The chief nodded. "Yea, verily," he said with authority. "Put down those Heinz baked beans cans and prepare for something truly savory."

T.'s mind had been distracted by the word "pedophilia," which he had come across in the family Krafft-Ebing, a book kept on the piano in his aunts' parlor, alongside the Congressional Directory and the Bible. He liked Krafft-Ebing's tall tales but, since he was flunking Greek in school, he had mistaken pedophilia for podophilia, a love of feet. Could *he* be classified as a ped since well as veal? This cast a kinky light on what had happened beside the crystalline spring. An old woman had had her way with him, causing him to break his binding oath to the Reverend Albert Hawley Lucas, headmaster of St. Albans and canon of the cathedral: to wit, he and the other lads in his confirmation class would save their purity—in jugs if necessary—until their wedding day when, joined to a little wife by Jesus, they could at last let rip. With all solemnity, he had sworn the Oath of Chastity, which he had now gone and broken ten ways to Sunday. Would Dr. Lucas, he wondered, accept his story of what had been, in effect, a rape at the hands of a white squaw? After all, it had been either rape or being skinned alive and boiled. Even the Episcopal Church would have to accept his terrible choice as the only sensible one.

By the time T. had worked all this out, a dozen braves, smelling like basketball players in a gym without windows, tore the blanket from him, hoisted him high and flung him into the pot with the maize and cauliflower, eggplant and kiwi fruits. Fortunately, the water was tepid by now.

"Hey," said T.

Whether or not it was his "hey" that set off the great bell or the bell his "hey," the braves froze into colorful attitudes beside the fire while the squaws froze as they went about their wigwam tasks, and where what had been a beautiful pristine vista of woods, plains, buffalo, mountains, T. now gazed at a somewhat dusty painted backdrop or diorama.

Exhibit time.

2

THE DOORS were flung open by human not wax guards. Tourists wandered into the hall where the fire no longer burned and the Heinz tins had vanished along with the Pullman blanket, while T., once more fully clothed and exactly as he had been upon arrival except, of course, he was now bull not veal unless . . . He frowned. Had this been another wet dream and not the real thing? He looked at the white squaw, who wore a sort of bandanna that hid her chestnut hair. Was it his imagination or did one of her painted plaster eyes wink at him?

"What're you doing in here, sonny?" asked one of the guards.

"On my way to see the Chief Director. Or is it Mechanic? Anyway, I opened the wrong door. By mistake."

"Be careful. Things ain't always what they seem around here. Why, some days when we open up, we find us a whole pile of bones round that campfire."

The other guard nodded. "It's a lot of crap them redskins not being cannibals. They eat *anything,* and that's the truth. Also, the chief's on Joe Kennedy's payroll."

This was a surprise. "How come?"

The guard chuckled. "During Prohibition, Old Joe used to smuggle his bootleg booze for Congress into this here exhibit, and the chief looked after it for him. Joe was a good tipper, you know." The guard winked unpleasantly.

T. made his way through a crowd of schoolchildren to the corridor at whose end shone a brass tablet: THE CHIEF DIRECTOR OF HISTORICAL EVOLUTION AND CERAMICS EVALUATION.

T. opened the door into a small anteroom with filing cabinets against the walls and numerous sepia-colored photographs of pots as well as charts showing how various pot-making civilizations came and went. The room was damp and musty; dust everywhere. Plainly this department of the Smithsonian had given up all hope of the Good Housekeeping Seal of Approval, so important for an organization ever needful of federal transfusions of money.

An ancient lady, wearing a man's jacket, white shirt, and tie, sat typing at a desk, notable for what looked to be one of the very first telephones ever invented.

"What may I do for you, young sir?" She was courtly as she turned from what must have been the prototype of the first Remington Rand, but then why else did the Institution exist if not for the preservation of such things as the bones of the first Cro-Magnon man or the original toilet of Sir Thomas Crapper?

"I've come to see the Chief Director of Historical Evolution and Ceramics Evaluation. I am T. from St. Albans."

"So the time has come," she murmured cryptically, her eyes not on him but on the inner door to the Chief Director's office. Then she cranked the telephone until a bell in the next room rang and she was able to talk into it. "Chief Director, the lad is here." A murmur of static. She put the receiver back in place. "You may go in. I would escort you but as you can see, I am blind." With that, she resumed her typing. Mysteries, thought T., not for the first time.

The inner office was magnificent, if dusty. Glass cabinets, streaked with the grime of ages, contained Ming, Han, and Tupper artifacts worth a king's ransom. Beneath a bronze Victorian chandelier, seated at a huge oak desk and writing with a quill pen, sat Abraham Lincoln.

"Come in," said the great man, a kindly smile breaking through his beard. "Take a load off your feet. We've been expecting you."

Awed to be in the presence of so distinguished a dead man, T. bowed low before seating himself on the stool to Lincoln's left.

"No," said Lincoln, anticipating T.'s question while adding carefully to his confusion. "I'm *not* President Lincoln. Though if I had *my* druthers he'd be here right now where he belongs in this pantheon to a great nation's past, present, and—now that you are here on time—future. But Springfield's got him and we'll never be able to spring them cold cuts, the Illinois legislature being what it is. 'Course, we've got his squaw, Mary Todd, and all the other first ladies but that's not the same thing, is it?"

"So what *is* your name, sir?"

T. noticed that the director had a mole in exactly the same place on his cheek where the dead president had had his mole.

"Lincoln." The director sat back in his chair and put his large feet on the desk. "Just a coincidence, of course."

"So you're not the president?"

"Well, he *is* dead, you know, and I am still very much, I hope, in action, with a thousand things to do. This office, as you can see, is a beehive of activity." From the next room T. could hear the blind secretary typing, tap . . . tap . . . tap . . .

"How does she do it, sir?"

"The typing? Oh, she has all the correspondence prepared in Braille. We have wonderful facilities for Braille here. Then, with one finger of her left hand, she reads the Braille while with the other hand, she touch-types. It's amazing the amount of work she gets done."

T. took a deep breath. "Storm clouds," he began.

Mr. Lincoln held up a huge hand. "I know. And that is why you are here. The Chief Mechanic—he was the one who phoned you in the dormitory—concluded, after an examination of all the data, that you possess—or, to be precise you yourself *are*—the key . . ."

"Key to what?"

"A good question. In the event you're *not* the key itself, you're *a* key to *the* key. Unfortunately, the Engineer's in New Mexico on the Easter holidays. But he's asked me to settle you in until he gets back and give you a brief course in ceramics and, naturally, the theory of history." Mr. Lincoln swung his feet to the floor with a crash; stood up; stretched. He appeared to be even taller than Raymond Massey. Then he opened a small door back of his desk to reveal what looked like a stove.

"That is a kiln," he said, "where we bake the clay that makes the pots . . ."

T. hated having things explained to him, even by Mr. Sofield, his favorite teacher at St. Albans.

"What have pots got to do with the unique crisis that faces mankind?" T. was stern as he said these words, all the while wondering, even as he spoke, just what they were talking about.

Mr. Lincoln turned to him with a melancholy smile. "Yes. I see it now. You are, my boy, the last best hope of dirt."

"Earth?"

"Dust, is the actual word I was searching for. The big problem of looking like Lincoln is that it makes me sound like him some of the time if not all of the time or indeed none of the time . . ."

The door to the office suddenly opened and Mr. Sofield marched into the room. Stanley Sofield was a plump small man with a long, pointed nose and bright eyes hugely magnified by thick glasses. Mr. Sofield knew the lyrics to every musical comedy written since Victor Herbert, but as he knew only one tune, "Chopsticks," the way that he could match any words to that single musical tune was truly eerie.

"Mr. Lincoln." Mr. Sofield feared no boy much less man much less an Abraham Lincoln look-alike. Hearty handclasps were exchanged. T. could tell that Mr. Sofield was suffering from a terrible hangover, but then every boy in their form could tell when their favorite teacher had passed a Dionysian night by the glassy morning-after look in those magnified eyes, not to mention the soft precision of his speech and the careful way that he moved so that his pain-wracked head might not fall off.

"We are in your debt, Mr. Sofield."

"Credit," said T.'s master, "must also be given the Reverend Albert Hawley Lucas, our headmaster and cathedral canon."

"Yes, indeed. Do sit down." Mr. Lincoln and Mr. Sofield sat in a black leather sofa while T. sat opposite in a straight chair as befitted a mere schoolboy, admittedly a boy unlike other boys, since he was now a nonvirgin and already hankering, bull-like, after ever more cow or Squaw. Could he— dare he?—slip into the Indian exhibit after the tourists had left? He kicked himself for not asking the glorious squaw how they could meet again without his being boiled alive. Erotic images flashed through his mind, obliging him to cross his legs as the two men discussed him.

"Frankly, I was going to flunk him." Mr. Sofield pressed his thumbs against aching eyeballs. "He couldn't— wouldn't—grasp algebra. He could, of course, if he spent less time on the baseball diamond. . . . Champion pitcher . . ."

T. wondered if he'd be able to start spring practice, or would he still be here, searching for the key to whatever it was.

Mr. Lincoln had—what?—read his mind? "No matter how long you stay here with us, and I'm afraid it could be years, when you leave it will be the same day as you came in. Time stopped out there for you. But in here time's at our service . . . forever!" He chuckled. Was this his idea of a joke?

Mr. Sofield withdrew a blue examination paper from his pocket. He gave it to Mr. Lincoln. "You asked for the notes that he made prior to arriving at the formula. Here they are. More like doodles." Mr. Sofield frowned, in quiet agony.

"Can I get you something to drink?" Mr. Lincoln was so-licitous. "Coffee? Tea? A boilermaker?"

"Gin," Mr. Sofield whispered. "A hair of the dog . . ."

"A martini?"

"Gin!" screamed Mr. Sofield. The scream started on a low note then rose to a crescendo so loud that Mr. Lincoln clapped his hands over his ears, while T., quite used to the elephant roar of hangover, hurried to a sideboard where bottles had been arrayed and poured Mr. Sofield a large gin, causing the horrifying howl slowly to abate. "Thank you," said Mr. Sofield in a soft ingratiating voice. He took a dainty sip from the glass held, like a mug, in two hands to control his tremor. Good Friday Eve was always a time of jollity in the bachelor masters' quarters of the lower school.

Mr. Lincoln was studying the mathematical notes that T. remembered scribbling, with half a mind, during the numbingly dull algebra exam for which he had done no homework. "This is hardly a trained ceramist's natural territory but I can see that the boy is a master of quantum physics, starting with $E = mc^2$ and then . . . and then . . ."

"Going on to $E = mc^2$ to the enth degree." The gin had brought the roses to Mr. Sofield's eyes. "When I saw his proofs—that is his sketch of how to prove his proposition—I realized that only the Smithsonian could handle so delicate and . . . well, astonishing a proposition."

"You did well, Agent Thirty-five." Mr. Lincoln smiled at T. "You didn't realize that your fifth-form master was an agent of ours, as you are, too, as of now—junior division."

T. was suddenly alert. He liked spy movies almost as much as he hated the FBI's dumb G-men. "Hey, that's pretty swell! Do we get to wear a badge?"

"Shut up!" shrieked Mr. Sofield, the prophylaxis of the gin for an instant ceasing to give protection, but T.'s quick refill of the empty glass restored good nature to that amiable rosy anteater's face. "Sorry, T. It's just that I expected better of you."

"What better than this?" Mr. Lincoln returned the mathematical formula to Mr. Sofield. "When you sent me the young man's material last week I had copies made. Top secret—eyes only—and called in session the Ceramics Evaluation Committee, to whom I then submitted these various formulae . . ."

"Ceramics Evaluation is really on the case?" Mr. Sofield sounded awed.

Mr. Lincoln nodded. "After two days, they came to the conclusion that if this new theory of derelativity can be physically demonstrated—it has already checked out mathematically—then we have a whole new ball game."

"Ball game" made T. think of the coming baseball season. He massaged his pitching arm. For once Woodrow Wilson High would have a good team. Victory would depend entirely on his right arm, a grave responsibility. But apparently other victories were now in view.

Mr. Lincoln turned to T. "You'll meet the committee in due course. For the moment they are still testing some equations, while I am busy trying to get the comptroller to give us funds to build a prototype bomb."

"Surely," said Mr. Sofield, happy and relaxed at last, "the War Department will provide the funds."

"In the end, of course. But these are early days . . ."

T.'s mind had abandoned the baseball diamond for math. "Bomb? What bomb?"

Mr. Lincoln rose to his full terrifying height. "War clouds," he proclaimed, much as Raymond Massey might have said *four score and seven years ago,* "are gathering over Europe while in Asia a dangerously small yellow race is on the move from its native Nipponese islands into the vast Asian hinterland of China where these bespectacled as well as dentally challenged savages have defied every order that we have given them to cease from and desist in their conquest and to henceforth do exactly as we tell them, for is it not as plain as a Chinaman's pigtail that we are a freedom-loving democracy and the very first as well as the very last best hope of man- and womankind? So should they persist in their disobedience, we must stop them, for their own good, by brute force— nay!—by sophisticated forces as yet undreamed of outside the walls of the Smithsonian and, of course, Dr. Einstein's lab in Princeton with its fun-loving appendage, Lawrenceville. . . ."

T. had considered going to Lawrenceville, a tennis-minded country-club prep school not unlike Princeton, its role model, but the three aunts in K Street had kept him in D.C., to keep an eye on him. Since Mr. Lincoln now seemed ready to swing into an endless State of the Union address, T. stopped him with: "My formula can be turned into a bomb?"

"With malice toward but one enemy and . . ." Mr. Lincoln sighed; then ceased and desisted. "Yes, a bomb of incalculable power. What you have done is found a way to release not only the power of the atom, which we have already tapped in Chicago, but the neutron as well."

T. had not the slightest idea what Mr. Lincoln was talking about. "I guess I hear where you're coming from," he said in a Joe Penner "Wanna buy a duck" voice. Would the—*his*— fair-skinned Squaw like his Joe Penner imitation? Should he—dare he—go back to the Early Indian Exhibit tonight when the tourists were gone? T. knew one thing: he couldn't live without her. "It all started," he said to Mr. Lincoln, who was now taking notes at his desk, "when I read the *Life* mag- azine story on Albert Einstein and his theory of relativity, which I thought real neat."

"You *understood* it?" Mr. Lincoln gazed at him over the pince-nez exactly like the one in the photo of him—or his double—giving the Second Inaugural Address.

T. tried to describe accurately what he had felt when he saw the famous equation spelled out and "explained."

"No, I don't *understand* it. But I can *see* it. I can sort of make a picture in my head about what it's all about, you know? I mean you've got this whole lot of mass and then there's energy . . ." As T. talked, he began to visualize what he was saying. Since he often lacked words to describe what he meant, he substituted numbers as they occurred to him, causing a pleasurable tingling in his mountain oysters and an overwhelming desire to piss, almost as pleasant in early stages as orgasm. Somehow the thought of light being electromagnetic radiation made a brilliant symmetrical picture in his brain, and then he saw how it was done—with more numbers and then more energy—and the atom itself could be broken to create further energy. He could also visualize a way to limit the chain reaction . . .

"Stop!" Mr. Lincoln's hand seemed stiff from trying to keep up with T.'s description of what he was seeing. "Explain how you can control the chain reaction so that the entire planet, solar system, doesn't . . . uh, short-circuit . . . Explode!"

"A simultaneous implosion?" T. could see in his mind the entire spectacular light show, centered on a man-made sun which could only be controlled by . . . A blinding flash in his head nearly knocked him out of his chair.

"Shit," he said, looking nervously at Mr. Sofield, who disapproved of the word, preferring the bleak "fuck" only when no student was within, he thought, earshot.

"I saw that, too." Mr. Lincoln's voice was low and frightened. "You *made* me see it."

"You're a trained physicist," observed Mr. Sofield, "like all Smithsonian ceramists." He turned to T. "This is all a front." He indicated the glass case of Ming and Tupper vases. "Abe here doesn't know a Sung bowl from a bedpan."

"Actually, there is nothing that I don't know about my hobby—my passion, really—ceramics." Abe was stern.

T. was watching the two men, rather coldly he thought. To what extent was he being had? He had known for some time that he had an unusual knack for turning numbers into pictures that he could study in his head as actions set off reactions. True, he had almost flunked algebra because it was so dim-witted a subject, but these formulas were as exciting to him as the Petty Girl in *Esquire*. What were only numbers to other people were landscapes and maps to him—and potential bombs, if that's what they wanted.

"O.K., guys," he said, carried away. "Try this formula on for size." He shut his eyes and saw a vast explosion in his head. It started just above the Capitol and then engulfed all Washington. Afterward, the Capitol and all the other buildings were just as they were, only the people inside them and in the streets had disintegrated, become ash. Although, as he proceeded, T. explained the numbers, Mr. Lincoln had stopped trying to note them. He had been left behind.

"The buildings—property—is unharmed while the people are all killed." Thus, T. translated into brief words what he had so spectacularly visualized and elegantly formulized.

"Didn't I tell you?" Mr. Sofield poured himself a vertical finger of gin. "He *sees* the equation in applied action."

"How do you do this?"

"I don't know. I just do. I guess it started with baseball. You know? Being able to figure out how a fastball can strike a batter out before it does."

Now Mr. Lincoln was pouring himself gin. "You've got the goods, my lad. This is the bomb we've been aiming for. You kill the people but save the real estate for the better angels and angles of our common nature."

"I'll drink to that." Mr. Sofield was now ready to drink to anything.

Mr. Lincoln then gave T. a map of the underground complex of the Smithsonian—laboratories, storerooms, offices
were all conveniently placed between the Castle on the National Mall and the various buildings parallel to it on Pennsylvania Avenue.

"I know you'll want to see the Hall of Aviation. Most boys
your age do." Mr. Lincoln then explained to T. just where
they were in the Castle and then where the staircases were
that would take him down into the warren of subterranean
corridors, one of which led to the Hall of Aviation: "Where
someone will be waiting for you. Someone you're going to
be pretty thrilled to meet if you're the red-blooded boy I take
you for."

Mr. Sofield staggered with difficulty to his feet. "Seldom,"
he said, speaking very clearly as was his wont when relaxing
at the end of the day or enjoying the hospitality of the likes
of Mr. Lincoln. "Seldom," he repeated for emphasis, "has a
lower-school boy held in his hands the secrets of war and
peace, of war or peace, of defeat and victory, of defeat
or . . ."

"And the war came." Mr. Lincoln could not bear to keep
his oar out of Mr. Sofield's competing aria. "None of us then
suspected . . ."

"Shut up, Abe!" Mr. Sofield's scream was now beginning
to rise, and Mr. Lincoln cowered behind his desk.

Mr. Sofield resumed his soft even hushed tone. "Defeat or
victory. Your formula, though accidentally stumbled
upon . . ."

T. thought the accidental part a bit much. Each night, between masturbation and sleep, in the creaking whispering
waxed linoleum-smelling dormitory, he would visualize mass
and energy and their atomic-neutronic components. In his
head, he always used a baseball diamond instead of a blackboard. On the three bases, the figure representing mass would

be so placed that when the batter encountered energy in the form of a ball hurled by a pitcher, mass got the full force of the ball. Basically, it was all pretty easy. There was no real mystery to it, other than why it was that he, so unthinkingly, had scribbled down his principal theorem in the course of a dumb algebra exam.

". . . accidentally stumbled upon, costing you, I'm afraid, a passing grade in algebra. Genius is no excuse for deliberately shirking the necessary quotidian tasks of our God-given mediocrity." Then Mr. Sofield, like a rundown toy, slumped back into the sofa and slept, and snored.

T. waved good-by to Mr. Lincoln, who had begun a new speech—what a bore he was, even if he really was . . .

The main staircase in the Castle was crowded with tourists going up while T. hurried down. Many of the younger ones wore shirts and hats decorated with the Trylon and Peri-sphere of the World's Fair in New York, which was, in T.'s view, ten times more interesting than the dull old Smithson-ian with its cannibal redskins and . . . The sudden thought of Squaw emptied his mind of everything else as it promptly en-gorged his weenie.

An almost invisible door at the foot of the staircase yielded to his tentative touch. He was now in a brightly lit area from which innumerable corridors led to hundreds of under-ground rooms and staircases. With Mr. Lincoln's map firmly in hand, he turned left; turned right. Stopped for a traffic light. Oddly, he saw no other visitors as he made his way through the underground maze, noticing how the floors, walls, and ceilings were painted in luminous vivid primary colors that reminded him of . . . of what? A sign that said PAWN MAY NOT TURN BACK AFTER THIS POINT was the clincher. He was on—or in—a vast Parcheesi set. Who else, he wondered, was also at play?

Finally, he found himself at the Hall of Aviation. A circular multicolored starting place for the pawns to make their way Home.

The hall was even larger than he recalled from a childhood visit. It was like a super airplane hangar with early airplanes hanging on chains from the ceiling. There were the Wright brothers' planes, very crude and papery looking. There was also the plane that poor Amelia Earhart, now missing in the Pacific, had first flown the Atlantic in. Then there was the *Spirit of St. Louis* that Charles Lindbergh, something of a hero to T., had used to cross the Atlantic. Lindy's great flight was always exciting to contemplate, as was the later kidnapping and gruesome murder of Lindy's baby that had scared every child in America, among them T.: he still had nightmares of a hulking dark-browed German climbing a ladder on a dark night to grab you out of your bed and carry you off to the woods where he'd smother you. Lindy was the hero of easeful flight. Lindy was also a character in every child's most fearful dream. At the moment, he was President Roosevelt's nightmare, busy making speeches saying that the United States ought not to go to war in Europe no matter how many storm clouds were gathering, no matter how bad Hitler and the Germans were. This was big of Lindy, T. thought, considering it was a German who had snuck up that ladder on a moonless night and stole and killed Lindy's son.

But where was the *Spirit of St. Louis*? Ordinarily it hung at the very center of the ceiling, the one thing that most visitors to the Smithsonian really wanted to see. But its place was empty.

T. looked around him. To his surprise the Hall of Aviation was also empty even though this was now a normal tourist day. What was up?

T. walked among the exhibits. One of them was a small weird-looking two-seater plane that his best friend in the dormitory had flown two years earlier in front of the newsreel cameras; the boy's father had something to do with aviation. T. often thought about this when the two were belly rubbing and talking of girls. If there was a war, T. knew that he would make a good pilot because of his pitcher's eyes—farsighted with perfect depth-spatial precision, unlike his buddy, who was so nearsighted that he had nearly crashed when landing the plane, a Hammond, according to the plaque.

A tall, skinny, boyish-looking man appeared from the far side of the hall. "Hi, T." The man also had a boy's voice. He looked like the ideal grown-up buddy if such a thing was possible. Luckily, T. was no longer on the lookout for a replacement for his dead father. Since the encounter at the Early Indian Exhibit, he was completely his own man now with no real problems other than how to get himself, at thirteen, a squaw on a regular basis. This was going to take some doing. Maybe the boy-man could clue him in.

"You know my name?" T. was beginning to get used to the idea that here at the Institution, if nowhere else, he was a person of consequence, thanks to Mr. Sofield's dumb algebra test.

"Sure. We all do around here. You're quite a kid." There was something very familiar about the tall stranger and his easy manner, which was a sort of boy-to-boy man-to-man mixture.

"Catch." A fastball came hurtling toward T. He caught it, instinctively, with his left hand and gave it a high spin in return, which his new buddy nearly dropped. "Hey, there! That's quite a spin you got. Looking for the *Spirit of St. Louis*?" The man pointed to the hook in the ceiling where the plane was usually attached.

"Yeah. I remember seeing it up there when I was a kid."

"Well, come this way. It's over here now."

At the far end of the hall, in a large open space, they found the famous plane, looking even smaller than it had the last time T. saw it.

"*You* put it here?"

Lindy nodded. T. was excited even though all along he had suspected that this amiable man was Colonel Charles Lindbergh, who had just come home from France where he had gone to escape American kidnappers as well as, some said, his American fans. In France he had invented an artificial heart of all things. Now he was home, warning the folks against getting into a war with Hitler. "When I'm in town I always like to come over and fly the old buggy around the hall."

"You *fly* in here." This seemed to T. unusually intrepid, if not just plain dumb.

"When no tourists are here, of course. Hop in."

As T. had never dreamed of flying with Lindy in the plane that had crossed the Atlantic, this was hardly a dream come true. More like a miracle. Heart pounding, he found a place for himself on a sort of jump seat.

"Is there enough room . . . ?"

But the noise of the propeller that Lindy had just spun drowned out their voices. Lindy hopped into the cockpit. Pulled the ignition. There was a roar from the engine. T. noted that the hall was bigger than it looked when you were just wandering around among the grounded aircraft. With a swoop, they were aloft. Lindy banked this way and that. T. felt he was going to fall out—or off was more his sensation—but the Lone Eagle, eaglet back of him, was mankind's acknowledged master of heavier than air.

"You like to fly?"

"Oh, sure! Yes!" T. now definitely planned on being a pilot in the coming war.

"You try." T. leaned over Lindy's shoulder and took the controls. Up-down-left-right. At one point they got so low that they nearly hit Amelia's plane, hanging from the ceiling. But T. swerved in time.

"Good boy," said Lindy. "You got an eye. Wish Amelia had had as good a one. She was a wonderful girl but . . ."

"What happened to her?"

Lindy shrugged. "Sooner or later most of us crash."

T. shuddered: would he crash, too?

After a double loop that set T.'s head spinning, they landed and Lindy taxied the plane to the spot where they had started. "Brings me to life again," he said, helping the dizzy T. out of the plane.

"How did you go to the bathroom when you were over the Atlantic?"

"Well, I had this bottle."

"I mean," T. blushed, "number two."

The Lone Eagle suddenly looked just like a teenage contemporary. He grinned when he said, "I sure felt sorry for those Frenchmen who carried me on their shoulders after I landed."

T. was thrilled. This was the sort of real history he liked.

"O.K., youngster, now we've had our fun, we go to work." Lindy unlocked a door back of the first gyroscope ever made and together they entered a large laboratory, full of machinery of the sort that T. had seen only at the World's Fair in the technology building and nowhere else.

"This is advanced physics," said Lindy. Then he greeted a half dozen men in white smocks; to a man, they were scientists, though what they were up to, T. couldn't begin to fathom. He assumed that since they were next to the Hall of Aviation they must be inventing new airplanes—bombers and fighter planes for the coming war that Lindy was, publicly at least, trying to prevent. He was all for keeping those war clouds that were gathering over Europe in Europe and American boys—like T., T. thought sadly—home.

After a round of greetings, a Dr. Bentsen took charge of the Lone Eagle and T. He led them to a corner of the lab, where what looked to be a movie screen filled one corner.

"We've developed this since you were here last, Colonel Lindbergh."

"What is it?" Lindy was always direct. Any other grown-up would have pretended he knew what it was.

"I'll demonstrate." Dr. Bentsen went to a panel filled with switches, levers, buttons. He pulled, tugged, pushed. The screen lit up. Mathematical formulas began to appear. Then quantum variations. T. had no trouble reading any of them starting with $E = mc^2$. As always, he could promptly visualize the meaning, in three dimensions only, of each formula. He had no idea how he did what he did. He just could; and did—especially when Mr. Sofield was writing dim-witted algebraic formulas on the blackboard. Boredom, T. assumed, was the trigger to his peculiar gift. He also had, for several years, a subscription to the one monthly magazine that any would-be quantum physicist must never miss a single copy of, *Popular Mechanics.* He kept his precious stash of scientific journals in his footlocker in the dorm, under the *Esquire* Petty Girls.

The screen began to fill up with more and more equations, each a variation on Einstein's initial theory of relativity. As the formulas kept being added to the screen, T. was aware that Lindy and Dr. Bentsen were watching him intensely. Why? To see if he could really fathom the—rough sketches is how he thought of what he was watching on the screen, very rough.

Suddenly he felt a jolt as if an electric shock had been applied to the back of his head. "Ow!"

"What?" asked Lindy.

T. shook his head, dizzy for a moment. "That one. The degree of uncontrolled fallout from a fission at a nuclear core. It's wrong."

"Wrong?" Dr. Bentsen was astonished. "How can it be? We got it straight from Princeton." Dr. Bentsen threw a switch on the right-hand side of the screen, just to the right of the theorem that had given T. such a jolt. He saw what looked to be a bona fide moving picture of a nuclear explosion: a huge ocean wave of light rising and falling. Looked to be to T. because, aside from knowing that the atom had been broken in a Chicago lab, T. also knew that no machine existed capable of putting those beautiful sketches—so real to his imagination—to the improbable physical test.

Dr. Bentsen turned to a panel containing various controls. "Now, watch this, Colonel. I'm going back to the exact moment of fission."

Where there had been a great sun-bright fireball on the screen, there was nothing at all but the empty air over what looked to be a stretch of cactus-growing desert.

"Now," said Dr. Bentsen, "we magnify." An atom's image, not visible to the human eye, started to fill the screen like a miniature solar system—and by no means miniature if it were allowed to keep on expanding until it was indeed the same size as the solar system or—larger? Was that possible? Was Earth's solar system nothing but an atom with ever, ever smaller components to the infinite degree? T. was getting a headache. The possibilities were too awesome.

Then Dr. Bentsen aimed what looked to be a bolt of lightning at the atom, which exploded, in very slow motion, over the desert, a kaleidoscope of colors against navy blue sky. There were now sensations—colors?—never before registered on T.'s retina. "Watch as the chain reaction begins within the nucleus." A series of small explosions was beginning and, T. duly noted, not ending.

"What's to prevent," he asked, "that atom you're opening up—the *way* you're opening it up—from setting off all the other atoms there are on earth and blowing us all up?"

Dr. Bentsen switched off the screen. "You sound just like Dr. Oppenheimer. He thinks there is a possibility that fission could be total but . . ."

"It's more than a possibility." T. was blunt. "You've got it all wrong. You got to anticipate . . ."

"You must drop Dr. Oppenheimer a line . . ." This was snide.

"Isn't he the guy at Berkeley?" Lindy was studying the various dials on the panel that controlled the screen.

"Cal Tech." Dr. Bentsen was sour. "The word is, he learned his physics at the Ethical Culture School in New York."

"Not the worst place . . ." T. decided that Lindy was more like a boy than an adult in the sense that he didn't chatter all the time, an answer for everything. ". . . for being ethical," Lindy concluded a bit absurdly.

"Don't worry, young man." Dr. Bentsen was only mildly patronizing. "Enrico Fermi has already succeeded in splitting an atom of a certain top secret element . . ."

"Uranium." Lindy grinned mischievously at T. "Only he didn't know what he was doing when he did it years ago back home in Italy."

"How," asked T., "did *he* control the reaction so everything wouldn't blow up?"

"Well, he didn't." Lindy turned a dial. On the screen was T.'s formula. "He was lucky. We were lucky. Now he's over here, at Columbia, and he thinks we can make us quite a bomb if the government will help out."

Dr. Bentsen turned to Lindy, a puzzled expression on his face. "I suppose you'll be against a government subsidy?"

"Anything for science, Brother Bentsen. I'm just against our getting into that war over there, because it's no more our business now than it was when my father was in Congress back in 1917 and voted no. Also, if this thing of T.'s works . . ."

Lindy pulled a lever. T.'s formula became a three-dimensional model of an atom; then, as the lightning bolt struck it, T.'s inhibitor caused a narrowing of the atom's full power. Instead of the ominously expanding fireball of the first model, this one remained focused, steady state.

Dr. Bentsen: "Amazing!"

"There's no risk, if you do it my way." T. had imagined this effect dozens of time, usually while pitching a game. Mathematical problems steadied his hand, helped arm and eye to concentrate totally on the placement and pitching of the ball; meanwhile, the secret part of his brain was equally focused on the numbers, like so many of those perfect musical riffs at home in Benny Goodman's clarinet.

Lindy took as much pleasure in T.'s triumph as T. did. "You'll get this off to Columbia?"

Dr. Bentsen nodded. "Berkeley and Princeton, too. Dr. Einstein rang this morning to say how impressed he was by this breakthrough. He couldn't believe a thirteen-year-old had thought of it, but then, on second thought, he said that he hadn't been much older when he figured out relativity, which meant that if he hadn't wasted so much time at thirteen playing the fiddle, he might have come up with a unified field theory by now."

"Einstein!" T. could not believe that the great man had studied *his* theorem, and got the point to it.

"As Smithsonian Director of Archaeology and Elemental Geography, I've given orders for a lab to be set up for you over there." Dr. Bentsen pointed to a corner of the room where plywood panels were being put in place to enclose a sizable office with its own screen and visualizing apparatus.

"Gosh," said T.

Lindy switched off the film monitor. "You've all got your work cut out for you. I guess you know that two weeks ago a couple of German physicists caught up with us. They'll be bomb making too."

Dr. Bentsen looked skeptical. "Dr. Fermi thinks not."

"Dr. Fermi doesn't have my connections. Their air force is superior to ours. Now they're in the race to develop the atomic weapons that will win us the war which, if I have anything to say about it, won't be taking place."

For T. these words, so quietly spoken, were like a trumpet blast. Could Lindy actually dispel those war clouds gathering over Europe? On the one hand, fighting in a war sounded pretty exciting, though he hadn't much enjoyed a picture book that he'd found in K Street—photographs of dead soldiers in the Great War. One of his aunts had lost her husband in France. T. wondered if he himself might one day fight in France, just in case Lindy failed to sweep away those clouds.

"Here." Lindy gave him a piece of paper with some telephone numbers on it. "In case you want to get in touch. Anyway, I'm going to be in and out of the lab here pretty regularly now."

With a wave, Lindy was gone. Dr. Bentsen shook his head. "He really thinks we can stay out of the war."

"Why can't we?"

Dr. Bentsen made a speech while T. investigated the lab that was being assembled for him by two technicians. T. asked one of them for a time projector.

Dr. Bentsen concluded his speech, ". . . and freedom and democracy will win. What time projector?"

"I don't know the technical name but it's what you've got in my bedroom. You know? Where Pennsylvania Avenue goes back and forth in time."

"Oh, that's just a trick someone thought up. . . . Who was it?"

He turned to a technician.

The technician shook his head. "That was before I signed on."

"A real nut as I recall . . ."

The technician said that he'd find what equipment he could, but, as far as he knew, only Pennsylvania Avenue had been recorded from what looked to be some sort of a lightscanner. "They say it starts with a bang and ends with a bang."

Dr. Bentsen was not interested. "*Your* job, my boy, is to perfect your model so that the atomic chain reaction doesn't get out of control."

"I've done that." T. disliked being called "my boy."

"On the screen. But soon they'll be trying out the real thing in Chicago and we don't want to lose the Windy City, now do we?" Dr. Bentsen chuckled at his own ready wit.

But T. was off on another tack. "You know that a *non*lethal bomb is also a snap."

Dr. Bentsen stared at him in amazement. "What's the point to a bomb that doesn't kill the enemy?"

"Scare him! Dissolve a couple of his cities but leave the people alone. Then say, next time we'll disintegrate you, too."

Dr. Bentsen was suddenly alert. "You can formulate such a device?"

"I already have. I can see it in my head—the numbers, that is." T. was not about to describe how he worked to anyone. Mr. Sofield was his first and last attempt; and Mr. Sofield had screamed his elephant's scream. T. vowed never again to explain his method.

When the technicians left the lab, Dr. Bentsen seated himself in a plastic chair while T. sat cross-legged on his desk. "We've already seen some of the numbers for a neutron bomb, which does exactly the reverse. The people die but the buildings are left intact. We call this the Realtors' Dream Bomb."

"Are you building it?"

Dr. Bentsen shook his head. "We don't really have all that much time. Fact, if what the colonel says is true, we may not have enough time as it is, to keep ahead of the Germans." He rose. "You keep on perfecting your formula. Then we'll see. . . . We're expecting a go-ahead any day now. Fermi's persuaded Einstein to write the president, saying this is our only chance to win a war fast, blowing up the people *and* the buildings."

———•———

After a lonely dinner of Virginia Smithfield ham and baked sweet potatoes, T. went to the window and looked down on Pennsylvania Avenue, a familiar enough sight in the early evening. Then he switched the thermostat to fast-fast-forward. Streaks of light and dark as months?—weeks?—years?—centuries?—passed: there could be no way of gauging time not yet elapsed but one thing was certain, the technician was right: the avenue did seem to end in a spectacular fireball. After that, T. picked up nothing at all, neither light nor dark. Nor any sound save an odd humming. Whatever device had been recording time's passage had either stopped recording, or there was nothing left for it to record. In which case, had he actually seen the end?

T. felt the small hairs on his forearms rise. Why, he wondered, hadn't the officials at the Smithsonian put two and two together? Here was proof that what they were all working on was going to end, sooner or later, in a very big bang—at least as far as Pennsylvania Avenue was concerned. But when? Plainly, no one had had the good sense to time this event. Also, how could you measure future time which does not, by definition, exist? What has not happened is not. On the other hand, earth light scanned at a great distance from the planet would show future as well as past unless, by looking up ahead, you changed it all: indeterminacy was the name of a—if not the—game. Yet there was that explosion somewhere in the undatable future. What to do?

T. decided. For now he would fulfill his mission and write some simpleminded formulas on how to limit nuclear fallout; also, if they would let him, a neutron bomb that would not damage human beings. But what he had to find out was whether or not the course that they were on would end all life on earth—soon. If, as he had begun to suspect, this was the case, he must find a moment in time from which he could alter what they were doing before it became irreversible.

T. lay back on the bed. Shut his eyes. Waited for the right picture to form. But all he got was a blue sky filled with equations. When he worked them out in his head, each ended in that terrible flash of light. This war must not take place, he repeated to himself Lindy's line. And slept.

—————

Days passed inside the Smithsonian while, outside, it was always Good Friday, or so Bentsen assured T. who still couldn't believe that two sets of time, involving him, were going on simultaneously.

"So I'm getting older at St. Albans and staying just the same right here?" T. was at his console while Bentsen sat at T.'s desk, smoking a pipe. After the first fairly bad impression, T. was getting used to Bentsen's brusque ways.

"That's about it."

"How?" T. flung a switch to demonstrate his latest formula for the preservation of buildings. A single nuclear device, based on his design, promptly blew up the entire earth—on the monitor. "I guess I goofed on that one." He was apologetic.

"We all make these little mistakes. But you can see why Dr. Oppenheimer keeps worrying about *un*controllable chain reactions."

T.—stimulated by the detonation of the whole earth—began to think yet again of Squaw. How could he get back to the Early Indian Exhibit without being scalped or cooked?

"Time has always been the weak point in Einstein's theory." Bentsen was in a pensive mood.

"It would have to be." T. cleared his screen. "Because nobody can live long enough to test it. We can only—what's the word—colonize today."

Bentsen chuckled into his pipe smoke. "Well, that's one way of putting it, only . . ."

"That was Minkowski's." T. had read everything that *Popular Mechanics* had written on the nature of time—not much. "Of course, you can simulate. That's why I really like the Pennsylvania Avenue tape, or whatever it is."

"Kids do." Bentsen managed not to sound too patronizing. "And it *is* fun seeing Lincoln's funeral and stuff like that but, basically, it's only entertainment, like a movie. I mean we can't interact."

T. picked at something called a cheeseburger that one of the staff had brought him. This was a new delicacy, almost as addictive as the Little Tavern hamburgers served all over town in a chain of green and white one-room shacks with peaked roofs. The Little Tavern hamburger cost twenty-five cents and wasn't very thick, but the greasy onions and slice of sharp pickle on a soggy bun was T.'s favorite food. He once ate nine in a row, gazing contentedly at the motto above the grill NOT THE BEST BUT BETTER THAN THE REST.

"Why not?" he mumbled through the cheeseburger.

"Why not what?"

"Interact. What would happen if I went outside during Lincoln's funeral?"

"You'd find yourself in Pennsylvania Avenue on a gray spring day in 1939."

Inadvertently T. shuddered. Had time really stopped just for him on Good Friday so that he could make it back in time—in Time—for baseball practice? Of course, they could be lying to him. After all, they needed his trick, which was how he thought of his ability to conceive and visualize an inexhaustible—infinite?—supply of equations.

On the other hand, T. was not much good at visualizing, or sometimes even understanding, the theories of others. He was having his problems now with Bentsen.

"So time is passing normally for me here. I arrived on Friday and it's now next week. Well, is last Friday still waiting around back there for me at St. Albans?" T. wolfed down the remains of the cheeseburger and took a swig of Coca-Cola, whose bottle reminded him of Squaw's body.

Bentsen looked uneasy. "Let's say there's someone just like you at St. Albans today, going out for baseball practice . . ."

"Then," T.'s logic was superior to that of Bentsen, "we *are* interacting with time. You've got me in two places already, so when do I get to meet me again, *before* I came here?"

"When you leave here, of course . . ." Bentsen kept on talking, but T. had stopped listening. He was beginning to feel that rush to his head which, usually, meant that he was going to come up with something he had not thought of before. Obviously there were multiple sets of time and, somehow, the Smithsonian had figured out a way to get him to come to work for them within a frame of time parallel to the one that he was living in at St. Albans. So if he could be on two tracks . . .

Suddenly, he started to visualize himself graduating from St. Albans. He would be seventeen in 1943. Six foot tall at

least. Slender. Muscular. In a fuguelike state T. began to op-
erate the console while Bentsen watched fascinated.

T. punched out Einstein's sloppy—certainly untested—
fourth-dimensional equations. Then he switched to visualization, adding the new numbers that flooded into his head so
quickly that he felt he might burst if he couldn't get them onto
the magnetic tape, which he now activated with a flourish.

On the screen, T. saw T. dressed in a black robe for graduation on a bright June day.

Bentsen gasped. "But . . . You *can't* do that! Einstein
doesn't allow for the capture of a future image that hasn't
taken place unless . . ." He stopped.

T. filled in: "Unless one is traveling at the speed of light,
which I'm now . . . uh, simulating." Although T. was enormously pleased at what he had done, he had no idea how he
had done it other than to throw on all power while lining up
space-time coordinates that, somehow, focused in on the
right place and time to produce a moving picture of himself
four years into the future.

T. decided that he looked pretty neat and grown-up; a tiny
nick on his chin was happy proof that he had started to shave.
Then he opened up the image so that he could see his classmates with their parents as well as Mr. Sofield slyly nipping
from a flask in the shadow of the chapel tower. All was going
to be as it should be except . . .

T. saw the bad news. Soldiers, sailors, marines mingled
with the graduates. A boy two forms ahead of T. was in a
wheelchair, legless.

"The war," Bentsen whispered.

"I guess I didn't stop it, did I?" T. switched off the console.

"I hope you've kept all your notes for what you've just
done." Bentsen was anxious.

"Yeah. They're already in the memory bank. Anytime you
want to see me on Graduation Day, 1943, you can punch it
out."

"Just how far into the future can you probe?" Bentsen was pale with, T. assumed, amazement.

"Well, if you sit here watching the screen for the next twenty years, you'll see twenty years' worth of St. Albans. No." T. anticipated Bentsen's next question. "You can't follow me for more than maybe an hour. Or anybody just yet. With a bit of luck—and enough energy—I was able to manage the coordinates for this one place and time."

"But how exactly did you do it?"

"If I knew exactly, I wouldn't be me, and if I'm not me I couldn't do it at all. For now, I can only get this one look into the fourth dimension up ahead. Then—well, the other three get in the way."

T. wondered if atomic energy could make it possible to travel as fast as light. If so, he could go anywhere he chose in space-time. But, for now, he was positive that he was just himself, all alone, and he now knew that whatever he might be accomplishing at the Smithsonian, he had certainly not stopped the war from taking place—or kept his friend out of a wheelchair. "But then how could I stop a war when I still haven't thought of anything except a bomb that all of you hate because it takes out buildings and not people?" He hadn't meant to say this part aloud.

Bentsen knocked ashes from his pipe: "Are you surprised? Your neutron bomb has got to be a hard sell at the War Department, where they want to kill the enemy."

"Civilians, too?"

"Why not? That's what the Japs are doing in China." Bentsen put away his pipe. "That's what Sherman did in the South when he burned up the cities. War is hell."

"So why don't we just skip this one."

"Don't listen to the colonel's isolationist crap."

T. couldn't stop thinking about the boy in the wheelchair. A boy his St. Albans self was probably at baseball practice with even now, four years before then.

Bentsen left. T. finished his Coca-Cola. Thought of Squaw. Began to feel horny.

A soft voice from the screen: "Veal."

T. looked to see which circuits had switched on. There were so many communication setups that he had still to explore much less master. He punched out a simple Comethrough.

On the screen, in full color, he saw Squaw: she was wearing an old lady's dress from the last century. There was nothing squawlike about her now. "Miss me?"

"You can see me?"

"Just the way you can see me. When they first wired the Smithsonian for electricity they put in this system. Heaven knows how they figured it out back then. Miss me?"

"I'm going crazy for you."

"So why didn't you come see me?"

"Those damned Indians, that's why."

"Well, I'm not always on the reservation. Anyway, tonight, after supper—it's the macaroni and cheese, really good here, believe it or not—go to the Old Western American Exhibit . . ."

"Not more Indians!"

"Just a few. Selling rugs. No problem. This exhibit takes place long after the one where we first met. Twenty years after the Civil War . . . Oh-oh." Bentsen was in the lab. T. switched to a beautiful shot of the World's Fair.

Bentsen looked at him suspiciously but said nothing other than, "The macaroni and cheese is one of our chef's specialties."

Mischievously, to show off, T. recorded on the screen a variation on $E = mc^2$. He was now beginning to regulate at will rather than by accident, in the case of Graduation Day, 1943, the simulation of Faster-than-Light Travel which he was certain that he could, in Time itself, cease to simulate and actually experience in the flesh.

"What on earth is that?" Bentsen was hurriedly making notes. It had been obvious to T. from the beginning that no one at the Institution trusted him except, maybe, Lindbergh.

"That's—working backwards—how I got forward to 1943, with just a scanner." T. punched out a few more teasing notes. "I think I know how to control mass at Faster than Light. If I can, I'll be able to travel back and forth in time . . ."

"Wait a minute!" Bentsen's hands were shaking as he copied the formula. But then T. switched off the monitor.

"I don't have it yet. According to this calculation, if I went in the flesh to 1943, my mass, arriving in that space, would blow up the cathedral and me, too."

T. went back to his room. He had a new idea: it had come, like all the best ones, unbidden.

The colored waiter, dressed as a Pullman car porter, brought T. his tray; he also gave T. a recipe for the salad dressing that was served, he said, in every restaurant car of the Pennsylvania Railroad. "It's got this secret ingredient. Your aunts will love it."

Before T. could ask the waiter how he knew that he had three aunts in K Street, the waiter was gone, leaving the recipe for salad dressing in his hand.

T. walked over to the window and looked down. The usual evening traffic; shop windows announced a special Easter sale. Time outside the Institution was keeping up with time inside. Would they—could they—really get him back to Good Friday, 1939, were he to stay all spring—or longer—inside? If they could, someone on the premises had already worked out the problem of Faster than Light. Who?

T. fiddled with the fast-forward button. Another funeral was coming down the avenue. Black crepe in the store windows. Thousands of soldiers, sailors, marines on the sidewalks while other troops, in formation, marched before and after the hearse. All flags at half-mast and, everywhere, large portraits, framed in black, of President Roosevelt. More proof that the war Lindbergh was so desperately trying to stop did not get stopped. So how did it turn out? No way of telling except that Washington hadn't been bombed yet. And everyone was still in uniform.

The macaroni and cheese was as good as advertised. The salad dressing . . .

T. looked at the recipe without interest; then turned it over.

On the back of the recipe an equation had been written in purple ink. Automatically, T. visualized the parts of the formula that he understood. But there were odd extrapolations unfamiliar to him. Someone—with purple ink—was developing Einstein's relativity theory to include, in more detail, the nature of time, how it bent back upon itself in space, the light retaining everything but as a reflection on film or—was it the real thing? T.'s heart pounded. He liked time-travel stories but until now he had seen no practical scientific need to move ahead or back of the clock other than to test Einstein's rather grand if skimpy assumptions about energy, mass, space. Now someone was working on the same subject that he had just puzzled Bentsen with. He would have to study this new theorem. Surprisingly, his mind did not initially visualize it. He put the recipe in his pocket. Best to let the brain idle its way to a solution. In his dreams, solutions came.

3

THE OLD WESTERN AMERICAN EXHIBIT occupied
the entire ground floor of a building that he had never
noticed before. But then that was the principal secret of the
Institution: there were far more buildings and exhibits—
above and below ground—than anyone suspected. In fact,
how much you knew depended, finally, on which map you
were given—or so Bentsen told T. in the lab when, somewhat
reluctantly, he gave T. a map totally unlike Mr. Lincoln's.

Once again, T. descended a flight of stairs into a well-lit
turquoise-painted Parcheesi corridor. The guards were wax,
which meant that it was after closing time and the general
public was gone. The public was something of a nuisance to
the "permanent personnel," as Mr. Lincoln referred to himself and to the other full-time employees and residents of the
Institution, who all lived, their addresses unnoted, in the
great consortium of buildings.

Four wax guards stood at the entrance to the Old Western
American Exhibit. Surprisingly, the double doors were open
and there was a blue blaze of noon light from inside. Cau-
tiously, T. set foot into the American past or, rather, what he
took to be its re-creation.

Although the Early Indian Exhibit had looked authentic,
this one was far more spectacular when it came to realistic detail. For one thing, no walls, no ceiling, no floor were visible.
Just a large western town with a brand-new railroad depot of
the sort shown in Westerns every Saturday at the Mercury

Theater. On the side of a parked railroad car, he read the magical phrase, THE ATCHISON, TOPEKA AND THE SANTA FE.

In the distance, past endless prairies, sharp mountains glittered in the bright sunlight. The air smelled of sage and woodsmoke, horse and cow dung.

Eyes wide, T. walked down the main street of the town, which was made of adobe . . . whitewashed mud-brick houses fronted by low arcades to shield passersby from the sun. Indians were everywhere, but they paid no attention to T. In fact, no one paid the slightest attention to him despite what must have seemed to everyone his strange costume.

Inside an arcade on which was tacked a sign that read LA FONDA, Squaw was waiting for him. She looked even prettier than he remembered.

"Veal, darling!" She gave him a big sisterly kiss on his cheek. "Welcome to Santa Fe."

"So that's where this is! It's sure some exhibit. Better than the World's Fair."

"That's because this one's more . . . well, the *real* thing. You know? It's also not yet open to the general public. The trustees want to keep it pristine, they say. Come on in. This is the first hotel in town since they put in the railroad last year, their last year, not yours, but come to think of it, mine too."

They entered a large room with heavy wooden beams overhead and a cedarwood staircase back of the registration desk. In leather chairs about the room, bewhiskered stout men sucked cigars, chewed tobacco, smoked, and talked in low voices. Several rose politely when Squaw entered. Was it T.'s imagination or did one or two glance at him in a knowing way? He blushed.

As they sat down, he wondered just who and what Squaw was. She had certainly been pretty cozy with the Indians back in Plymouth Rock days; of course, they were basically a plaster exhibit except when animated. T. shuddered at the thought of the stew pot he had so narrowly escaped. Now Squaw was very much at home in what a calendar back of the reception desk indicated was the year 1846. "Only it's not really 1846. This is all taking place something like forty years later. But the trustees like 1846 because that's the year the Smithsonian was founded and the railroad got here." Two fashionable ladies entered the lobby, accompanied by a very young army officer.

"What are they dressed as?" T. stared at the women, who ignored him as they followed the young officer into the dining room.

Squaw stared at them narrowly. "They are dressed as of the height of fashion for this year which is . . . Oh! Look at that one's shoes! Made in Paris. This is 1886 and I look such a fright."

Squaw seemed genuinely upset by her costume, which didn't look too different from what the girls were wearing. "The awful thing about visiting these exhibits—particularly the live ones—is there's no way those of us from other exhibits can ever find the right clothes to wear, much less accessories. I'd kill for those shoes!"

"So—what is *your* exhibit?"

"A perfect bore. You'd hate it."

"So—*what* is it?"

"Handicrafts. Tea!" Squaw commanded a black waiter who might, depending on the year, be a slave or, more exciting, someone who had gone and freed himself and lit out for the territory of New Mexico.

"I wonder if Billy the Kid's anywhere around?" T. had a thing about Billy, his kind of boy, at least according to what little he could learn about him from the movies.

"Oh, he's been dead maybe five years now. Shot not so far from here. I've even met Pat Garrett, who plugged him." Squaw gave T. a dazzling smile.

"They let you—at least your exhibit lets you—just go around and visit all the other exhibits?" T. was growing more and more curious about Squaw. Had she been put in charge of him by Mr. Lincoln or by the trustees or whoever ran the Smithsonian? Or was she just a fun-loving girl who liked to moonlight from Handicrafts, which did sound pretty dull.

The waiter brought tea, which Squaw poured for two. T. wondered how she was going to pay the waiter. But then, as they were both just exhibits, perhaps they wouldn't bother.

Squaw read his mind, no hard thing at the moment. "I told you all of this is really real, where we are now, not like the place where we met."

"Why is this real and not that?"

T. was beginning to visualize the time formula, if that was what it was, in purple ink on the back of the salad dressing recipe. He had got the hang of time raised to the nth power but . . .

"You'll have to take that up with the trustees. I've only been part of the Institution since 1886 . . ."

"How did you join?"

"Well, Veal dear, you can't just join, they . . ." She stirred sugar into her tea, frowning. "What happens is they join *you* is the best way of putting it. I was pulled in as historical . . ."

"Are you someone famous like Pocahontas?"

"*Historical Handicrafts,* I should have said. Yes, we do have Pocahontas in the Jamestown Exhibit. You know, she lived for a time in London and, oh, the airs she puts on! Anyway, Veal, you're on board, as Mr. Lincoln likes to say, because of your mathematics, which I don't entirely understand." She opened her handbag. A tag dangling from the handle identified it as Reticule Late Nineteenth Century. So Squaw really was in Handicrafts. Veal had feared she was a Nazi spy or, perhaps, a New Dealer, anathema in K Street.

"I have instructions to take you to a priest in a pueblo on a mesa near here."

"Not all that near," said the young officer last seen entering the dining room. "But I'll get you there, ma'am."

"That's nice of you. The trustees . . . ?"

"Mr. Lincoln, actually." Gravely the young man shook T.'s hand. T. noticed on the right sleeve a tag which said Marine Corps Second Lieutenant Circa 1846.

"You're part of the Military Exhibit . . . ?"

"Isn't Veal quick?" Squaw looked mischievous; and desirable. T. wondered, darkly, if this young man was a potential shadow on his potential happiness. Was Squaw flirting with him, too? Or—horrible thought—did she have a lover in every exhibit? Would he be ruled eventually out of competition on grounds, if not of size, of age?

"Yes, sir. I'm part of that exhibit. And you can bet they don't let us out all that much, which means it gets pretty dull, talking to nothing but soldiers and sailors, most of them from wars long after me, like the Civil War and the Great War. Now that one really sounds scary."

As they walked down the main street of Santa Fe, the gentlemen would raise their hats when they saw Squaw and each lady would smile and incline her head.

"How come they seem to know you if you're not from out here?"

Squaw laughed. "I suppose they aren't taking any chances. Who knows? I might be the wife of the new governor of the territory . . ."

"More likely daughter, ma'am."

"You are so gallant, Lieutenant." Squaw tapped his chest with her forefinger. T. was engulfed in rage; frustration too.

The lieutenant stopped at a livery stable. A sign read: HORSES, BUGGIES, CARRIAGES, HEARSES FOR RENT.

The lieutenant went inside to talk to the owner. Several shy Indian children gathered in a circle around Squaw and T., and simply stared. The bright blue weather, so unlike muddy springtime Washington, put T. in a good mood again.

He was ready now to go *mano a mano* with the lieutenant for Squaw's affection. After all, he was close to six feet tall, too, with golden fuzz on his cheeks, at least just by the ears—sideburns-to-be.

"We'll need a carriage," Squaw said. "You know, Tom wasn't much older than you at Buena Vista, where he killed all those Mexicans and got commissioned a second lieutenant in the field by Jefferson Davis himself."

"It was Zach Taylor, ma'am," the lieutenant called out from inside the stable.

"Wasn't Davis Civil War?" T. remembered that much even though he had hated American history as taught by the Canadian, Mr. Pratt, who disliked the United States almost as much as he did the boys in the school, particularly the ones in the lower school dorm of whom T. was Mr. Pratt's self-appointed nemesis.

"Yes, darling. But before the Civil War there was the Mexican War and Davis was in that one, too. So were Grant and Lee and a lot of the other young men who became generals in the Civil War. And Zach Taylor who got to be president."

"I can't say I like our history class all that much. Those dumb wars—and those dates, always those dates." As T. spoke, he suddenly realized that dates—time itself—had suddenly become his life's work.

A lady and a gentleman in a carriage bowed as they passed Squaw, who waved cheerfully at them.

The lady in the carriage said, "Will your sister be coming for the wedding?"

Squaw smiled and nodded.

"You must be very important," T. began.

"I *was,* yes. Now about those dumb wars as you call them. They were pretty exciting, at least for the boys, and then if it weren't for the war, we would never have ended up with the whole continent, the middle part anyway, and California . . ."

"I'm going to stop the next war." Why on earth, T. wondered, did he keep saying what he was thinking?

Squaw stared at him with bright, intense hazel eyes. "Yes?
Go on."

"No. I just said that to impress you, I guess."

"I'm surprised. Because you're too young to have had the
chance to be a hero, like Tom at Buena Vista. I would have
thought you'd want your own war, too."

T. was relieved when the hero of Buena Vista reappeared,
seated on the buckboard of a carriage next to an old man
who drove four horses with a series of shouts, whistles, and
snaps of his whip.

"Get in, ma'am. Sir. We're off to Otowi."

Sun. Intense blue sky. Desert. Clusters of silver-barked
trees wherever there was a stream or a well. White people
lived in adobe houses set back from the rutted dirt road. Indian villages were built against—or into—the sides of abrupt
hills whose tops were flat. "Like tables," said Squaw. "That's
mesas in Spanish, tables."

The carriage began its ascent of the first of a series of
mesas, like steps to a pyramid. Halfway up Squaw said, "Stop
here."

Here was the first of several steaming hot springs set in
otherworldly formations of gray rock. The carriage came to
a halt. Tom leapt to the ground and helped Squaw down. T.
followed.

"I'm going in the water over there." Squaw pointed to a
high boulder which, apparently, shielded from view a pool.
She grinned mischievously at them. "You boys keep to your
own pool. I won't be long." Then she was gone.

The lieutenant pulled off his clothes. T. did the same, en-
vying the young man his superior development but not en-
vying him the jagged red scar that began at the base of his
neck and ended at the base of his spine. As T. followed Tom

into the hot sulphur-smelling water, he couldn't take his eyes off the scar—a red snake of a scar crisscrossed with smaller scars where stitches must have been.

"Buena Vista. A souvenir," said the lieutenant, aware of T.'s morbid interest. Tom submerged in the pool while T. took a standing dive; then he made the mistake of opening his eyes underwater, and shot quickly to the surface, eyes burning.

The lieutenant laughed as T. rubbed his eyes beside the steaming pool. Nearby, they could hear Squaw splashing about in her pool.

"What was it like, Mexico?"

"We killed a lot of Mexicans."

"They nearly killed you." T. looked at the naked Tom as he leaned over a large tumbleweed where he'd put his clothes. As Tom took a baseball from his tunic, T. noted morbidly that the red gash looked like the Mississippi River whose delta ended between high white buttocks. What on earth had it felt like when bullets struck him? Was Tom knocked out? Or did he lie there in a daze, surrounded by dead Mexicans, or by other American boys, all bleeding to death if not dead?

"Catch," said Tom. He threw a crudely made oversize baseball at T. who automatically caught it, to the lieutenant's surprise. But then how could the older boy know that T. was the best schoolboy pitcher in the Washington, D.C., area? They threw the ball back and forth, ever faster, until T.'s special spin caused it to fly from the lieutenant's hand.

"How did you do that?"

"I guess we've learned a few things since your day." T. picked up the ball. "How old is this?"

"I don't know how old anything is at the Smithsonian, including me. But we invented the game they call baseball down in Mexico during the war. Some of the lads who came along after us are really good at it, and the Great War boys tell me there are now professional teams that use a much harder ball than we ever used."

"You play a lot with the other guys?"

"Well, we don't have too much to do as exhibits go. I guess the trustees think that since we're trained soldiers we might try to take over the place, so even when we're not just dummies, we're usually encouraged to stand around with our fingers up our asses, like the Great War boys say. Now *that* was some war, with poison gas and those funny airplanes. We didn't even have balloons in our war. I hear there's another war coming?"

T. shook his head, beginning to feel a bit sick to his stomach. The sight of the young lieutenant's perfect body with the gash down its back was setting off inner alarm bells. "When did you die?"

Tom laughed. "I'm just a dummy. So how could I live much less die? Frankie looked up my record and she says that I barely got through that day at Buena Vista. I wouldn't know. I don't recall much about anything except joining the marines in Charleston, South Carolina, not much older than you. And then there was this girl who . . ." He frowned. "I don't have much memory left. A lot of it just gets knocked out of you, along with your life. The others from the different wars before and after me, they don't recollect a whole lot neither. I mean we're just an exhibit, after all, a popular one, you might say . . ."

"Who is Frankie?"

"Me!" Squaw was standing on a boulder looking down at the two naked boys. "Get dressed."

Blushing, they did. "It's not as if I don't know you both pretty well."

T. was now beginning to feel, if not in charge of the situation, in a new relation to the situation. "Why does he call you Frankie?"

"I was christened Frank. My father was crazy. I changed it to Frances so everyone calls me Frankie. Zip up your fly."

As T. zipped, the lieutenant, already clothed, watched with interest. "What's that?"

"A zipper. It's something new they just thought up, like Jockey shorts . . ."

"You boys and the latest fashion!" Squaw was now in the carriage ready to go.

"I got to tell the First World War lads about this. No buttons! Why, we could be on dress parade in no time at all with those things." The lieutenant was now beside the driver.

As the carriage started, T. suddenly registered what the lieutenant had said. "*First* World War means there's going to be a Second World War, doesn't it?"

"And a third and a fourth. Don't fret, Veal." Squaw put her hand on T.'s thigh. He experienced a familiar tingle in his groin.

"He called you Frankie."

"I let some of the boys do. I was a bit of a tomboy back in Buffalo, New York."

"How many . . . uh, boys, do you know? In the Military Exhibit?"

"A dozen or two. Who counts? It's all the same really, the sex."

T. was shocked. Somehow he had thought that the grown-up world was like the movies, where a good woman loved only one man and if they weren't in a weepie movie with Bette Davis they got married and ended up together once George Brent was dead or in prison. Of course, Squaw might not be a good woman. He'd read a few fairly sexy novels by Thorne Smith, all about "free" women but, somehow, Squaw seemed so old-fashioned. Or was it just the clothes.

"Dear Veal." She was suddenly sisterly, though her hand was now in his crotch. "Don't you get it? We are all just dummies in the different exhibits and the Military Exhibit—for me—happens to have the sexiest dummies of all."

As they approached the top of the mesa, the road became narrow and rocky. Tall juniper bushes on every side and the air sage scented. "That's right," said Tom. "The Military Exhibit is nothing but us, wearing a lot of uniforms from the French-Indian wars through the World War."

T. noted a slight hesitation before "world." How could Tom know there was going to be another world war?

"But," said Squaw, "they take only old original uniforms, which they dress you darling dummies in. Then, once they've done that . . . Well, Veal, I don't know how to explain this to you but all the soldier and sailor boys who wear these uniforms start out as dummies but then, after exhibit hours, they get to be whoever it was who wore their uniform originally. But like Tom, they are all basically the same dummy so they've all got pretty much the same body."

"Oh," was all that T. could think to say. At least Squaw didn't have to worry about intimate things not fitting. He visualized the very real young man in the hot spring, who seemed near perfect in the flesh except for . . . T. pushed her hand out of his crotch. "You're trying to kid me again. If you've . . . been with him, you've seen that scar down his back."

"Grisly, isn't it? A piece of a cannonball hit him. He died of infection a day later, which is what most of them did back then."

"He's really dead?" T. looked at the very alive youth on the buckboard.

"Of course he is. They all are, for heaven's sake—or I should say, for the Smithsonian's sake. The Institution has simply given us all a sort of historical extension, you know, as exhibits."

"When did you die?" T. was starting to feel a bit unreal himself.

"That's for me to know and you to find out. And *never* ask a lady her date of death." A sudden jolt of the carriage flung them into each other's arms. Squaw certainly didn't seem even slightly dead.

"There's a guest house at Otowi," she whispered, between kisses.

The dirt track was now a flat stony road. In the near distance, T. could see a village centered on a pond. Blue smoke from chimneys. He could make out a Spanish mission church and a cantina-style bar with wooden swinging doors.

"Do they all have that scar on their back?"

Squaw now had other things on her mind. "Do all who have what?"

T. repeated himself.

"Of course not. Each, if he was killed or wounded, has his own special scars. But most of them survived the wars in one piece. Anyway, I try to avoid the damaged ones . . . except for Tom. Naturally, there's a lot of trial and error because they're all so horny they won't let on before you get them out of those uniforms and by then it's too late."

"I still don't get it."

"The *uniform*, Veal!" She sounded irritated. "This dummy"—she pointed to the lieutenant—"began as a flawless standard dummy, just like all the others, until they put him into an 1846 marine's uniform and then the dummy became—what else?—the boy whose uniform he's wearing . . . the Hero of Buena Vista is who he was. He also became the same age the marine was when . . . you know."

T. found all this highly disturbing. He understood the exhibit with the dummy Indians and he had come to accept the fact that they did come to life—of a sort—after hours but . . . "What about memory?"

"Memory?" Squaw sighed. "In Tom's case there can't be too much before he got the uniform he's wearing. But I'm

tr'ld the military boys talk quite a lot together after lights-out.
They tell each other things. You know? About the wars.
Being hurt. Then things—memories—start to come back, or
so they say."

"About dying?"

"Who can ever know about that?"

"But . . ."

"Oh, do shut up, Veal!"

The carriage had stopped in front of the small adobe mission church. Nearby, Indian children played in the dust while
thin dogs slept under lacy green peppertrees.

The lieutenant helped Squaw down.

"Stay here, you two." Squaw entered the church while the
driver of the carriage unharnessed his horses. Women in
black came and went as if there were no strangers on the
scene. Even the children ignored them.

"Can they see us?" T. turned to Tom, who was mopping
sweat from his eyes: the direct sun atop the mesa was fiercely
hot.

"Why not? They get to see a lot of visitors."

"Here?"

Tom nodded. "Kind of a popular place lately."

Tom threw the baseball. T. caught and returned.

"Why? Why popular?"

Tom sat down in the shade of a peppertree. "I'm afraid
they never tell *us* much. Why should they? We're only the
troops."

"But you must know the people out here. Like those two
women you took into the dining room."

The lieutenant looked embarrassed. "Well, I knew them
from before . . ."

"Before what?"

"Before Mexico. I was all set to marry the mother of the
blond one. Then . . ."

In his mind, T. saw stars; with a roar, metal tore into Tom's body. "But you never came back, to marry her."

The young man frowned. "No. When she heard I was dead she got married and had our child—the girl you saw with her half sister. Then they moved to Santa Fe. Funny. We'd intended to move out here after we won the war and got all this new land. So she and her . . . new husband came anyway, with their little girl along with mine."

"What did you tell the mother, when you finally saw her?"

"Oh, that it was all a misunderstanding. War Department made a mistake. I told her how when I got out of the marines, I tried to find her. Couldn't. Anyway, she died, too. Now I come to visit my daughter. She thinks I'm her mother's cousin, who takes her to the dining room at La Fonda."

As Tom spoke, his face was crushingly sad and T., only six years the marine's junior, realized he was just a boy like himself.

"Do you think they know you're dead *now?*"

Tom smiled. "Well, if you want to be finicky, we're all dead, including the girls you saw me with this morning."

"You mean they are by the time I get to the Smithsonian in 1939?"

"1939!" Tom whistled. "That's almost a hundred years after Buena Vista. Of course, I know a lot about what's happened in between then and now. We've got a sailor who is—was—in the navy this year, your year. He even got to see the World's Fair. I'd love to see that."

"How did he end up in the exhibit?"

"Fell off his boat and drowned." Tom shrugged. "Something dumb like that. When we get naked after lights-out he sort of shines. You know? Sort of green from drowning . . ."

"Get naked?"

The lieutenant grinned. "Well, we've got all sorts of games we play together when day is done."

"Sounds wild."

"Mostly rassling. But at least we don't kill each other all over again, the way the Rebs and the Yanks had to kill each other off first time around. We're more buddies. Then some of us visit other exhibits, like this one."

"What's Handicrafts like?"

But Squaw had appeared from the church. "Go on in, Veal. The priest wants to talk to you."

"But I'm Episcopalian."

"He's not going to convert you. You go on now while I take a nap in the carriage, guarded by this gallant young officer." Tom grinned.

T. was jealous. "Are you an important person's wife?" he asked, unpleasantly.

"I'm only twenty-two," she said. "And don't ask personal questions."

The interior of the church was cool and dark and smelled of stale incense. There was a horrendous wood carving of Christ on the altar with realistic-looking blood painted on his face and side. T. thought of Tom; shuddered.

"Buenos dias." A voice rang out. Then the man attached to the deep melodious voice appeared from behind the altar. He wore a black robe and carried a lighted candle in his left hand while with his right he took T.'s hand and, instead of shaking it, led him to a door in back of the altar.

"We'll be more comfortable in my lab," he said.

T. was not prepared for a large well-lit laboratory with interesting if not exactly modern equipment. The lamps, he noted, were kerosene. Electricity hadn't yet arrived in this time and place but batteries had: a modern console was blinking on a table.

"I'm Father Lamy," said the priest, taking his place at a cluttered refectory table. "No relation to the archbishop."

"Oh," said T., trying to look knowledgeable. What, he wondered, was an *arch*bishop? "But he has been most kind to me. In fact, he has been so kind that he has not taken the slightest interest in my work here and, of course, he hasn't a clue that I'm a Fellow in good standing of the Smithsonian."

"Are you from here—the here whose now we're both in—or, are you from back then and I'm visiting you from my now?" Time, T. decided, was getting more like a pretzel than anything else.

"You might say that I'm allowed to straddle the two though I'm very much what you'd call 'then.' I was born in 1851. But, as you must have noticed, the Old Western American Exhibit is unique. Two vectors cross, in time, on this mesa. Eventually, when advanced computers become available to me, I may be able to figure out the process, but since you're still at 1939 I can't go beyond that year except in theory, and theory is just theory until demonstrated, as you demonstrated so brilliantly for Dr. Bentsen and Colonel Lindbergh."

Apparently a bona fide resident of the New Mexico Territory in the 1880s was in full communication with the 1939 Smithsonian and vice versa.

"Do you actually know Dr. Bentsen and Colonel Lindbergh?"

"The doctor, yes. The colonel—like you—only by reputation." Father Lamy's smile was canine yellow and his eyes looked as if they might shine red in the dark.

"*I* have a reputation?" T. fished.

"Indeed you do! The entire Smithsonian, past and present, were mightily impressed with your breakthrough equation. That is, as far as it *seems* to have broken through. Your science is astonishing, but then anyone who can see clearly what is already self-evident in the way of time and space is classified as a genius. The secret is in the adverb—'clearly.' You're still too young to see darkly, grown man's usual condition. Einstein was very young, too, when he broke into a mystery that has always been as plain as the sun at noon. But it took an unclouded youthful eye to see it and, of course, he only broke into a part of it, as you have into another part and as I am trying to do."

T. looked past Father Lamy to a blackboard on which he could see—really see for a change—$E = mc^2$ next to his own time-variant to it as well as a half dozen other formulas which he promptly memorized so that he could visualize them later.

Father Lamy knew exactly what he was doing and appeared pleased. He tapped the bottom equation with his forefinger. "I'll be curious how you . . . visualize this one. I'm having my problems with it."

"Well . . ." T. was flattered to be taken so seriously, or at least his peculiar gift was being taken seriously. He himself had very little science beyond what he could "see" but not always interpret.

T. approached the blackboard, eyes on the chalked-in series of symbols. As he got closer and closer, the blackboard ceased to be a square of slate and became a deep black night of unlit space. The symbols blazed like Arctic lights against the darkness. "Beautiful," he whispered.

"What is?" Father Lamy was standing beside him, staring intently at, apparently, nothing.

"Can't you see? Space. Lights."

As T. drew ever closer, he became aware that the lights were not fixed like stars but in motion, writhing in the blackness like snakes, countless fiery snakes that, as he got as close as he could, became so many intertwining strings of light, with no apparent beginning or end.

"Tell me what you see. Exactly." Father Lamy's voice was urgent.

T. did his best. Finally, he put out his hand to touch the nearest string. He felt a shock go through his system. An instant of dizziness. Then . . .

"That was a real breakthrough," said Bentsen.

To T.'s amazement he was in his own laboratory with Bentsen beside him. T. blinked his eyes, suddenly dazzled by electric light. "Where's Father Lamy?"

"Back in his church in eighteen hundred and whatever it is. I've been monitoring the two of you and when I saw what you were on to I got you back here with, well, *almost* with the speed of light. Our ultimate dream. You recall the formula on his blackboard?"

T. nodded. "In fact I had it in my pocket all along." He pulled out the recipe for salad dressing. There, on the back, in purple ink, was the formula. "Someone put this on my supper tray."

Bentsen frowned. "Too many people are coming to similar conclusions at the same time. This means we're about to make a huge leap forward in our evolution." He held up the menu. "If this works out, it will be on a level with the invention of the wheel."

"Fire is more like it," said T., getting into the spirit of the thing. "Whoever is using purple ink has discovered what life is. . . . Death, too, I guess. What . . . well, everything is."

Bentsen nodded. "We don't have the words yet to describe concepts never before dreamed of. But if those strings of light are what the universe is made of. And if we were to isolate any one of them and follow it from one end to the other . . ."

"Wrong." T. was no longer shy with grown-ups. "The ends connect. The strings are really loops that . . . Circles, you know? Like snakes, they swallow their tails."

"Are you sure?"

"Couldn't you see?"

"Not what you saw." Bentsen was grudging.

"It's beautiful but . . ." T. was practical. "I can't see what we can use any of this for, right now."

"Use follows knowledge."

T. punched out a series of variations on his console: let the machine do the dull math. But the machine did not seem to know what to do with the odd intervals between the snake-clusters—areas of what looked to be lightless nothing. T. was too distracted to focus his attention.

"Who's Father Lamy?" he asked.

Bentsen shrugged. "Just who he says he is. We made contact with him when we set up the Old Western American Exhibit. He's a genius, too." Bentsen nodded a bit sourly at T. "But he hasn't got much to work with back there . . ."

"Why not bring him here?"

"We don't have the technology to get people ahead of their time frame. *We* can visit them but they can't visit us, with one exception, which is still top secret."

"What goes one way can go the other." T. saw the flaw and wondered why Bentsen hadn't.

The physicist looked a bit uneasy. "Well, yes, it's theoretically possible but . . ."

"What about the exhibits? They're from old time."

"We only get the odd wave on a different frequency, not the whole construct or person. Anyway, they're essentially dummies."

"What's been done once can be done again."

"It's not really my field. Why don't you ask Father Lamy next time you pay a call?"

T. thought wistfully of the good time that he had planned to have with Squaw. Now the marine lieutenant was going to enjoy her while he was back in the salt mines at the Castle. "Where," he asked, "is Handicrafts?"

"Handicrafts?" Bentsen looked surprised. "There's no such exhibit. At least none that I know of."

T. got out his Smithsonian map and, sure enough, there was no longer any such exhibit. Just a section of the Parcheesi board with the label, in green, BLOCKADE, where HANDI-

CRAFTS had been. Then he turned to Bentsen. "How can I get directly to Father Lamy without having to go back to Santa Fe first?"

"Couldn't be simpler." With suspicious ease, Bentsen demonstrated on the monitor, and T. was relieved to know that for at least this one exhibit the space and time coordinates were easily mastered, and you could enter at any point you wanted during the late 1880s in the Santa Fe area of New Mexico Territory. Somehow, this particular fragment of space-time had been annexed by the Smithsonian.

"Why didn't they pick someplace more . . . well, interesting?"

"Because, for our purposes, this is the right window on the right time and place. Ask Father Lamy. He'll explain . . ."

"Since he's in an exhibit, he must be a dummy."

Bentsen smiled. "Old West is a *very* special exhibit, a sort of cinema verité." As T. had almost failed French, he dropped the subject. He waved to Bentsen and got himself back to the mission church. Apparently, Father Lamy had never noticed his departure, much less return. He wondered if he could also get back to Good Friday at St. Alban's on his own. "By the way." T. tried to sound casual. "Do you use purple ink?"

"No." Then, as if by association, Father Lamy raised the blinds of the window, revealing a sweep of desert that stopped at the purple mountain range of the Sangre de Cristo back of Santa Fe in its low valley. "You know, I never tire of this view. This proof of God's existence."

"Oh," said T.

"Yes, oh, I'm working secretly on my own port of entry for the Smithsonian, starting from here. I daydream about the wonders of your world. The wonders of 1939."

"They don't seem so wonderful to us. I like it back here. You know? Indians. Horse and buggies. Billy the Kid. What are you doing?"

Father Lamy was now replacing the window with a sheet of blue-tinted glass, using an old-fashioned crank to raise the one and lower the other.

"It must be awful, not having electricity."

"I'm used to it. And Dr. Bentsen does send me batteries for the console, though the principle of how *they* work is beyond me."

When the blue glass was in place and the light in the room grew dim, Father Lamy made some adjustments that involved more cranking.

Then—the view changed. The desert slowly gave birth to a large wooden building with a high roof and a verandah, supported by smooth round wooden columns. Military-style barracks surrounded the central building. Suddenly, a troop of Boy Scouts on horseback galloped into view and rode straight toward the mission church.

T. recognized his friend from the dormitory; the boy's family had been threatening to send him west to school. Now here he was, riding up to the window and then *through* the window.

"Watch out!" T. yelled.

Father Lamy was soothing. "We aren't really here. For them, that is. Don't worry. They're going to ride straight through us."

So they did. T.'s friend, a blond youth, looked straight into his eyes and said to his horse, "Come on, Two-bits." Then Two-bits and his rider passed straight through T. and out the other side of the mission church.

Father Lamy beamed. "That's about as close as I can get to your time with such crude equipment. I aimed for 1939 and this must be—maybe—1940."

"I don't see any sign of a war yet."

But Father Lamy was now cranking away and the mounted Boy Scout troop vanished. Then all the buildings, except the big one, were replaced by modern buildings, going up at a great rate right before their eyes.

"It's about here that I start to lose the picture. I get as far as what looks like a whole brand-new city where there used to be a boys' school when I'm blocked. I can't seem to go past this . . . whenever it is . . ."

T. gave a shout and dropped to the floor as the window was filled with a huge sunlike burst of light and smoke and dust.

"Don't worry." Father Lamy was calm. "It's only a reflection. Won't hurt your eyes."

T. got to his feet just as the fireball began to rise in the air on a stalk of flame. "So they're going to make the atomic bomb."

"So it would appear." Father Lamy cranked a few more times and the erupting light dispersed as night fell back of the blue glass. "That's where the show stops."

"Why can't you go into the next thing?"

"The batteries aren't strong enough." He replaced the blue glass with the old window and the view of a sunshine desert day of long ago. "I sometimes think Dr. Bentsen doesn't want us to go beyond a certain point, which is not much later than 1942, 1943. That's another problem. I have no way of pinpointing anything."

T. was depressed. Thanks largely to Lindy, he had been counting on the war, somehow, *not* taking place. Now it seemed that it was unstoppable. No one was going to spend the kind of money currently being spent for a superbomb without enjoying the bang.

"The archbishop thinks Armageddon is at hand."

T. usually slept through Bible class. But Armageddon had made an impression. "End of the world?"

Father Lamy nodded. "The archbishop and I will miss it— we will have left too soon—but you won't."

T. started to see numbers, sines, cosines, tangents in his head. Usually it was figures that started him thinking in vivid pictures but now he had gone into a kind of reverse: the nuclear explosion that he had witnessed through the blue window was filling his head with equations.

"Got a pencil?"

Father Lamy leapt to his feet, a very curious expression on his face; he found T. pencil and paper.

Quickly T. wrote down what he saw in his head. A series of progressions. Each more alarming than the other . . . When he stopped he was shaking. "Armageddon's right," he said not to Father Lamy but to himself. "I've got to get back."

———◆———

Dr. Bentsen and Lindy sat wide-eyed as T. explained exactly what would happen once Chicago's nuclear device was finally set off in the New Mexican desert.

"I don't know all the technical language," he said, aware that he didn't know *any* technical language, since none existed for him outside his own true language: numbers and all those other signs that stood for things seen and unseen. "But"—he used his monitor to produce visual effects on the screen—"here's what will happen when . . ." He punched out the moment of activation. The screen blazed with light, much as it had in Father Lamy's church. But then T. allowed it to continue past the arbitrary frame that had contained it in the mission church. The effect was like one Roman candle setting off another as the nuclear sun's energy was dispersed into countless smaller suns, filling the entire screen with a galaxy's worth of tiny stars.

"Chain reaction." An unfamiliar voice spoke just behind T.

"Yes." T. turned to see who was there. A lean, sharp-faced man with a boyish crew cut was staring intently at the screen.

Bentsen was on his feet.

"Dr. Oppenheimer. This is an unexpected honor . . ."

"I don't know about the unexpected part—or even the honor, Colonel Lindbergh." Oppenheimer shook Lindy's hand. Then turned to T. "Well, you really are the prodigy they say you are."

"Thanks. You're in charge of all this, aren't you?"

"Yes. We're taking over the Otowi mesa. There's nothing there now except a boys' school. Top secret, of course. You'll be with us, I hope."

T. thought of his best friend, bored to death at the school. "As long as I don't have to go to that school."

Oppenheimer's smile was thin and not particularly human. "That school will soon be gone. Then we start our work . . ."

"I hope you're already at 'our work.' The Germans also have a program." Lindbergh held up a copy of the *Evening Star*—HITLER WELCOMES SCIENTISTS.

"So Dr. Einstein told President Roosevelt. I'm recruiting scientists, too." But Oppenheimer was entirely focused on T.'s equation. "Take me through this, please." The great professor from Cal Tech was now the student.

T. did as requested. Oppenheimer asked no questions until T. had finished. Then he shut his eyes, as T. often did when he wanted to *see* a concept clearly, uncluttered by the world around him. "What set you in motion?"

The question was unscientific but since it was exactly the sort of question that T. would have asked, he felt at home. "The word Father Lamy used, 'Armageddon.' "

Oppenheimer's eyes opened wide. "That would do it for me, too, if I had your gift. The Hindus have the same concept of total annihilation. Only for them it will be Shiva, an aspect of Vishnu, who will put out all the lights at the end."

"Whoever's in charge," said T., "the whole world blows up when you set off that bomb you're planning to build."

"Yes," said Oppenheimer, with no apparent emotion. "That's my calculation. But no one else agrees."

Bentsen was sweating in the cool lab. "Does one atom really set off the next and then the next . . . ?"

"And there's no more world." Lindy was to the point. "So how do we control the chain reaction?"

"I don't know." Oppenheimer was suddenly gloomy. "I must talk to Fermi and Bohr."

"I've already worked out an inhibitor," said T. "Fact, I showed it to Colonel Lindbergh and to Dr. Bentsen."

He turned to Bentsen. "Why didn't you pass it on?"

Bentsen stammered. "I'm sure I did. Airmail special delivery from Postmaster Farley's post office. The receipt is . . ."

"Show me now," Oppenheimer said to T. He was polite.

T. pointed to a weak point in the connective tissue—as he thought of it—between the atoms. "If the connecting . . . highways could be broken down or walled off at the moment of detonation by the same fireball . . ." T. was sweating as he quickly transferred the theorems from his head to the screen and then into its memory bank. Oppenheimer and Bentsen watched while Lindy, whistling tonelessly, wandered about the lab, looking at the models of uranium atoms in various states of distress.

Later that night, T. lay awake in his bed. Although he had worn himself out in the lab, he was still not sure if he had made a useful contribution. Obviously, neither Oppenheimer nor Bentsen was prepared to pass judgment without further testing. A horde of quantum physicists would be consulted, since disintegrating the world by mistake was not exactly what President Roosevelt had in mind when he got the money, secretly, from Congress to set up what was now being called the Manhattan Project.

On the other hand, the *Second* World War—as opposed to the just plain European or Japanese wars—must not, in T.'s urgent view, take place because, for reasons he could not yet visualize, it would have almost the same effect in the end as the chain reaction in the desert. There would be a slower, subtler, but no less deadly effect. Why he was so certain of what would be was one of several interlocking mysteries. Had some hidden area of his mind zeroed in on a flaw in the plan? Or was he simply reacting to that sudden glimpse of his graduation day in 1943—of a uniformed classmate in a wheelchair?

That night, T. dreamt he was being detonated like an atom, bits of his mind tearing loose, hurtling away from the center, each meson an autonomous shining self—losing touch with all the others. He was suddenly no longer T. He was a myriad. A galaxy where once he had been singular, himself.

4

CONTRARY TO what T. had been originally told, time was actually passing at the same rate both inside and outside the Smithsonian. Bentsen had brought a copy of the *Evening Star* to work and he had left it—carelessly?—on a table in the main lab. The date was May 1, 1939. Hitler had conquered Czechoslovakia. Roosevelt had asked Congress for even more money, for war.

"I've been here over three weeks." T. stood beside Bentsen, who was typing out a circular memo on the lab's principal screen. The entire project, from Berkeley to Chicago to the Smithsonian, was now checking out T.'s alarming discovery.

"It certainly must seem like that." Bentsen arrived, as T. knew he would, at a wrong conclusion. "To you, that is. Time moves at a different pace in here."

"At the *Evening Star,* too. Look at the date." T. held up the newspaper. Bentsen frowned. "Now," said T., "I've got three aunts in K Street and baseball practice is coming up . . ."

"When you go back, I promise you will be joining our old friend Good Friday all over again, just as if you never went away."

"But what must they think *now* when I'm really gone?"

"But you're not. As far as they're concerned, you never went away."

"Proof?" T. knew that he was a far better conceptual scientist than Bentsen; he also knew that there were a great many rules and regulations at the Institution that Bentsen knew better than he ever would.

Bentsen turned to a dark young woman in a white uniform like that of a hospital nurse. "The future time tapes." She began to fiddle with the dials. Once again, T. saw himself at seventeen, graduating from St. Albans on a bright June day.

"We're in your debt for this mysterious breakthrough into the future." Bentsen tried to be gracious. "That is you, isn't it?"

T. had to admit that the images were authentic looking. "Let me," he said to the lab girl. T. began to work the controls.

Bentsen looked alarmed. "Are you sure you can handle that? This is our only machine for scanning future light . . ."

T. had stopped listening. The theory of tracking old light was, essentially, his inadvertent contribution to Mr. Sofield's algebra class. A sort of doodle like the one that could preserve from radiation buildings but not people. Bentsen's team had come up with a useful scanner of old light but, as far as T. could tell, no one had yet advanced beyond a focus on his graduation day. Whoever had scanned Pennsylvania Avenue seemed to have gone further, if seeing was believing.

T. refocused the picture. Got a close shot of Mr. Sofield, slightly plumper than he'd been in 1939. He was taking a furtive swig from a silver flask. T. laughed. "So far it all *looks* right. Now"—he turned to Bentsen—"how do I *enter* the picture?"

"You don't. This hasn't happened yet, and when it does happen, you—as you are now—won't be there, as we can plainly see."

"But if I *were* there?"

"You would be two people . . ."

"Or the same person at two different ages. Why can't I, by reversing the coordinates that get me back in time-space to Father Lamy, go forward—in the flesh—to Graduation Day?"

"Because where he was *is* to us—old light that has already been recorded, ready to be viewed or reviewed."

"So if I can get back here from there why can't I keep going forward to Graduation Day?" On the monitor T. watched himself as he took a lovely dark-haired girl in his arms and kissed her on the lips. They were standing somewhat apart from the others, in the shadow of a copper beech. The grown-up T. had got rid of his black robe and was looking pretty neat in blue blazer and white duck trousers.

"Boy." T. whistled as he watched his future self with . . . his future wife?

Bentsen was getting impatient. "From 1880 or whenever to 1939 is perfectly normal. We're traveling on the same road we took to get back there. But we can never go beyond where we started, which happens to be right now. The fact that the technology exists—and I don't really understand it, not my field—to show future images does not mean you yourself can go forward. It is the Great Contradiction. If you're not in that picture to begin with, you're not going to be in that picture, ever, except as a seventeen-year-old."

T. switched off the monitor. He had had enough of Bentsen. He also had the beginning of an idea, something truly radical, a brand-new approach to time-space. He picked up the *Evening Star* and looked for the funny papers.

But when Dr. Bentsen left T. alone in his lab, he dropped the funny papers and began to master, as much as he could, the scanning machine. It had been assembled on the same principle as the Pennsylvania Avenue diorama as well as Father Lamy's single light strand containing the Otowi mesa space-time. But T.'s attempts to go forward kept ending in a sort of visual static. Had it been a fluke, to jump ahead so that he could at least get a two out of four dimensional look at his future self? Or could he now add the third and fourth dimensions to the other two?

T. kept fiddling with the fragment of himself in 1943 and found that he could adjust the picture the way they did in movies, filling the screen with a face or pulling back so that he could see the whole school and graduating class with the unfinished cathedral on the hill. He was beginning now to see how he could break through to a three-dimensional time by . . . A familiar face filled the monitor.

"Veal, darling." Squaw looked mischievous, and a lot like the dark-haired girl at his graduation. "I lost you."

"I got caught up in Father Lamy's experiment. What happened to you?"

"We spent the night at this wonderful inn. Then I did some shopping down in Santa Fe. Turquoises." She held up a brooch. "Pretty?"

"Where did you get the money?"

Squaw giggled and seemed suddenly closer to T. in age. "Well, I guess you'll know sooner or later. This is my home time, the 1880s. So I've got plenty of pin money. Poor Tom's penniless because he's from so much earlier. How do you like operating *my* space-time light-scanner?"

T. was astonished. "You invented this?" He twiddled a knob and Squaw started to disappear.

"Stop that!" The voice was faint. Quickly he dialed her back. "That's better," she said, herself again. "When they brought in Mr. Sofield's algebra test with your equation, Dr. Bentsen couldn't believe what he saw while Mr. Lincoln, well, he's more an administrator and ceramist than physicist, and didn't have a clue as to what it was all about. Anyway, I said, let's get him over here and here you are."

"How did you learn so much physics?"

"Have you any idea how much time we exhibits have on our hands? The poor lieutenant has learned all of Shakespeare by heart and he doesn't even like Shakespeare. But I do. Especially when he plays Romeo . . ."

"I get the point." T. was sharp. "But you need some help on all this . . . I mean you can't just pick it up out of a book."

"How did you pick it up?"

"I didn't. I *see* it first. Then figure out—with figures—what I saw."

"I work with Dr. Bentsen in the evenings, after the exhibits close down, after you've gone to bed. This is a recording by the way."

"Where can I see you . . . How?"

"Why don't you do the official Smithsonian tour? It's time you got to know your new home. End of message. Over and out, Veal darling."

The screen was dark.

———•·•———

The Military Exhibit was a particular favorite with boys, T. noted, wondering if all the torn battle flags, old muskets, and Great War artillery was being deliberately used to get them in the right mood to go fight in the trenches of France again. Lindy, usually so mild, had told T. and Bentsen that he'd like the entire exhibit closed down. Bentsen had looked pained. But he was not about to argue with a national hero who was also on the board of regents.

T. actually enjoyed the exhibit, which started with the French-Indian wars and a majestic plaster Indian labeled King Philip whom T. had read about and then promptly forgot in Mr. Pratt's class.

The hall was lit by a long, gray, glass skylight. The tourists moved clockwise—chronologically—around an oblong hall that resembled the waiting room of a train station. Each of the many wars on display had its own section, with maps, banners, weapons as well as life-size soldiers, sailors, and marines wearing uniforms of the period.

In a row on the wall opposite the entrance was, first, the French-Indian wars; then the Revolution, with a number of highly bizarre flags. Apparently they had had trouble designing an agreed-upon national banner. T. quite liked the one with a twisty snake and the legend "Don't tread on me" but, in the end, the stars and bars had won the day and there sat the kindly Betsy Ross, stitching away in her rocker even though Mr. Sofield had said she had had nothing to do with the flag, while the Canadian, Mr. Pratt, of course said that she had. Since history always involved too many versions and misunderstandings, it had never had much attraction for T. He preferred the demonstrable truths of mathematics and the demonstrable lies of quantum physics that sometimes hid stupendous truths.

After the Revolution—whose exhibit contained General Washington's field tent and bed, both a bit on the fancy side—came the War of 1812 and the Mexican War.

A group of Boy Scouts were listening to a scoutmaster who told them how the evil Mexicans had dared attack the United States and how President Polk had finally declared war when the treacherous Mexicans crossed the Rio Grande into Texas. At the battle of Palo Alto, General Zachary Taylor drove them all back home to Mexico where they belonged in the first place.

T. felt a bit queasy when he saw a beautifully detailed diorama of Buena Vista, with the positions of the American and Mexican forces. He could also hear the scoutmaster's annoyingly nasal voice.

"Although outnumbered four to one, General Zachary Taylor's men defeated the army of Santa Anna in February 1847."

Next to the painting of the battle there were a half dozen dummies in the uniforms of that year—and day? One of them wore the dress uniform of a marine lieutenant.

"Tom?" T. whispered into the pink plaster ear.

"Come to pay us a call?" Tom's whisper was faraway but T. heard him clearly. The Boy Scouts were now moving on to the Civil War, a subject of continuing interest to Washington boys, since the Confederates had nearly captured the city whose population then was just the way it was now, pro-Southern.

"You can see me getting hit in the picture. I'm to the right of that big hill where the cannon's going off. Well, that's supposed to be me, just below, in all that smoke."

T. studied the picture so carefully that he began to become a part of it, smelled harsh gunpowder and dust, and sweat and something awful and sweet.

"Blood," whispered Tom. "It was all over the place. But we won the day and ole Zach Taylor got to be president. Course I was gone by then. Out of the picture, like the Great War boys say."

"What would you have done if . . . if you'd stayed *in* the picture?"

"Like I told you. Gone to settle the territory we stole from the Mexicans. You see Frankie?"

"Not since our trip to Otowi."

"That's a scary place."

T. looked around to make sure no guards were looking. Then he touched the back of Tom's tunic. "Can I look?"

"Sure. That's what we're here for. To be looked at."

T. slid tunic and shirt up several inches and there, on the pale plaster dummy's body, was a painted red scar like the one that he had seen in life—or whatever Tom's state was. T. readjusted the uniform.

"There's a Confederate boy in the next exhibit with no balls. We rile him about it. Take a look."

"No thanks." T. was feeling light-headed: loss of blood? Fumes from battle?

". . . last thing I saw was up there, by the church—see?—I'd been at the back of this cantina with the other marines when I saw the captain up ahead go down, and so I ran to get him and got him—alive, too—he lived to be real old someone told me, I forget where and when, but not me 'cause—

as I was dragging him back I heard this artillery from up there on the hill and when I turned to see what was going on, I was hit like a mule's kick in the small of the back and I saw every sort of star and moon while they drug us both out of the line of fire and then . . ."

But T. had heard enough. Tom was still whispering last earthly memories as T. moved on to the Civil War Exhibit, to the Spanish American War, to the Philippine Pacification—what on earth was *that* all about? A number of wars seemed not to have gotten into the St. Albans history book.

T. liked the uniforms, by and large; the dioramas, too—huge paintings of battles carefully reconstructed, including a 1914 city of Veracruz where President Wilson had sent American troops for reasons that the usually informative placards forgot to mention. But there was a picture of the bandit, Pancho Villa, played by Wallace Beery in a wonderful old movie that had just been reissued. Half the dormitory was now imitating Beery's accent.

The Great War was pretty grim stuff, and T. moved, as quickly as he could, to pass it by, but then morbid fascination caused him to pause at a life-size trench with poison gas masks stacked up and barbed wire strung this way and that. There were no bodies as there were in the picture book at K Street. Plainly, the Smithsonian was not about to show future warriors just how awful that war had been. As a result, the Boy Scouts thought it was all pretty exciting, and spoke knowingly of Richthofen and the other flying aces.

Between the Great War Exhibit and the exit there was a large empty space. Room enough for yet another exhibit? Apparently. To T.'s alarm, behind velvet roping, several men in blue suits were measuring the space and making notes. Something was definitely up. T. thought of the nuclear explosion as viewed from Father Lamy's church. Had that been a mere simulation or a real look at what was, very soon, to come?

"In the unlikely event of another world war," the scout-master was saying, "there is enough space here for a really bang-up exhibit. But one thing you boys can count on, you'll never fight in a foreign war. President Roosevelt has said so."

As usual, there were a number of boos at the mention of the president—Washington boys tended to be Confederates first, Republicans second, and New Dealers never.

T. was about to leave the exhibition hall when he noticed several dummies in a cluster by the door. They were dressed in up-to-date modern uniforms. One was a sailor—the green one who had recently drowned? There was also an aviator, wearing, for some reason, a cavalryman's leggings; then a soldier and a marine and a figure in a green-and-brown loose-fitting uniform, some sort of camouflage, with two hand grenades attached to his belt.

Since this dummy had been propped up by the door, T. was able to get a good look at him. Yes. Something was definitely up. T. had assumed that there was a fifty-fifty chance of stopping this second world war; yet here they were already putting the uniformed dummies into place long before the Americans had fired a single shot. Who had given the order for this exhibit? Suddenly, T. was both angry and alarmed; events were taking their mysterious course without him even though he had been persuaded that in the matter of war or peace he was destined to play a crucial role. Or was he being conned?

T. noticed that the back of the camouflage uniform was torn away, revealing the dummy's back, which had a jagged hole in the plaster that extended through to the stomach, an opening as large as a basketball.

The voice started. It was a whisper, like Tom's. "You got to get me out of here."

"Out of the exhibit?"

"Out of where this happened. You can. Nobody else can."
The hoarse voice was oddly familiar.

"Where did it happen?"

But, at that moment, one of the men in blue suits hurried over to T. "You shouldn't be here, sonny. We're just trying out some new-style plastic models . . ."

"For the next war?"

The man in blue had noted the torn back of the dummy. "What next war? This is the Peacetime American Military Exhibit. We're the best in the world. Undefeated. Invincible. From the halls of Montezuma . . ."

"He's a marine, isn't he?" T. pointed at the dummy, which the man in the blue suit was now dismantling.

"I don't know how this one got mixed in with this peacetime exhibit. Sometimes maintenance is really careless. This belongs with the Great War group . . ."

As the marine's head vanished beneath a burlap wrapping, he whispered, "Save me. Save us."

T. was halfway to his laboratory before he realized why the marine's voice had sounded so familiar—it was his own voice.

———◆———

T. returned to his corner lab, nodding absently to Bentsen, who was in his own section playing what looked like a pinball machine.

On T.'s desk there was a recipe for macaroni and cheese, courtesy of the Smithsonian kitchens. He turned it over and read, in purple ink, "Yes, it was you you saw, what to do?" Then a feathery signature that T. could not decipher. Someone was playing games with him.

If only Lindy would show up and help out; but he was off making speeches. Meanwhile, according to the *Evening Star*, it was now June and the king and queen of England were coming to town to see the president.

T. rang Mr. Sofield. Since it was five in the afternoon, T. could hear the tinkle of ice.

"Mr. Sofield. It's T."

"Are you home in K Street?"

"Should I be?"

"Don't ask me what you should or shouldn't be doing. You said you were going home to your aunts before summer camp."

"Listen. I'm still here in the Smithsonian . . ."

"Smithsonian?" Then Mr. Sofield said to someone, "Yes. You can freshen it while you're up. No ginger ale this time." In the background, the Victrola was playing "Deep Purple," an awful song that Mr. Sofield loved. "Of course I remember all about you and the Smithsonian and that astonishing theorem of yours. Naturally, I had to flunk you in algebra but Mr. Lincoln—could that've really been his name?—was certainly impressed with those doodles of yours and . . ."

"Stanley!" Very rarely did T. address a master by his first name, but this was summer vacation as well as an emergency. "Have I been living in the dormitory and going to school ever since Easter?"

There was silence on the other end of the line; then a tinkle of ice like "Jingle Bells" or Stanley's own special rendering of "Chopsticks."

"Don't you remember?" Mr. Sofield sounded wary.

"Don't *you* remember when it was agreed that I go to work here that when I was finished, no matter how long it would take me, I'd go back to where I started on Good Friday, 1939?"

"Yes, I recall what Mr. Washington said . . ."

"Lincoln . . ."

"But I do know that as far as I can tell you've been right here all this time and we beat Woodrow Wilson High though I can't understand why Dr. Lucas wants us to play ball with the local high schools instead of with other prep schools, the way we used to. Papa Chasseau thinks Lucas is a secret communist."

T. was developing a headache. Was Mr. Sofield as dense as he seemed? Was he drunk? Was T. himself off his rocker? He interrupted, firmly, he hoped. "I've been there all this time . . . ?"

"Right up to the June Commencement. Then that night I took you to the Capitol Theater to hear Artie Shaw . . ."

"How was he?" T. was momentarily sidetracked.

"*You* said he was great. Now." Mr. Sofield took a deep breath; pulled himself together. "I'm sure that Mr. Jefferson told us . . ."

"Lincoln . . ."

"Whomever. Whoever. Do as I say not as I . . . uh, say. We were told that when your work was—is—oh, what a problem we're going to have with tenses this year—finished at the Smithsonian that you would return to the exact moment you arrived there, on that particular Friday. Well, all I can say is the Great Emancipator kept his word. You have never been gone from here except for that one short trip by cab on the Easter weekend."

T. stared at the monitor in front of him. As of today, his day, Pennsylvania Avenue was suddenly visible. In an open car, in vivid color, the red-faced president Roosevelt towered over the small brown-faced king of England beside him. Sweating crowds were waving American and British flags.

"I can see the parade for the king."

"From the Smithsonian?"

"Yes. Only we get it on a monitor. Like television—remember?—the thing they showed at the World's Fair. Listen." T. was beginning to lose all grip on reality. "Am I any different?"

"Different from what?"

"From before Easter. That isn't me, you know, the one you've been seeing for the last three months."

"Of course it's you." Mr. Sofield had now pulled himself together. "I can't say I really believed it possible when—you-know-who said you'd be restored as you were once your work was done with, but then, obviously, your work was completed and we got you back without a break in the semester for either of us."

"Stanley, I'm still here, and it's June here and it's June there."

"For a genius—which is what *they* call you—you're a bit slow, dear T. You're still there because they still need you. When they don't need you, they'll send you back, as they already have done from *our* point of view. Oh, these tenses. Dear God. And you barely passing English. Anyway, don't worry. You'll be back."

"But I'm getting older here. I've got two hickeys."

"You've got two here, too. Now we bachelors are about to propose a toast to the king and queen." Stanley broke the connection.

On T.'s way back to his room, he noticed that the door next to his was ajar. He pushed it open; the room was empty. The boy who had looked like him was gone. He wondered now why he had never tried to get to know him. Were the other five gone, too?

T. knocked at the door next to the empty room, which was opened by a sleepy version of himself. "I was asleep," said the other T. "Come on in."

The room—like the boy—was identical. "So," said T., "who are you?"

"Who are you?" This wasn't helpful. The other T. offered him a Coca-Cola.

T., briefly, explained their situation to his look-alike.

The other T. did not seem very interested. "Yeah. I guess we all know that much."

"All?"

"The six of us who live in these rooms, only we lost one the day you moved in."

"You think he's the one that got sent back to St. Albans?"

"I don't think *anything* around here. It's not worth it. We play basketball down in the basement mostly. You're the one things happen to. We're what they call the pawns in that Parcheesi game they got in the basement." T. wondered if he talked with quite as heavy a southern accent as his . . . copy?

"So you weren't with me in the Indian exhibit?"

"So who's you? *We* saw it, if that's what you mean. Kind of dumb, those plaster models."

"And Squaw . . . ?"

"Lot of ugly squaws, yeah."

"Frankie?"

"Who?"

T. was relieved that he was still a single entity and not, like an amoeba, one of seven exactly identical parts with a shared memory. "Who's responsible for all of us?"

"Beats me. You play basketball?"

"Yeah. Who were you before you came here?"

"You." The other T. named the three aunts, as well as Stanley Sofield's favorite booze, Queen Anne Scotch.

"You remember everything I did all my life?"

"I guess I do as much as you do or anybody ever does. What pisses us off is the hanging around we have to do, while you're having all the fun."

"Am I?" Suddenly T. found himself tapping an old memory. "When velocity is so great, two things at different times are at the same time."

"Minkowski," replied the other T. Then the boy frowned. "Who's Minkowski?"

"It is possible that you *in yourself*"—T. was making pictures in his head—"and I, *in myself*, at a certain velocity, turn into just shadows and only a kind of union of the two of us retains an independent existence?"

"I can see why you flunked that algebra test, the one *I'm* going to have to retake. You've got the screw loose, I guess. Anyway, I think the one from the empty room next to yours is the one back at St. Albans."

"So when did you—all of you, that is—get here?"

"Don't know. Can't remember. I guess when you did. But we still can't figure out why Dr. Smithson needs so many of us. One's more than enough, I'd say. Particularly the one who's a genius, which is you. We're all just the same, kind of average except at baseball. Of course they take a lot of tissue from us in the labs. To make more clones, I guess, though God knows why—or maybe I should say Dr. Smithson knows why."

"Dr. Smithson?"

"He's this English guy who gave the United States all that money to build this place so as to, you know, civilize the country."

T.'s mouth was suddenly dry. "But . . ." He swallowed; hard. "He's been dead over a hundred years."

The other T. laughed. "Well, you know what the old-timers around here say? 'You can't be fired from here just 'cause you're dead.' "

"You ever see Dr. Smithson?"

"No. But I know where his office is. It's under the basketball court. There's a sign in front of it that says HOME. You know, where the game ends when the winner's four pawns get to home base."

———•—•———

Squaw was waiting for T. in his room. Thoughtfully, she had taken off all her clothes and so they were able to begin promptly, the way he liked it, without all the buttonhole, knotted-ribbon foreplay that jangled boyish nerves. Then . . .

Exhausted, they lay back on the bed. "Darling Veal," she murmured in his ear.

"Squaw," he whispered, not the easiest word to whisper he decided.

"Did you visit the exhibits today?"

"Just the military one where I saw Tom. I talked to him, sort of."

"Ghostly, isn't it? The way those dummies can talk to you like that. I stay away when they're on exhibit. But when they're not, they can be loads of fun."

"Where do you meet?"

"Different places. In Santa Fe. La Fonda's nice. I go there with Tom. And sometimes with this Confederate captain I like. He was at Fredericksburg. Not much older than you. What did you and Tom talk about?"

T. was not aware that he'd said anything. "I must have been talking to myself. I mean that's what I've been doing all morning. The boy two doors down from me. He's me, without the math."

Squaw was now in the bathroom, tidying up.

"I can't think why they need so many of you. *I* might, of course." Squaw laughed, a very sexy laugh.

T. never tired of watching Squaw, *his* squaw, as well as Tom's, and now a Confederate captain's and the young Early American brave's and . . . Could she possibly be one of those nymphomaniacs he had read about in a book one of the boys had smuggled into the dorm?

She came back into the bedroom, carrying a wet towel; she tidied him up, which excited him.

"Don't," he said. "I better do that." T. took the towel; he wondered why Squaw had hair under her arms while none of the ladies in the movies ever had any. Was this the fashion in 1886? He was still trying to think of a way to ask her that

wouldn't sound rude when she said: "As far as I can tell"—
she pulled on her slip; she wore no bra—"you're an experiment. Nothing like you has ever happened around here
during my time. So I suppose they brought you in for that
awful bomb . . ."

"But they couldn't care less about my saving most of the
people while blowing up the buildings."

"Angel Veal, the whole point to war is to get your hands
on the buildings and to get rid of the people who live in
them. Anyway, according to Dr. Bentsen—that old lecher,
how he does come on!—you're really needed, he says, according to Dr. Oppenheimer—now *he's* quite attractive if
you like older men—because you can show them how to
limit the something-or-other reaction."

"Chain reaction. Yeah. That was easy. They're all pretty
dumb, you know. Einstein isn't, but then he's off on this
wild-goose chase, trying to explain everything. A *unified* field
theory. Well, if he could just begin to see what I see in my
head, he'd give up. There's no such thing. How could there
be when there's no unity?"

Squaw was staring at him with awe. "How do you . . ."

"I don't know *how* I do it, but I do it. Everything out there
is sort of all the same but with special differences that don't—
aren't supposed to—add up. At least in the really dumb way
most people add and subtract. Listen . . ." T. had not meant
to tell Squaw about his encounter in the Military Exhibit.
Too scary, the more he thought about it. But he couldn't help
himself.

"I'm listening, Veal."

"There was this dummy by the door, next to the Great War
Exhibit, and he had this hole in his back, worse than Tom's . . ."

"Don't." Squaw shuddered. "I know most of us are dead
and gone long ago except you, of course, and the tourists and
the daytime personnel but even so, it's best just to accept
things as they are and not go snooping."

"I think," said T., a new thought forming, "that I'm here to snoop. Anyway this dummy started that awful whispering like the other soldier boys . . ."

Squaw was now looking very pale, as if she was going to be ill. "Let's order dinner, in the room."

"Well, he wanted me to get him out of wherever he was. I guess he meant wherever he was when he got killed, and he sounded so familiar, you know? Like I knew him."

"Did you? Do you?"

"Yeah. He's me."

There was a long moment as Squaw, now fully clothed, sat at the dressing table and arranged her hair. T. waited to hear what she had—been instructed?—to say. A view of the vast Parcheesi board beneath the Castle and the Mall popped into his head. BLOCKADE in huge red letters on a bright yellow square.

"Veal. I think you're getting in over your head here. Yes, you're a genius and all that and the lab people are very grateful for your help and all that, but there are things we're not supposed to know."

"Then why"—T. was suddenly pedantic—"do we know them?"

"Accidents happen even in the best run universe."

"So whose decision was it to bring me here and make so many copies—pointless copies since none of these other me's knows any physics?"

"Mr. Lincoln's in charge of the day-by-day administration . . ."

"What about Dr. Smithson?"

Squaw turned from the dressing table mirror to face T. directly. "Dr. Smithson died in England long before even I was born."

"One of the boys told me he had seen him." T. lied in a good cause.

Squaw laughed and rang for the waiter. "That's all an act, for the tourists. I didn't know they still did it. Someone dresses up as Dr. Smithson and shows the tourists around this reproduction of his original laboratory back in the 1820s."

"Under the basketball court?"

"What in the name of heaven is a basketball court?" Squaw was mysteriously amused.

"Down in the basement. It's where the boys play."

"Your duplicates?"

"That's right . . ."

"Maybe I should take a look at *them*." Squaw suddenly sounded like Mae West in the movies.

"Why bother when you've got me?"

The waiter appeared and proposed meat loaf with mashed yellow turnips and creamed pearl onions.

———

For the next few days T. worked so hard in his lab that he was in bed each night before Squaw and the other exhibits came to life. He also talked several times with Mr. Sofield, who reported on the activities of his St. Albans self. Presently both the other T. and Mr. Sofield would be off to summer camp. T. thought wistfully of the many long days on the baseball diamond, never to be his.

Work was now going so well that Dr. Oppenheimer paid him what the aunts would call a courtesy call.

"I think you've eliminated, well—minimized, the risk of an uncontrolled chain reaction."

"I've eliminated it entirely because . . ." T. punched out the basic equation on his monitor. "Well, look." Atom after atom broke serially until T.'s control stopped them on cue.

Dr. Oppenheimer seemed convinced but, as T. had discovered, he was something of a nervous Nelly, unlike Professors

Fermi and Bohr, who had sent T. a joint telegram of con-
gratulation, doubtless saving money.

"So I guess you won't be needing me anymore." T. was
tentative. On the one hand, despite fun with Squaw, he was
just about ready to go home if not to the Parcheesi Home;
but only just about ready because he was now—he could
feel the familiar tingling—on the verge of a breakthrough
in time-space. If successful, he might yet stop the fast-
approaching war. The president had only that morning sworn
a mighty oath: there would be no war involving the United
States. This meant, as everyone in Washington knew, that
there would be an all-out war any minute now.

"Well, from my point of view"—Dr. Oppenheimer lit his
pipe—"your job is done, well done, too. Your other project . . ." He paused.

"Eliminating buildings but not people . . ."

"Is simply not in the cards. I like it. But the War Department doesn't."

"What about the president?"

"That's not the sort of thing that interests him. Anyway,
he's busy running for reelection next year."

"A *third* term?"

"Yes. *We* stay out of politics." Dr. Oppenheimer gave him
a warning look.

T. wondered just how far he dared go with the great man.
If he were to alarm him, he would be dismissed from the
Smithsonian. That was certain. T. made himself sound offhand. "You know, sir, I've been doing some work on space-
time . . ."

Dr. Oppenheimer indulged in one of his rare thin smiles.
"How you youngsters love the notion of time travel."

This was, T. thought, pretty condescending, but he played
dumb. "Well, I can't say that I don't like the idea, but as a
question of quantum physics I think we can go beyond, way
beyond, Einstein's general relativity theory."

"Why not? Go to it." Plainly T. was losing Dr. Oppenheimer's attention.

"You see, sir, he's wrong about so much. He doesn't accept indeterminacy and that's the name of our game." T. abandoned caution. After all, he *saw* what others could only enumerate. "The universe is random even if it were a universe and not a multiverse. Max Planck was starting to get it right."

Dr. Oppenheimer was staring at T. "Where did you study all this?"

"Well, if you know how to read *Popular Mechanics*—you know, the magazine—it's all in there in a messy kind of way. One thing that seems true is that there is no real difference between past and future in quantum physics. I think I know how to reverse the motion of particles to what was." T. smiled nervously. "That's why *I* am T."

Dr. Oppenheimer was frowning now. "You were named for the T. that reverses the direction of motion of all particles? For Time itself?"

"Nicknamed."

"By whom?"

"By me."

"This is not really my field . . ." Dr. Oppenheimer trailed off; then with wonder, "*Popular Mechanics*. All right. T., you're here. See if you can outdo Einstein."

"I need some new equipment. I've made a list." T. opened the drawer to his desk and took out a yellow legal-size pad that he gave the doctor, who whistled when he saw what T. had written.

"This is about a hundred thousand dollars' worth of equipment!"

"The War Department . . ."

"Won't give you a penny unless my colleagues and I approve this and we won't."

"Why not?"

"Aside from your lack of standing, we have too little time as it is to develop the bomb before Hitler does."

"But if my calculations are correct we can reorganize time, or at least a section of it, and prevent the war."

Dr. Oppenheimer smiled and shook his head. "You mean go back in time and smother baby Hitler in his crib?"

"Too corny and, I suspect, on this particular highway, there would be another one just like him, maybe even worse. But I do think a number of events could be so changed at one of the—well, crossroads along the way so that we'd then have no war where nuclear weapons were developed and used."

On the word "crossroads" Oppenheimer had suddenly sat up very straight. "What is a crossroad in time?"

"Just that. As past events veer in one direction, history takes one of a number of roads. In our case the road is leading to a second world war and to nuclear weapons, which, with or without a chain reaction, will eventually destroy the planet for us."

"Shiva." Dr. Oppenheimer shuddered.

"I don't know anything about Shiva. But I do know I'm going to need help with the history of the road we're on now so that I can pick the right crossroad when I come to it and then change things . . ."

"No one has ever been able to interact with the past. We can look at it for what it is now, old images on old light, but to . . . Well, T., to enter what *was* would require energy close to light's speed."

T. nodded. "One hundred eighty-six thousand miles per second should do the trick. Anyway, someone right here has already interacted. At least once."

"I think there was such a case. A botched job, I believe. Anyway, it was more accident than science, which means no . . . highway." Dr. Oppenheimer shook T.'s hand warmly. "You'll be getting a special citation from the president and a scholarship to Cal Tech, though I think it might be wiser simply to give you the *Popular Mechanics* chair in quantum physics."

T. was now desperate. "Look. If I can raise the money, fast, can I set up my own lab?"

"How do you mean to raise it?"

"That's my business, sir."

"Well, if it costs *us* nothing, go to it." At the door, he paused. "Shiva is the Hindu god who will destroy this cycle of time . . . this highway . . . and then, without us, who or what will measure time? What need for T.?"

Dr. Oppenheimer left. T. addressed the wall. "Funny how they don't see what's right here." He touched the wall. "Us but not us. The mirror universe is always next to us."

———•◦•———

The blind secretary welcomed T. by name. Did she recognize his voice? "Mr. Lincoln is expecting you. Do go in."

T. entered the office, where he found Mr. Lincoln at his desk with several large dark volumes open before him. He seemed to be weeping, or, perhaps, it was just a standard District of Columbia allergy. As T. entered, he blew his nose.

"So what is this matter of some . . ." Lincoln looked at T.'s note to him. ". . . urgency?"

T. sat in the chair opposite the world's leading authority on ceramics and spoke of his urgent need for equipment.

Lincoln heard him out; then observed, "Dr. Bentsen has already filled me in on some of the details. Certainly, within our very limited budget, you know how Congress is, we cannot request anything—in your department, that is—which does not hasten the astonishing even fundamental day we go nuclear."

"Suppose"—T. took the plunge—"that I paid for the equipment."

Mr. Lincoln smiled a kindly smile. "I didn't know schoolboys got so much allowance nowadays."

"They don't." T. gave Mr. Lincoln the Briggs Bank statement.

Mr. Lincoln whistled when he saw the size of the deposit. "Who gave you all this money?"

"The bank. By mistake."

"Oh." Mr. Lincoln seemed relieved. "Then they've probably corrected their error by now and got it all back. These things happen, you know. According to Carl Sandburg—a magical writer"—Mr. Lincoln tapped one of the books on his desk—"President Lincoln was afraid no one would take the new dollars—the so-called greenbacks—when they were first issued because he didn't realize that the value of money depends entirely on the confidence people have in the persons or country issuing it, not on the paper itself."

"How true," said T., wondering why hardly anything Mr. Lincoln said ever made much sense except when he was on the subject of pots.

"Suppose," said T., fearful that Mr. Lincoln was going to read aloud from Sandburg, "the money is still in my account. Suppose I then turned it all over to the Smithsonian as a gift. Then, as a Junior Benefactor, I could have my equipment, couldn't I?"

"That would be highly irregular. Give me your checkbook." T. complied. Briskly, Mr. Lincoln spoke to the blind secretary on the intercom. "Get the manager at Briggs Bank and ask if check number"—Mr. Lincoln read off the number of one of T.'s blank checks—"to the amount of one hundred thousand and one dollars will be honored as a special bequest to the Smithsonian Institution."

Then he put down the receiver and began, as T. knew that he would, to read.

" 'Evergreen carpeted the stone floor of the vault. On the coffin set in a receptacle of black walnut they arranged flowers carefully and precisely . . .' How marvelously poet Sandburg sings his lays! and these, my boy, are lays mightier than Homer's . . . 'they poured flowers as symbols, they lavished heaps of fresh flowers as though there could never be enough to fill either their hearts or his. And the night came with great quiet. And there was rest. The prairie years, the war years, were over.' " Mr. Lincoln had been reduced by Mr. Sandburg to tears. He blew his nose like a trumpet. "Never again," he sobbed, "will there be such a man, or such a poet to sing his lay."

The blind secretary poked her head in the door. She was triumphant. "Bingo, Mr. Lincoln. Bull's-eye. They fell for it hook, line, and sinker."

"Never," murmured Mr. Lincoln so softly that T. could barely hear him, "give a sucker an even break."

"The hundred thousand and one bucks are, even now as we palaver, already entering the Smithsonian piggy bank." The blind secretary shut the door. Mr. Lincoln opened his desk drawer and removed what looked like a diploma with a huge red and gold seal. Then he wrote in T.'s name and rose to his full awesome height.

"My boy, you have just become a Junior Benefactor, first class, of this Institution. Cherish this document and the distinction for which it stands, one nation totally invisible under glass . . ."

"What if the bank finds out their mistake?"

"Finders keepers is the first law of species as well as of specie." Mr. Lincoln smiled contentedly. "Besides, the money is for the heart of the nation—the Smithsonian, the holiest of all our tabernacles with, may I say, the finest trust lawyers as ever gave chase to the swiftest hearse."

Bentsen had already been told by the comptroller's office that T. now had a hundred thousand and one dollars' worth of credit for his lab. He was suitably amazed.

"I don't know how you got the money out of them, but here's your audit sheet."

T. looked with pleasure on the numbers next to his name. "When can I start ordering?"

"Now, if you like." Bentsen showed T. how to fill out the proper requisition forms. "But you won't have enough room here for everything."

"I know," said T., who already had a plan for his new lab, far away from the sharp and not always friendly eyes of Drs. Oppenheimer and Bentsen.

Once the paperwork was done and an "especial" War Department hurry-up seal attached, T. said, "You know I haven't really seen half the exhibits here."

Bentsen looked at him blankly. "Exhibits? You mean the old junk for the public? Mr. Lincoln's pots. The Persian rugs."

"I saw the Military Exhibit."

Bentsen chuckled in a most disdainful way. "They won't have the space for what we're coming up with." He lowered his voice, though there was no one else except T. in the lab. "A *nuclear* submarine. How does that grab you?"

This war, T. said to himself, yet again, must not take place.

In the Hall of Aviation he half hoped to see Lindy but there was no one there except the guards, closing up for the night. Presently the exhibits would be coming alive.

T. hurried along the Parcheesi basement to the Military Exhibit. He was going to need Tom for what he had in mind. But he took a wrong turning—or did the wrong turning take him? There seemed to be, in the final analysis, no entirely wrong turnings at the Smithsonian: the Parcheesi game had been fixed.

T. climbed two flights of stairs and found himself in the Hall of Presidents. There were still a few tourists wandering about and the living guards had not yet been replaced by wax.

Like most boys brought up in Washington, T. disliked politics in general and officeholders in particular. Since at least a quarter of the boys at St. Albans were political children, there were many lively fights between the "cave dwellers," the politicos' contemptuous word for native Washingtonians, and the outsiders that the even-year elections brought to town in ever greater hordes. Now, in joyous preparation for war, a huge super War Department was being planned, while the cardboardlike "temporary" Great War naval buildings were being shored up.

Only T. could stop this, he thought grimly, because only he had the means and a plan . . . except that the plan was really nothing much more than a notion. In principle, he knew how to enter the past, but where and when and then— *what* to do? Long ago Einstein had been exciting on the subject of time-space, making it sound as if the past-present-future *could* interact. But then, according to T.'s reading of an article in *Popular Mechanics,* Heisenberg had grasped the randomness of quantum mechanics, opening a door in T.'s imagination, already hooked on relativity as opposed to Einstein's cop-out for unity, which was, T. knew, the last thing that the universe—that word again! try multiverse—was all about.

Confronted by a large statue of George Washington, T. suddenly had one of his hard-to-tell-where-they-come-from flashes. The four-dimensional coordinates of time-space were suddenly clear to him. Once he had the energy to transfer mass, himself, he could not so much enter as *cross over* into one of innumerable parallel pasts. Presently, he'd have the energy. Then . . .

T. stared at a pair of Washington's stockings in a glass case. The general must have been enormous. T. then looked with no particular interest at the various images of the first president that began the exhibition, which, fittingly, ended with a small portrait of the current president, so much detested in K Street and by Lindy and, if he was as eager for war as people said, by all the versions of T., which, if the dummy was to be believed, were going to end up with a basketball-size hole in their common back.

The second flash came to him as he stepped in front of President Buchanan, a celebrity at St. Albans because, nonentity that he was elsewhere, his niece Harriet T. Lane had given a building to the school and her portrait occupied the place of honor on the black wood paneling of the school's entrance hall.

Buchanan had white hair and a sort of crick in his neck. He had never married (the boys feared the worst), and so Harriet had acted as his hostess. Gazing into Buchanan's benign sheeplike face, T. suddenly realized that the colony of time into which he had been born (or to which he had been arbitrarily assigned?) was itself being manipulated—even as he stood in the Hall of Presidents—by someone else. For a moment, his face became icy cold and he thought he was going to pass out. Then, shakily, he sat down on a bench next to Buchanan and opposite the curator of pots himself, Abe Lincoln.

T. collected thoughts that were starting to scatter. He studied the gloomy president in the painting before him. He was reputedly dead, while his Smithsonian counterpart was more or less alive and a bit of a dope except at fund-raising. Of course, the manipulator need not be in the Institution. There was the crew-cut, thin-lipped Dr. Oppenheimer from Cal Tech. He knew all of the interested parties—admittedly few—whom T. had also met or studied. But Oppenheimer had no grasp of something as elementary, to T., as chain reaction, something your average master of time–space could have worked out upon the easily accessible curvature of light, which was more or less like a movie in its dull two dimensions.

No. Whoever was playing with time was, of course, playing with T. as well. The whole business of getting him to the Castle on Good Friday, with a promise to return him home at the instant of his departure, was typical of what someone who had worked out a part of the theory might think do-able. But there was much more to the theory than his rival—enemy?—seemed to know. There were all sorts of signs, as well as sines and cosines, that T. had been unconsciously read-ing since his arrival, and they indicated, like so many alarm bells, that his rival was more at sea than either suspected. The business of a half dozen versions of T. was the sort of error that an amateur would make. One would have been enough, at a time. At a *time*. At *any* time. At *this* time. At *that* time. Time? T. had a giddy feeling that he was beginning to surpass his rival. Was it Dr. Bentsen? *He* almost knew enough. If only poor Lindy had any gift for this sort of thing . . .

T. entered the Assembly of First Ladies, a row of headless dummies in their inaugural finery. Back of each dummy was a portrait of the original lady in her gown.

T. was struck by how small and dumpy most of the girls had been. Mrs. Washington was a sort of dwarf, wide as she was high. Only Mrs. Roosevelt, up at the far end of the line, was tall and impressive.

Dutifully, T. made his way past the dummies. The outside light was now fading into evening, and the tourists were gone. Presently, the guards would be replaced by wax.

At about the middle of the line, T. heard a familiar whis-per. "Veal."

In front of T. was a headless dummy like all the others ex-cept that this one had a tightly cinched-in waist, long gloves, and a sheer covering over the shoulders which made her look as if she had nothing on when she was actually swathed like a mummy. T. stepped behind her to get a good look at the painting of the original, which turned out to be Mrs. Grover Cleveland, born Frank Folsom, daughter of Cleveland's law partner in Buffalo. When she was old enough, the sign said, she had changed the fanciful Frank to Frances, but the whole country persisted in calling her, lovingly, Frankie, while her husband called her Frank. In 1886, she married the twenty-second president in the White House. The president was forty-nine. Squaw was twenty-two.

As T. read, he heard a woman to his right say, very distinctly, "Chicken hawk!" T. looked at the portrait of the first lady after Squaw and there was Mrs. Benjamin Harrison, wife to the twenty-third president and the woman who had welcomed him to the Smithsonian. According to her sign, she had been a preacher's daughter.

Then T. heard a second "Veal." This one from just beyond Mrs. Harrison. He moved on to the next dummy, which proved to be a second Squaw, as of 1893.

"I knew all along, after Grover lost to Harrison in 1888, that we'd win the next election. And so we did!" Squaw's voice was becoming more and more distinct as the natural light in the hall faded and the headless ladies began, mysteriously, to gleam and become . . . real?

"After we lost to the Harrisons, I told the servants in the White House"—this came from the twenty-two-year-old Frank, also known as Frances, Folsom Cleveland—"you keep everything in apple-pie order now because four years from today the president and I are coming back."

"Vile, abominable chicken hawk!" Mrs. Harrison, as new lights came on, was human again; fat filling up her bodice and puffed sleeves while small red eyes glared at Squaw, who simply laughed. "Jealous, Caroline?"

"You disgrace us all."

"Do go home, Caroline. And switch on the electric lights if you dare." Mrs. Harrison flounced through a door just back of her; then slammed it hard.

T. saw that, all up and down the line of first ladies, shadowy doors had appeared back of them, rather like the doors to the rows of old houses in Lafayette Park across from the White House.

Down the line, at the far end, Mrs. Washington waited, head held regally high, as two liveried black men holding candelabras opened the door for her to enter.

"Does this go on every evening?"

"Yes. But we all keep strict union hours, thanks to Grover, the workingman's pal." Squaw was going through her handbag. "Let's hope I haven't left my key inside. If I have, we'll have to get in by way of our second administration." She pointed to her older self, two doors up the line, who gave a friendly wave as she disappeared into the second administration house.

But Squaw found her key and let T. into a handsome front parlor that may or may not have been like one of those in the White House as of 1886. Carefully, she turned up the gas lamps, illuminating a number of pictures of Buffalo, New York, hometown to her and the president.

"Gosh," said T. "It's like . . . an old movie."

"Well, I can't say I've ever seen an old or even a new movie but I do know about magic lantern shows. I can't think why, but I still prefer gaslight to electric light. More flattering, I guess." In what must have been her wedding gown, she looked young and playful. "You know, right after we left in '89, they finally put electricity in the White House, and the Harrisons, a pair of rubes hired by Wall Street to impersonate a Mr. and Mrs. President, were so scared of it that they never dared switch the lights off at night, so they'd spend the whole night every night all lit up until the staff came in the morning to turn them off. Grover!" she called.

From the next room, a man's voice. "Yes, dear. I'll be right in . . ."

"He reads all day. But at least he comes home. I don't think Mrs. Lincoln has ever seen her husband since she got here, while Mrs. Washington prefers her hen parties. They really are so stuck-up, those original girls, except for Dolley Madison, who's full of jokes and is very nice to us later first ladies, unlike Mrs. Monroe, who thinks she's Queen Victoria. Anyway, those girls at the end of the line stay pretty much put, just as those of us in the middle stick together, except for Caroline Harrison, of course, and then there's Mrs. Roosevelt, up there at the end of the line, so lonely. But, of course she isn't really *entirely* there, since she's still very much alive and living in the White House."

"How does she do both?"

"The same way, I suppose, that there were all those versions of you for a while. After all, there are three of me. Here I am twenty years old . . ."

"Twenty-two. I'm a mathematician, Squaw."

"Then there's me up the line as I was six years later at Grover's second inauguration. She's the one that Mr. Cleveland really prefers because they have so much more in common, you know? Like all those years together in the White House."

"Where's the third you?"

"Living in Princeton and very, very old."

"So you're not dead?"

"Not yet."

"What happens to you here when you're finally dead in Princeton?"

"I *think* I get a lot more memories. We both will. The other Frances that is. We'll know everything the old lady got to know after we checked in here." Squaw looked mischievous. "Grover says she's remarried. To a Princeton professor. An archaeologist. Grover seems so offhand but he's really terribly jealous." Squaw picked up a photograph of what looked to be a plain middle-aged version of herself. "That's Mother. Emma Folsom. Everyone thought Grover would marry her, *including* her. Then he announced I was the one. Oh, what a scandal that was."

An Irish butler brought them lemonade and cake. "Even so, it's funny how different we are. We're the same person yet we seem to have different memories of almost everything that we do share in common, like growing up in Buffalo, or like the day when we were eleven and Father was thrown from his buggy and killed and Mr. Cleveland, his law partner, looked after Mother and me—us."

"Does your . . . the other Mrs. Cleveland, go gadding around like you do?"

"No, Frankie is much too much the dignified first lady and politician to have . . . adventures."

For an instant, "chicken hawk" reverberated in T.'s head. At least Squaw was taking full advantage of the institutional facilities, of which his chickenhood was one. "I got the money," he said.

"For the lab?" Squaw knew of his hopes.

"Yeah. Only I want to get everything out of here."

"Too much Dr. Bentsen?"

"Too much all of them. I thought maybe I'd set up near Father Lamy at Otowi. He's on the right track, too, but way behind, of course, stuck back in . . . when was it we saw him?"

"Eighteen eighty-six. That was the summer I married President Cleveland. Right after, I took a trip out west to see some relatives, and met you."

"No. You met me here."

"But I also met you there, in my time not your time."

T. was now getting a clearer picture of what it was Minkowski was *seeing* when velocity became so great that two different things, though at different times, become the same. T. was 1939. Squaw was 1886. Luckily for him, whoever had prepared the Old Western American Exhibit had given T. permanent access to 1886, as well as to Squaw, who actually belonged there, and to anyone else who visited the exhibit. Unless the whole thing was some sort of a simulation for the general public. Otherwise . . .

"What would happen if I burned down old Sante Fe?"

"But you didn't."

"But I could. So wouldn't that show up in newspapers and history books?"

"Really, Veal! Don't be childish! That's the old what-if game. You know? For want of a nail something or other was lost. But it doesn't work when the track is down and the track is already down back there for good. You can't affect it. No one can."

Why, T. wondered, was she so certain? Grover Cleveland entered from the next room. He was a perfect cube of a man, wide as he was tall, with a walrus-style mustache; he wore an orange suit and carried a thick book in one hand. "Happy to make your acquaintance, Master Veal. Mrs. Cleveland speaks very highly of you, sir. Very highly indeed."

T. was somewhat awed as the great man shook his hand. "Gosh," he said, "I've never met a president before."

"Well, around here it's hard to meet anything but." Cleveland sounded a bit sour. T. wondered if he—if any of them—grasped the fact that they were just a lot of names in the history books. Of course, Squaw knew what was what and she decided to take the whole thing as a joke; she was also having too much fun with all the soldiers and Indian boys in the exhibits to fret. No wonder Mrs. Harrison was green-eyed with envy.

"Sit down, my boy. Frank, I'll have some whisky." As Squaw prepared him a drink, Cleveland held up the book. "Allan Nevins. Have you read him? He's written a splendid biography of me. Lot of mistakes, naturally, when you're writing about what went on long before your own time." Cleveland opened the book to the title page. "He published this in 1932 . . . Which was . . . ? How long after I moved in here?" T. began to get gooseflesh. When you came right down to it, he was trapped with a bunch of ghosts.

"Darling Grover, you died in 1908. My heart broke." Squaw gave him whisky.

Cleveland turned to T. "As you might imagine, we presidents spend a lot of time reading the latest biographies about ourselves."

"I know," said T. "Mr. Lincoln is reading Carl Sandburg for about the fifth time."

"Crackpot," said Cleveland.

"Sandburg or President Lincoln?"

"Neither, as far as I know. No, I mean the functionary in charge of pots here at the Institution. I can't think why the management doesn't get him to change his name and shave off that beard. President Lincoln may have been a Republican and an unsavory lawyer for the railroad magnates, but he was nothing like this imbecile."

"Sir, were you in the Civil War?"

"No, Master Veal. I had two brothers in the war, which left me with a mother and two sisters to support. I bought me a replacement for a hundred and fifty dollars. You could do that *t* en."

"Thank heaven!" Squaw gazed at her husband fondly. "The reason Grover was such a great president was that he wasn't one of those terrible generals that came after Mr. Lincoln, every last one a crook!"

"Not all of them, dear." Cleveland seemed a kindly man.

"Do you see a lot of them, sir? The other presidents?"

Squaw laughed and answered for her husband. "They *never* see each other except by accident . . ."

"Now that's not exactly true, Frank. General Washington and Jemmy Madison are thick as thieves. Then there are the special convocations when we get together."

"In a blue moon," said Squaw.

President Cleveland put down his empty glass; picked up his book. "I've got to show Frank this. The other Frank, that is." He chuckled. "Professor Nevins calls me 'John Bunyan's Valiant-for-Truth transferred to the nineteenth century.' Nice to have met you, Master Veal." He kissed Squaw's cheek. "I'll be having supper at the other house. Can't think now why we were so hard on those poor Mormons with all their wives." Then he was on his way up the line.

T. was wide-eyed. "He's got two houses and two wives. The other presidents must be really jealous."

"About the two houses, yes. At least Ben Harrison is, that second-rater. To have to live between *two* Cleveland houses kills him. On the other hand, any married president who served two terms is going to end up with two wives, one for each inaugural gown that's on display here. But he'll have only the one house as they all served continuously, without a four-year break, like us."

"So each has a younger and an older model of the same wife."

This sounded like too much to T.—like having three aunts in K Street.

"Not always. Poor Mr. Wilson had two different wives. As of now, the second one is still alive, but when she joins us— first she has to hand over her dress to the exhibit—it'll be hell for him. You see, the first Mrs. Wilson was Miss Meek and Mild and died in the White House while number two is a battle-ax. I can't wait to pay a call on the two of them."

"So the first ladies do see each other?"

"Oh, yes. We're not at all like the boys, who are so prickly about who's who, and who's just rated the best biography." Squaw smiled sweetly. "I must say, I haven't seen Grover so pleased in a coon's age—with Mr. Nevins."

T. picked up a model of the Statue of Liberty from the piano.

"That," said Squaw, "was stuck in New York Harbor in October 1886, right after I got back from Sante Fe. Very French, isn't it?"

"They all know you there, don't they?" T. suddenly had an idea.

"I'm usually incognito. But, yes, I suppose they all do because I have to have Tom or another military aide when I go anyplace alone. Come on to bed."

Squaw led him by the hand through the president's library and then into a bedroom with a view of the South Lawn of the White House as it had looked in 1886.

T. was nervous. "Suppose Mr. Cleveland comes back?"

"He won't. He'll be with me—the other me, in the other house. And even if he did, he wouldn't care. That is one of the advantages of being . . ." Squaw stepped out of her dress.

"Being dead?" T. unbuttoned his shirt.

"Being an exhibit is a more gracious way of putting it. After all, we're pretty lively when we're not on display." She held his hand. "Yes, I'll help you move your lab to the mesa."

———◆———

Bentsen was not pleased. "I can't think why you'd want to leave here where we have everything you could need." But everything that T. would need had so filled his small lab that Bentsen and T. were obliged to sit on wooden crates.

"I have asthma," said T. "The air's wonderful out there in New Mexico . . ."

"How can it be? It's just an exhibit like all the others. You've got the same air-conditioning there that we get here."

"No. It's real, that place."

"To you." Bentsen was cryptic. He then offered T. more space in the main lab but T. firmly declined.

Since T. was not eager to revisit the Military Exhibit—he was still spooked by the backless boy—Squaw volunteered to get him Tom as well as a pair of soldiers to help load the equipment onto the train that left from the Train Exhibit for the Indian Territories. T. had already spoken to Father Lamy on the monitor. The priest was delighted to have him as a neighbor. "You can use the old church building," he said. "It's just across the road from me. I've also got some interesting news for you."

Two nights later, T. and Squaw, very handsome in her traveling outfit and very much first lady of the land, boarded the presidential car of a westbound train that would, eventually, link up with the Atchison, Topeka and the Santa Fe.

They were greeted by a dozen stout officials of the railroad, each wearing a silk top hat. In the cars anything that was not gilded was red plush. Crystal chandeliers lit the drawing room, bedrooms, galley as well as a bathroom with a huge marble tub.

"Does the president always travel like this?" T. was thoroughly impressed.

"Grover *never* travels like this. He hates the railroads. The source of all corruption, he says. But I'm not so high-minded."

The officials wished Mrs. Cleveland a pleasant journey, and respectfully withdrew. A black steward brought them coffee. T. was not aware that the train had left the exhibit until the car was filled with daylight.

Between lovemaking and sight-seeing, the long trip seemed very short indeed. Late-nineteenth-century America proved to be a fairly empty place. Except for the big towns, there were no electrical or telephone wires. But in the towns through which they did pass, wires were everywhere, like strings of spaghetti, crisscrossing every which way.

"When was the telephone invented?" T. sat back in a swivel armchair, large feet on the mahogany windowsill.

"About ten years ago, I think. There certainly weren't any when I was a child. We still see Mr. Bell every now and then. Fact, I think Grover helped him become an American citizen. He's from Scotland but lives here in Washington—or he *lived* in town, as you'd say—where he's a regent of the Smithsonian."

Over lunch in the swaying dining car, Squaw said, "Speaking of telephones, after you left the house the other evening, I paid a call on Mrs. Franklin Roosevelt. She's always a bit edgy with us, what with her not only being alive like only a handful of us but, unlike any of us, she's still in the White House. Well, she couldn't have been nicer even though she was on the telephone talking to herself in the White House. Then, when she hung up, she looked very grim. 'I was talking to myself, Frankie'—she always uses my nickname. I suppose because I'm so young. Also Grover was the first president her husband ever met. Franklin was just a boy and he says that Grover said, 'Young man, I pray, for your sake, you will never be president.' Naturally, Grover denies the story, as if he'd remember anything so trivial. Where was I?"

T. spoke, mouth full of steak. "Grim. Telephone. Mrs. Roosevelt."

"Oh, yes. There's a rumor that the Germans and the Russians, what's his name and what's his name . . . ?"

"Hitler and Stalin."

"Are going to make an alliance and if they do it's the end of France and England, as if anyone in our day—out there . . ." With a sweep of her hand she indicated a small town where the church was on fire and a horse-drawn fire wagon was spraying water all over the church and the excited bystanders. "That's all we really cared about in our day, a church catching fire. England and France were so far away. Now they want us to go over there and help them fight their wars. Scandalous! Grover was fit to be tied when we first heard about the World War and you can bet he grilled Mr.

Wilson when he finally got here. I remember him saying that the peace Mr. Wilson forced the Germans to accept would mean another war in twenty years. And now here it comes, right on schedule."

Wilson. Woodrow Wilson. Since that's when and where it had all started, could that be where the new war might yet be nipped in the bud? No first war, no second war. But where, T. wondered, was the crossroad in time, with its bud, ready for the nipping?

T. and Squaw spent a memorable night at the La Fonda Hotel. Then, the next day, they were obliged to part. "I'm here in my own time," she said, "and I have to dedicate a bridge or maybe a river if there's enough water. So you and the boys go on to the mesa. I'll try to join you."

Tom and his Civil War assistants, Yank and Reb, filled two wagons with equipment. T. assured the puzzled drivers that the machinery was for agricultural use.

Once out of town Tom, Yank, and Reb took off their shirts to get tanned. "We never see the sun in our dumb exhibit," said Reb, a languid long-haired youth from Atlanta who had died during the siege. T. was longing to find out what it was like to be alive one minute and an exhibit the next but the boys were pretty closemouthed when it came to discussing something so intimate as life's bloody end in war.

But they were not in the least shy when it came to swimming in the icy spring at the base of Otowi mesa. It was Reb who started speculating whether or not they would have the time—and opportunity—to find girls on this trip. Reb had two neat holes above his left nipple while Yank had a long scar from navel to groin. "Just missing the family jewels," he said, rising from the spring. "How long're you gonna need us, Captain?"

T. liked being called captain. But from the look of their fatal wounds he had no urge to play soldier for real. Would he ever be obliged to?

"Get me out of here." T. could hear the whisper of his exhibited self in his ear.

"Only a couple of days, to set things up."

"Great," said Tom. "We'll have time." He turned to the others, drying off on the rocks. "Lot of girls in Otowi."

"Who takes your places in the exhibit?" Anything to do with the time factor was now part of T.'s essential puzzle.

"We do," said Reb.

"But you're here."

"We're also there, too," said Tom. "We could stay up here a year but then when we reported back for duty it would be just like when we left. Don't ask me how it's done."

I sure wish I could, thought T. Somehow his "rival" was already using velocity in order, specifically, to propel these boys—as well as himself and Squaw—from one coordinate in Smithsonian time to another, while each self continued, simultaneously, to occupy other points. Question: was real time *outside* the Smithsonian equally manageable? There was a T. look-alike off to a New England summer camp while T. himself was establishing a lab in the New Mexico Territory as of 1886. But was the T. in camp really T. or a sort of—well, dummy?

The boys were talking now of sex but in a far more polite, old-world way than the boys in the dormitory did in 1939.

"What would happen," asked T., "if one of you got a girl pregnant back here?"

"I suppose," said Yank, thoughtfully pulling at the fleshly connection between 1864 and 1886, "she'd either have the baby or else eat ergot like they do back home in Nashua and get rid of it early."

"But if there was a baby, then it would be all out of sync with its own time."

"That's too vexatious for me, Captain," said Reb. "But it seems to me if it's born here it belongs here, no matter how long its daddy's been dead."

Tom frowned. "One of the ladies said that we men are 'safe,' her words, because we're like mules once we got killed. We go through the motions real nice but there's no result."

"What ladies?" T. was intrigued.

"Now, Tom, you shut up. That ain't nice to talk about." Reb was blushing from his chest bone up.

Yank laughed. "Nothing to be ashamed of. Years ago a bunch of us in the exhibit formed an escort service, you know, to look after the first ladies and Barbara Fritchie and Betsy Ross and all the other ladies they have on view. After all, women got needs just like men and so that's what we're there for, as well as decoration."

T. had never heard of anything so outlandish, not even in the obscene comic books that made the rounds of the dormitory. "You mean they pay you?"

"Well," said Yank, "we'd sure charge if we were living in a money economy but as we're basically dummies we do like we're told, and get a good meal thrown in maybe, particularly at Dolley Madison's. She's fun for an old lady."

T. turned to Tom, who looked embarrassed. "Does Frankie . . . Mrs. Cleveland use the service?"

Reb gave an authentic Rebel yell. "If only she would! Every lad's hot for Frankie, but she just goes and picks and chooses as she pleases. She was hipped on Injuns for a while. And then old Tom here pleasures her . . ."

"That's enough." Tom started to button his tunic.

T., remembering that he was their captain, quickly dressed and hopped onto the buckboard of the first wagon. Tom sat beside him. The other two boys mounted the second wagon.

"Mrs. Washington, too?" T. couldn't imagine that majestic old lady ever naked, much less being "pleasured" by a soldier.

Tom laughed. "No. She's much too high and mighty. Some of them don't play around much. Of course they seem lots older to you than to us. Actually, they're all the age they were when they first came to the White House and got inaugurated—when they was in their thirties, maybe forties . . ."

"What about the presidents? What do they do?"

Tom blushed. "Well, there *are* a couple who use the escort service pretty regularly . . ."

It was T.'s turn to blush. "No. I meant what do they do for girls?"

"Oh." Tom was relieved. "The exhibits are full of girls. Early American girls. Indian girls. Black slave girls. Eskimos are considered really hot. And of course they all like the idea of going with a president, any president, in fact."

For the hundredth time T. wondered who was actually in charge of this intricate system known as the Smithsonian Institution.

5

⚜

IT TOOK FOUR Old Western American Exhibit days to install T.'s laboratory in a ruined adobe church opposite Father Lamy's mission. The boys were surprisingly adept with modern machinery and understood almost as well as he the principle of the batteries that would power the entire lab. "But then," as Tom pointed out, "at night we do a lot of comparing notes with each other. Fact, every time there's a new arrival like the green sailor from your years we quiz him about all the latest weapons and gadgets. For some reason, Civil War boys are the best with the machines. That's why I brought along a couple. But then most of the lads are right quick, except for the ones from the Revolution—thick as boards, they are."

At the end of each day, the three soldiers would head for a cantina in Otowi town while T. and Father Lamy had dinner in the priest's quarters. Black beans with rice was T.'s favorite.

In a sense, each was working in the fourth dimension. But, since neither quite understood the other, T. was already planning to do a total scan of Father Lamy's string of light, where earth's human space-time occupied a small section.

"If I can isolate the one, dealing with our time on the planet, I can then go back—or forward—and make changes."

"It's odd," said Father Lamy, chewing a red pepper without wincing. "I only want to look ahead while you only want to go back."

T. was not about to give away his game plan. "Well, it's in the past I expect to find, you know, a turning point that might be—uh, corrected. In that case, any future *you* might be looking at would be only temporary."

"I want to see as far as I can up ahead." Father Lamy wasn't listening. "I want to know how the story ends. The Cherubim. The Seraphim. The Great Trumpet . . ."

"It is going to end all right." T. always got gloomy when he thought of what he was certain would happen even though he had no evidence other than the Pennsylvania Avenue tape, which might be nothing more than a kind of movie.

"If it does end, I'm not sure we'll be able to tell." Father Lamy drank black coffee. Through the window the mountains of the Sangre de Cristo range were rosy in the sinking light. "I also doubt—though naturally I wish you luck—that there is any earthly—or heavenly"—he crossed himself—"way for us to interfere in time. After all, God made all this only the one time."

"With some real funny results." T. had not cared for religion since Dr. Lucas taught him the catechism.

"Let's say obscure results, like science itself. Then, as a sort of afterthought, God came up with us, to fine-tune His show."

T. changed the subject. "A lot of people at the Smithsonian keep hinting around at how there was this one case of an intervention but no one will tell me just what it was or how it was done."

Father Lamy cocked his head and frowned; then he crossed to a small instrument panel in the wall beside the door and switched on a device that filled the room with a low humming sound. "We're being electronically bugged," he said. "The head office likes to know what everyone's saying. But with what I call my hummingbird, no one can understand a word we say in here."

"Head office?"

"Down in the basement of the Castle. There's a sort of shrine to Dr. Smithson where the board of regents meets and so on. No one knows much about what goes on there and as far as we can tell they pretty much keep out of our way, while, heaven knows, we don't bother them. Anyway, after the fire in 1865 . . ."

"What fire?"

"The Castle caught fire and most of Dr. Smithson's collection of minerals was destroyed and a lot of his writings, too— notes on natural phenomena, chemistry, everything. He was a universal scientist who left a fortune to the United States even though he'd never set foot in the country. I suppose he liked republics because he himself was the bastard son of an English duke . . ."

"Is he buried in the basement?"

"That's the legend." Father Lamy chuckled. "Actually, no one's buried down there as far as I know. Anyway, the fire took place, I think, shortly after President Lincoln was shot, and one of Dr. Smithson's colleagues—quite crazy, everyone said—in all the confusion of burning minerals and stacks of research, managed to work out a way of increasing velocity that then made it possible for him—who knows how? he left no notes—to get himself to Ford's Theater an instant before the bullet struck President Lincoln's head. Only everything went wrong. He had intended to save the president and get him out on Good Friday, 1865, and into June of that year at the Smithsonian so that Lincoln could continue his second term in peace. But just as he pulled the president into *his* space-time, the bullet collided *but* did not penetrate. So what he ended up with—*we've* ended up with—is a highly concussed Abraham Lincoln, an addled version . . ."

"In charge of pots." T. had suspected all along that Mr. Lincoln was indeed the original President Lincoln.

"Also creative bookkeeping. Anyway that was the one and only intervention in the history of our race, save for the miraculous moment when God raised up His Only Son . . ."

Later that night, in the bed at the back of the ruined adobe church, T. and the newly arrived Squaw made love; then, as she began to comb her hair, she said, "If only Grover and I could've stopped the Depression in his second term, he could have gone on and had a third term, just like Roosevelt's about to have next year."

T. dried the sweat from his body. The night was unexpectedly warm. Through a crack in the adobe, a fragment of bright moon covered them with an icy silver light.

"Think I can go back and stop the Depression?"

"If Grover couldn't and he was there, I don't see what anyone else could've done. Of course the real villain is Harrison . . . Veal!"

In the moonlight Squaw's eyes looked like polished silver.

"What?"

"Why do you care so much about all this?"

T. wondered why he always sounded just like a ventriloquist's dummy on the order of Charlie McCarthy or, maybe, a parrot, whenever he said: "The war must not take place."

"What do you know about this war that no one else does?"

"A lot of things—as far as quantum physics go. But I also know what Dr. Oppenheimer only *thinks* he knows, too. In time—pretty soon in time for us—nuclear weapons are going to kill off the human race."

"Something's bound to." Squaw was indifferent. "But I doubt it's going to be as soon as all that. Anyway, everything's now been invented and nothing that gets invented ever goes unused."

"But just about anything can be uninvented—at some point in the past."

"Kill Einstein on his way to school? Veal, all of his ideas— as you know better than I—have been around for too long a time."

"I know." T. was glum. "You can't change the course of science. At least I know I can't. But I think I can stop the Second World War."

"How?"

"That's for me to know and you to find out."

"Aren't we cute? But why of all the wars we've been involved in are you so much against this one?"

"Because I'm going to be killed in it. Like Tom at Buena
Vista."

Squaw put her arms around him.

———••———

For most of the two Julys, 1886 and 1939, two Julys that had
now coincided for T., he was at work in his lab, with only
Father Lamy for company and, sometimes, assistance.

T. was deeply intrigued by the string theory of all matter,
including "life" as it was called at the Smithsonian and in lay
circles elsewhere on earth, as well as on who knew how many
other planets as yet unlocated in the infinitude of parallel uni-
verses.

T. was now being bombarded with the sheer busy-ness of
life and everywhere-ness. When his projected equations produced pictures or even mere pictograms, life in its infinite va-
riety was seething hotly out there in the cold, racing from
some unknown center to . . . More and more did the Milky
Way, T.'s home galaxy, resemble an ejaculation of sperm into
the by no means empty womb of space. It was clear to him by
now that there was no beginning and no end to anything; just
the heat and the cold, and ever new creations and—if not,
ever, extinctions—transformations, metamorphoses.

"There is no nothing," T. announced to Father Lamy in
the mission church lab.

"There had to be when God . . ."

T. frowned; it had been agreed that Father Lamy keep his
sky-god opinions to himself, since neither science nor common sense could support the notion of nothing emerging
from nothing. Something had to come from something and

the *thing* in question was forever—an infinite cloud of restless dust as far as T. could grasp. When he first started brooding on the matter of creation, T. realized immediately that the human brain was so constructed as to be absolutely unable to make the slightest sense of the whole. As we start and stop so, for us, the cosmos must start and stop. But he could also see that his own reasoning was crippled by the built-in limitations of a two-lobe human brain, with its peculiar hang-up on beginnings and endings when it was change that was the nature of nature. But just as he felt he was on the verge of grasping the whole, everything seen and sensed fell away. Back to Go. "We ask all the wrong questions." T. pressed the button that summoned up the string of light which represented their small planet's brief life as a sphere. "And that's why we keep getting all the wrong answers."

"There was a man, born the son of a Virgin . . ." Father Lamy was dogged.

T. was equally dogged; and annoyed. "I was confirmed by Bishop Freeman himself in the cathedral and I knew then that everything to do with that story is not only useless but designed—only your heaven knows who or what did it and why—to keep us from finding out anything that we actually need to know."

"Perhaps we don't need to know the things that you think that *you*—for now—want to know." Father Lamy was a good sport, but his religion had made him a largely useless scientist. The basic questions had all been answered for him in advance: it was a wonder that—when his faith was napping?—he had managed to stumble on those strings, unmentioned in Genesis. But since he could not deal with them, it was up to T., in the present at least, to make as much of this tantalizing glimpse as his limited but not entirely blinkered brain could imagine.

T. drank an 1886 Coca-Cola, which had the drug cocaine in it, according to Squaw; then he played *their* string on the monitor: first, up and down and then from side to side. The human race took up a very small part of the whole, which he narrowed down to a shining arc on the screen. T. then marked, digitally, the first humanoids at one end, followed by ever-increasing bright cities that flared up and then burned out as the string continued to bend.

T. pressed for full power. The entire shining string was now visible against black. Only what had been an arc had become a circle.

"Look!" T. was delighted. "The snake swallows its tail at the end. This proves Einstein's curvature of space . . ."

Father Lamy was edgy. "The Indians have a creation legend somewhat along that line . . ."

"I'm sure you'll talk them out of it." T. enjoyed making fun of Father Lamy. He was a bit like the hopelessly unscientific Mr. Sofield.

"This is only conjecture, after all." Father Lamy indicated the screen.

"No," said T. "It's the real thing. The only problem is can we ever understand it." Or *use* it, he thought to himself, grimly.

The next day T. locked his lab door. Squaw had gone into Santa Fe to prepare for a wedding. T. decided to think. This was best done by taking a long walk across the mesa. Dry heat. Ice blue sky. Smell of sage. Juniper. He knew he was close to something. The obvious was right in front of him, only he couldn't see it yet.

Problem: first to make a change in the past. The light string, enormously magnified, could pinpoint any instant in space-time. The theorem that he had devised for Dr. Oppenheimer to keep one detonating atom from setting off random explosions within other atoms could also be adapted to provide sufficient velocity for a human being to go either backwards or forward in time and, once located in the desired space-time, he would be able to synchronize with the speed of those already there for a limited period—the limitation being the amount of power he could produce to provide him with sufficient velocity needed to do what he had to do and return to his home time-space.

Second problem: what historic event must he affect in order to prevent whoever it was that had got the United States in the First World War that was now rapidly turning into the Second? President Cleveland had promised to give the matter some thought. "I think I can identify the culprit," he had said.

As T. theorized, he stumbled over the remains of a round pueblo building. He swore aloud as he landed on all fours in a juniper bush.

An elderly man in a costume of the period helped T. to his feet.

"Sorry." T. wiped his hands on his trousers.

"No doubt you were cogitating on some great matter to do with time." The man gave him a knowing look.

"Well, yes, sir, I was. You know me?"

The man nodded. "We all do, of course—which is to say I know *of* you. I'm Spencer Fullerton Baird."

They shook hands. T. must have looked mystified because the old man laughed and said, "I'm secretary of the Smithsonian. As of now, that is. I'm also the U.S. Commissioner of Fish and Fisheries."

"Not many fish out here, I guess."

"There are some lovely trout streams. Anyway, I'm mostly interested in birds and snakes." Mr. Baird sat down on the low adobe wall and motioned for T. to sit beside him. "I was traveling in these parts, in the line of duty, and I thought I'd look in on you."

"But you're 1886, aren't you?"

"That's right. And you're half a century ahead of me. But we've always maintained a special sort of calendar at the Smithsonian. You know, to keep track of what's going on, or will be going on. It was Dr. Smithson's notion originally. All rather crude, I'm afraid, but we do get a very *general* idea of what's going to be going on. Obviously your years are highly significant for us." Mr. Baird pointed to a large rattlesnake sleeping on a rock in the sun. "That snake, rather a handsome *Charina bottea,* is resting on what will one day be the so-called Big House of the Los Alamos Ranch School for Boys . . ."

"I know," said T. "A friend of mine's going there right now. In 1939, that is. He hates it."

"Well, tell him, if you're in touch, the school will be gone by 1940. The government's taking it over and they will build the atomic bomb over yonder where those cottonwoods are." Mr. Baird frowned. "But from this point on our calendar is a bit muddled."

"Because someone is rearranging the sequence of events."

Mr. Baird smiled. "You're a very bright young man. But then maybe . . ."

"It's me?" T. was tentative. "Maybe I'm the one who is trying to change events, to stop the war."

"If you have, you've started a bit late."

"In real time," said T., "there is no late, there is no early."

"True."

"You know, Mr. Baird, everyone tells me over and over again how we can't go back and change events. Well, here you are, in your own time, meeting me who has come back here and who could, theoretically, blow up Los Alamos . . ."

"No. No." Mr. Baird was firm. "Technically, this is not 1886 but an exhibit. It just *seems* like the real thing. A masterful job of re-creation, if I may congratulate my successors. You seem totally real to me even though your parents haven't been born yet . . ."

"O.K. This is a sort of movie. Well, in this particular movie the curator of pots, one Abraham Lincoln, was pulled out of Ford's Theater just before the bullet struck his head . . ."

"Just *as* the bullet hit him, but before it penetrated the skull. He was—is—totally gaga, sad to say. We'd so hoped he could serve a second term but . . ."

T. was not interested in 1865 politics. "The point is someone did interfere in time and got him out, a bit on the late side so . . ."

"The means I used—yes, I'm the culprit—were highly crude and had less to do with time than space. It was the day after the assassination, when we knew—or thought we knew—exactly what the murderer, Booth, had done. So I intervened, with the help of Joseph Henry—he was Smithsonian secretary before me. We were just barely able to visit what was then yesterday, under certain crude laws that no longer obtain. We also had to know the exact moment that Booth fired his pistol. Unfortunately, the press got everything wrong. This meant when we arrived in the presidential box, the audience was laughing . . . it was a dreadful play, which I'd seen only a day or two before. . . . Unfortunately, Booth was *ahead* of us instead of the other way around. Our coordinates were set at the entrance to the box, so we were only two or three yards from the president's chair when . . . Oh, it was a nightmare! I stumbled over Mrs. Lincoln, who screamed. The pistol went off simultaneously with my pulling the president out of the chair. Then Mr. Henry shoved Booth over the ledge of the box, causing him to break an ankle on the stage. By then, we had hurried what we thought was Mr. Lincoln into the next day but it was no longer he."

In the middle distance the rattlesnake was now swaying on his rock. "Who was it?"

"We have multiple selves. You are not the same you that I first met a few minutes ago, nor am I who I was."

"Like all those versions of me back in the Castle?"

"In a sense. But that was a mindless trick, if I may say so." Mr. Baird was disapproving. "Anyway, the Mr. Lincoln that we got was the one whom the bullet had struck in the back of the head but not yet killed. He was—is—needless to say, not much of anyone anymore. He does have an eye for ceramics, and he does like to read about the Mr. Lincoln, and since he has a natural gift for administration—almost five years as a wartime president—the Institution keeps him on while the real, the *final* Abraham Lincoln can be found in a funeral vault at Springfield—in a different universe, of course."

The rattlesnake vanished down a sandy hole. "How has Lincoln stayed alive all these years?"

"He hasn't. He's been a dummy for some time, I fear. So"— Mr. Baird gave T. a knowing glance—"we still haven't properly solved what it is you want so much to do, which is to enter time at the right point and alter history. And now I'm warning you what happens if you arrive a half second too late."

"You came," said T, "as close as I will . . . need to come." T. was beginning to visualize a new set of time-spatial coordinates.

"I will say one thing." Mr. Baird was on his feet. "Starting with your arrival at the Smithsonian, there is now nothing but confusion in the records."

"I'm sure that's Einstein's effect, not mine."

"No. *He* was anticipated. You weren't. You're not even supposed to exist."

"But I do." T. suddenly shivered—a cold breeze had risen in the hot sun.

"I daresay Dr. Smithson would have approved."

"Is he down in the cellar, under the basketball court?"

Mr. Baird laughed. "A nice old ghost story. But what we do have down there are some of his papers, saved from the fire of 1865. But here comes the First Lady of the Land." He rose; removed his hat; bowed low to Squaw, who was mounted sidesaddle on a great horse, the loyal Tom beside her on his cavalryman's horse.

Squaw leapt to the ground and shook Mr. Baird's hand. "I thought you were up at Woods Hole, looking at fish."

"No. I'm here, looking at reptiles. And meeting our young friend."

"He's very ambitious, isn't he?" Squaw smiled at T., who wondered if there would be any objection from Grover Cleveland if he were to marry her. After all, Cleveland was already in possession of Frankie aged twenty-seven and, considering his sedentary life in the Hall of Presidents, he hardly needed two versions of the same wife. T. wondered just how to bring up the subject to Squaw, who was explaining to Mr. Baird how, the more she thought about it, "Veal—that's what I call him—is on the right track. There's no real need for this war, not like Mexico."

"Wish you'd let *me* know what need there was for that one," muttered Tom, but Mr. Baird was dispensing what Mr. Sofield, something of a radical, called "conventional wisdom."

"These wars, so far, have benefited us greatly, Mrs. Cleveland. In my own lifetime, we've doubled in size. We've also helped the Latin Americans to find their way, no matter how stumbling and hesitant, toward Democracy and Freedom . . ."

"I am," said Frankie coolly, "the first lady of the United States and I need no seminar on the greatness of the land over which my husband presides. But with this mid-twentieth-century war, weapons now exist to blow Washington off the face of the planet and, Mr. Baird, if Washington goes—and it's sure to go either in this nuclear war or the next—the Smithsonian Institution goes with it. That means that all memory of you and of those two headless dummies of me in that idiotic exhibit will have been forever erased."

All three were taken aback by Squaw's vehemence. Mr. Baird rallied first. "Dr. Smithson's review of the future does show eccentric lapses in the continuity but . . ."

"To hell," said Squaw, "with Dr. Smithson's tea leaves. He knew nothing about the future but, thanks to T., we're starting to get glimpses, and it looks pretty bad."

"If I may say so, ma'am, it don't really matter one way or the other. Everybody's got his Buena Vista coming, you might say." Tom struck a philosophical note.

"You say so, I don't." Squaw was brisk. She turned to T. "Mr. Cleveland would like to talk to you. He has a plan. Good day, Mr. Baird."

Mr. Baird raised his hat and bowed to the president's wife. Squaw mounted her horse and T. jumped on Tom's horse, just back of the saddle.

"I'll show you the way out of the exhibit," said T. "I've found a lot of shortcuts since that great ride on the Atchison, Topeka and the Santa Fe."

———•·•———

Grover Cleveland was still wearing his orange suit when Squaw and T. joined him in his study. T. also noted how clear and easy on the eyes gaslight was. He wondered if the Frankie—or did he call her Frank?—in the second Cleveland house minded the time Cleveland spent with her earlier self. If she didn't and if the president really preferred the company of the second Frank to the first . . . Of course, they could simply go on living in sin, but . . . ?

Frankie kissed her husband's fat smooth cheek. "You know Grover was the first president since Buchanan to be clean-shaven. Starting with Lincoln, it was nothing but one ghastly beard after another in the White House."

T. sat in a straight chair opposite the president while Squaw went into the bedroom to change out of her riding habit.

"I confess, Master Veal, that I am not at ease with the sciences in general and with what is going on around here in particular." Cleveland was drinking beer from a pewter mug. Foam had turned white his walrus mustache.

"Well, sir, from what little I learned about you, in American history . . ."

"No doubt viciously partisan! After all, Wall Street pays for most of the better schools and universities, so you've doubtless been taught that a high tariff is a good thing?"

"Well, sir . . ." T. had no idea what Cleveland was talking about.

Cleveland wiped his mustache with the back of a fat hand. "But I suppose you boys are a lot more interested in how I finally defeated Geronimo—the Apache chief—and settled him and what was left of his tribe out in Oklahoma. Can't say he was particularly grateful but . . ." Cleveland drifted off. "Nevins—this historian—is wonderful. He gets just about everything right except the details." Cleveland chuckled. "If history is in the details then there can be no history because who could ever know those details unless he was actually there? But it *is* possible to grasp the whole, which must be the way the poet works, I should think, being a lawyer myself."

Cleveland moved the orange cube of his person around in his chair so that he could face T. directly. "I've been reading everything I could get my hands on, on what happened in the years between me and Wilson." He shook his head, frowning. "Very odd sort of history—our history—to my mind, that is. Naturally, Wall Street got the country away from me and back to the Republican McKinley—personally, a dear man, by the way, and then to Teddy Roosevelt, a sincere sort of hypocrite who passed the job on to poor Mr. Taft. Then Teddy turned on Taft and that's how we Democrats got back in with Wilson. That was some four years after I arrived here as an exhibit."

Beside Cleveland's chair there was an intimidating pile of history books with dozens of slips of paper inserted between their pages. Squaw liked to boast that her Grover was the hardest-working president in history. T. could believe it, though what presidents actually did, other than throw out the first baseball of the season, had always been vague to him. Sign things, he supposed. Declare war. Put on Indian feather headdresses.

Squaw joined them, looking fresh and very young. "I've now come to the conclusion"—Cleveland shut his eyes and blew out his mustache, rather like the sea lion at the zoo; then he opened his eyes wide—"that when Wilson, my fellow Democrat, sad to say, became president in 1912—and got re-elected in 1916—that he, and he alone, got us into the European war in 1917." Cleveland picked up one of the books; opened it to a marked page. "He will then trick the Germans into surrendering while the Allies trick him into letting them bankrupt Germany, which will, in revenge, twenty years later, produce this remarkably wicked man—if the most recent books can be believed—this Leon Trotsky, who will, even as we speak, if Mrs. Roosevelt up the line here is to be believed, take on the whole world in a war with terrible new weapons."

"It's not Trotsky," said T. "He's Russian or something. It's Adolf Hitler, who's a German and has this Charlie Chaplin mustache."

"I stand corrected, Master Veal. All events after my own life have . . . well, an aura of unreality to them. For me, naturally." He took a great swig of beer. Squaw frowned disapprovingly. She was always trying to put Grover on a beerless diet.

"I could never have conceived it possible for the United States to send a military force to fight in a *European* war. We solemnly vowed in the Monroe Doctrine to stay forever out of their hemisphere if they stayed out of ours. Then Wilson maneuvers the U.S. into a war against Germany when the few Americans who were at all interested in Europe would probably have wanted to fight *alongside* Germany against England and France. If only I had been still on the scene in 1917!"

"Well, darling, you weren't." Squaw placed the pewter mug out of Cleveland's reach. "But now we are . . . once again 'around,' in a manner of speaking. So why don't you go up the line and talk to Mr. Wilson?"

"Can't stand him. So self-righteous, so . . . Anyway, what's done is done."

"But," said T., "what's done can now be undone."

"Remember, Frank, when he was inaugurated as president of Princeton?" Cleveland sounded dreamy. "That was around 1902, when we were already settled in Princeton. Mark Twain wore this white suit, down the front of which he'd spilled whisky, and . . ." Cleveland stopped his own story, picked up another book. "Well, it was only eight years later, he gets himself chosen by the bosses of New Jersey to be governor and then, two years later, my friend George Harvey gets him nominated as president and Teddy Roosevelt makes him president by splitting the Republicans when he runs against his personally chosen successor Taft . . ."

"Mrs. Taft still doesn't speak to the Roosevelts." Squaw sighed. "We've had some mighty chilly tea parties just up the line."

". . . and so Wilson becomes the first Democrat since me to win. Now, young Master Veal, if you want to keep Mr. Wilson from becoming president I can give you the time and the place where you can—what is your phrase?—nip him in the bud. I'll also give you the scissors." Cleveland opened another book. T. could see a great many marginal notes as well as a number of Xs and arrows, like a theorem.

Cleveland was most lawyerly. "On Sunday morning, June 25, 1910, the Wilson family is going to be at Lyme, Connecticut, while my old friend, the editor of *Harper's Weekly* and kingmaker-to-be, George Harvey, is at Trenton, ready to fix the deal between the Democratic bosses and the pure high-minded Professor Wilson. Harvey will telephone Mr. Wilson that it's urgent he come to Trenton. But Wilson wants to enjoy the cool of Connecticut. After several more urgent calls, Wilson agrees to come down to Trenton on the Sunday but then finds there are no trains. So Harvey sends one William O. Inglis to Lyme, to collect the White Knight and drive him over a number of bad roads so he can meet the big city bosses and conclude his pact with the devils who will make him governor of New Jersey. Once elected, he will then double-cross the bosses, and move on to the White House." Cleveland shut the book.

"If he is to be stopped, you must pay him a call no later than nine A.M. that Sunday morning. Inglis won't arrive, as far as I can tell, until just before noon. So you'll have three hours to talk Mr. Wilson out of running." Cleveland was looking now at his wife.

Squaw looked alarmed. "You want *me* to talk to him?"

"He won't listen to a boy. But he'll listen to the widow of President Cleveland."

T. was delighted with the old man's gift for detail. He only hoped that he would be able to get himself and Squaw to the exact cross section of space-time. One good thing about Minkowski's famous diagram: you had all the present time you needed for trial and error before you got to old time.

"Now, Master Veal, what I have to tell Mrs. Cleveland is not for your innocent ears."

"Is it really . . . *awful?*" Squaw's eyes were gleaming.

"For Mr. Wilson, yes. But not for the likes of me." He turned to T. "When they found I had an illegitimate child, I surprised the press by saying, 'Print the truth.' They did and to everyone's surprise, except mine, I was elected anyway.

But Mr. Wilson is too serious a hypocrite ever to be honest. We shall scare him off."

Then the Clevelands both sang: "Ma, Ma, where's my Pa? Gone to the White House. Ha. Ha. Ha!"

———✦———

T. entered Bentsen's lab to find his colleague and associates listening to the radio. The president was talking about neutrality; and about his own deep-seated hatred of war, which he had seen, or so he said.

When Bentsen saw T. he said, "Well, it's happened. The Germans attacked Poland and England's declared war."

T. went into his former lab. Bentsen followed him. "The prediction is that we'll be in the war in a matter of months."

"Not much time."

"No." Bentsen misunderstood him. "But the buildings at Los Alamos are going up. Dr. Oppenheimer's in charge. So we're still ahead of the Germans."

"I thought the president just said we're going to stay out of all this."

Bentsen's smile was tolerant. "He'll stay out until November 1940 at least. That's when he expects to be reelected. After that . . ." Exuberantly, Bentsen pressed a button and the simulated fireball filled the screen. "Your work will be remembered," he said, the entire spectrum of fission–light reflected in his face. "Without your contribution, Dr. Oppenheimer would still be fretting about that nuclear chain reaction. Now what are you going to be doing out there in the wilds of New Mexico?"

T. noticed an envelope addressed to him. The writing was spidery and the ink used was familiar purple. As he opened it, he said, "I'm playing around with space-time."

"Science fiction." Bentsen was dismissive.

"No, it's science, all right. But it needs a fictional sort of mind to employ it."

"Like yours?"

But T. was no longer listening; he was reading the letter. *"May I compliment you—in advance—on your coming break-through into new areas of time-space previously unexplored? Your ability to visualize first and then demonstrate both mathematically and practically is unique and was so noted here at the Institution's center when you—idly? I think not—made your by now famous— among those few who matter—equation at the expense, alas, of a passing grade in algebra. In due course, Mr. Sofield has promised us you will have the opportunity to take a makeup exam and so will continue your academic career triumphantly until Graduation Day in June 1943.*

"As you have already glimpsed that particular day, you are aware that the president who has this day sworn to us he will not involve you Americans in war, will have by then, done just that. Also, as you have correctly surmised, you will fall a victim on March the first 1945 and your uniform—and dummy—will become a part of our Military Exhibit, like that of your friend Tom as well as your friend in another exhibit, Mrs. Frank or Frances Cleveland. This sort of half life I assure you as one who knows from both experiment and experience is by no means to be despised. But for a genius like you to leave so prematurely your natural habitat in space, the United States—and, in time, the last three quarters of the twentieth cen-tury—would be to deprive you of a valuable life, valuable to the human race as well as to you yourself.

"Although I am nowhere near so advanced in quantum physics as you, I am aware that you are on the verge of making great changes in our history not to mention in our common sense of time itself. The general view of what is to come was first projected in 1822 as a secret addendum to 'On the Composition of Zeolite,' in which, under cer-tain circumstances, this hydrous silicate swells . . . But that is an-other, cruder look at the nature of time now superseded by your

*development of Einstein's rough theory. I look forward to your com-
ing adventure in New Mexico. My 'zeolite' view is coarse, even
muddled, but I suspect that the future is, literally, yours for a time if
not time itself which you may yet prove is nonexistent. I look forward
to making your acquaintance when you return from New Mexico—
and 1910. (How far, far in the future these dates are for me as I
presently indite them!)*

"*I remain your obedient servant in the service, each of us, of science and of our common race.*"

With a magnifier, T. read the signature: *James Smithson.*
Then, under the name, a scribble, "*Yes, my laboratory is beneath
the basketball court where the Parcheesi board appears to conclude
with the comforting word HOME.*"

T. folded the paper and put it in his inside blazer pocket.

Bentsen was trembling with curiosity. "Who was that
from?"

T. let him tremble. "A colleague."

Then T. went to his room and telephoned Stanley Sofield.
There was the familiar clink of ice and, in the background,
the noise of a radio.

"We're listening to the war news." Stanley sounded mildly
tipsy.

"We're staying out, for now, aren't we?" T. knew that
Stanley had a soft spot for Franklin Roosevelt.

"Well, that's what the president *has* to say, what with all
those isolationists in Congress. What's happening in the
Castle?"

"We're busy with . . . you know. Listen, how am I doing?"

"You've grown an inch. The upper school has accepted
you this fall. Funny talking to you there and seeing you almost every day here. How's it done?"

"It's called cloning. Only I'm the one who's really me and
the one at St. Albans is a copy, a recent one, cooked up under
the basketball court here in the Castle."

"Just pour it straight into my glass, Pratt," was Stanley's response. There was a clatter of ice. Then Stanley sighed. "Mother's milk! Now, T., I wish you'd talk to yourself here. You—*he*, that is—is talking about quitting school and joining the marines."

T. felt suddenly shaky. He took a deep breath. "I can't. He can't. Anyway, we won't be fourteen until March. You have to be seventeen. With parental permission, too." All of this had been explored by the boys in the dormitory the previous summer when war clouds were gathering over Europe.

"I'm afraid he's big enough to pass for seventeen. Now, if you could talk to him . . ."

T. was beginning to see a—if not the—shape of things to come. But then he recalled that on Graduation Day he was seventeen and still in school.

"When are you coming out of there?" Stanley made it sound like prison.

"I don't know. But when I do, you'll never know the difference."

———◆———

Father Lamy was fascinated by T.'s new ability to examine used light. It took several days of trial and error to arrive at the exact time and place when—and where—Squaw and T. were to make their appearance in Lyme, Connecticut.

T. had made an entire whitewashed adobe wall in his laboratory into a window-doorway to 1910. The window aspect was easy enough. He used the same two-dimensional light-scanner that he had used to show him Graduation Day.

At the throwing of a switch, a two-dimensional green lawn was visible where the adobe wall had been.

"It's so lifelike!" Father Lamy was duly awed.

"That's because it *is* life—or was when it was and now is again just for us. This is the easy part. Like running a movie.

Only this movie won't be made until twenty-four years from now—that is, for you—and twenty-nine years ago for me."

The Connecticut sky in the spring of 1910 was a milky blue. A willow tree swayed in a mild breeze. Then a lean figure approached them, walking so jauntily that he seemed, at one point, to be doing a dance step. He was also whistling. He wore a flat white straw hat and a tweed jacket with a yellow rose in the buttonhole. Now he was so close that they could see the gleaming pince-nez and the ponderous jaw of Woodrow Wilson, president of Princeton College, awaiting the call to glory.

"Will you be using the Einstein-Podolsky-Rosen paradox?" Father Lamy tried to keep up with all the latest literature.

T. tried not to sound superior. "That's 1935. This is 1939. I've gone past it."

"You've gone past Einstein?"

"Yes. But that's what science is all about, isn't it? He goes as far as he can, then I ride on his back, sort of, and go on a bit further. Actually I can't wait to demonstrate this to him. They say he's read my notes on synchronicity and told Dr. Bentsen that he'd have to see it demonstrated to believe it. So, let's do it! Third dimension coming up."

T. threw the third switch. The dark musty-smelling ruined church was suddenly filled with warm scented air. New-mown grass. Honeysuckle. Sound of birds in the trees. Woodrow Wilson looked as if he was about to step out of his world and into theirs. But then he stopped; frowned; polished his pince-nez as if he had seen something he was not quite certain of. T. feared that that something was T. himself who was not only one foot away from Wilson, but so close that he could smell the cologne that Wilson was wearing.

"Mr. Wilson! Mr. Wilson!" A man's voice sounded just beyond the willow trees and Wilson turned away from T. "I'm down here, Mr. Inglis!" he said in a loud voice.

Then Wilson started up the lawn just as a sweating red-faced young man came into view. Wilson motioned for him to stay where he was. They met beneath the willow tree.

"Incredible!" Father Lamy gazed with awe at the not-very-interesting scene from the future.

"I guess your first look up ahead is always pretty astonishing." T. tried not to sound patronizing.

Father Lamy put out his hand toward the vista before them. But the hand was stopped by what felt to T.—who was doing the same thing—a powerful wind that repelled anything that wanted to penetrate it. He had had the same sensation once when, flying in a small plane, he had stuck a hand out the open window only to have air pressure shove it back inside.

"Well," said Father Lamy, eyes bright, "you have three dimensions at your command. What about the fourth?"

Now would come the test of a velocity that must be so great that it could place anyone using this entrance into a spring day in 1910 and onto the same plane as Lyme, Connecticut. Although the Smithsonian, by other—still mysterious—means had managed to bundle Abraham Lincoln out of the box at Ford's Theater, no one, as far as T. knew, had ever done what he was about to do, which was to take a pair of Einstein's paradoxes and synchronize them.

"O.K. Get ready." T. pulled the fourth switch. Nothing, as far as he could tell, happened. "Come on," he said to Father Lamy. Then T. stepped onto the green spring lawn. Father Lamy, moving with tiny nervous steps, joined him.

"Another world!" Father Lamy took a deep breath: it was certainly a world different from the one of mica sand, obsidian shards, juniper, and sage in back of them, or so T. hoped, for he could not see where they had come from. The lab was now as one with a large rose garden.

Sudden thought: Suppose they could not find their way back? Or suppose the generator that was creating their velocity failed? Father Lamy would turn into a very old man while

T.'s chromosomes would split into two packets and rejoin his parents' ovaries and sperm wherever they might be on this cloudy June day. He did his best not to panic.

While Father Lamy collected rose cuttings, T. moved back to where the lab should be and was relieved to find that what looked at first like a common cloud shadow on the rose terrace was indeed the lab entrance.

As T. crossed into the familiar adobe room, he called to Father Lamy, "Come on back."

Once both were inside, T. switched off all four dimensions. Then he examined his stopwatch to get the time right. Checked his personal time against the timers on his generator. He could now return, whenever he wanted, to the exact moment that Woodrow Wilson appeared beneath the willow trees. Just before Wilson's appearance, T. and Squaw would be ready for him and, for the first time along this string of light, human history would be seriously altered.

Apparently, Father Lamy was now thinking similar thoughts. They were seated in the mission church, eating very hot tamales and drinking very strong coffee.

"You have gone far beyond Einstein . . ."

"I've only demonstrated what he theorized." T. played modest. But, of course, he knew that he had done something unique, thanks to a supply of zeolite which had arrived from Dr. Smithson with exact instructions on how to use this extraordinary source of power for the generator: "Which will then be increased a millionfold," Dr. Smithson had written.

"This means, of course"—Father Lamy munched on a dried red pepper that would have set fire to T.'s digestive system—"that others will travel in time, too."

For once, T. missed a point. "But it'll take some time for the Germans or even Dr. Oppenheimer to be able to do what I've done."

"What," said Father Lamy, suddenly pedantic, "is the key to what you've just said? The key phrase?"

T. played it back. Got the point. " 'Some time.' Yes, I get it. We could have a visitor right now from the year 2000 and he could come back here with his space gun and zap my machine and I'd never get through to Mr. Wilson. Or, worse, let us get through to 1910 and then zap our generator and leave us stuck there."

"Exactly. Now that you've made it possible—in this now—everyone is going to be traveling back and forth, altering the past, affecting the future. Well, suppose someone really wants this world war you don't want. What's to stop him from stopping you?"

"Randomness." T. was beginning to see pictures. "If I'm effective, he'd have to find me here at this instant. That's needle in a haystack time." But no picture registered on T.'s mental screen.

"Are you sure?"

Father Lamy had succeeded in spoiling T.'s lunch. T. belched thoughtfully. "Well, who will ever know what never was?" This was not much of an answer, he knew.

Although T.'s breakthrough was quite enough for any one hundred scientists' lifetimes, he found it far more difficult to get through to Woodrow Wilson than he had found it to get to past time. The telephone number for the Wilsons in Lyme was not in his name. Given time, T. could have gone around the neighborhood until he found the right number so that he could make an appointment for Wilson to meet Squaw at the crucial minute. But that would have used up more generator energy than he was willing to. He thought that perhaps a letter from Squaw might do the trick, but where could he buy a stamp with no old currency? And what about the postmark? Squaw had no idea where her real self happened to be that spring.

It was Father Lamy who made a sensible contribution. "Get her to write a note saying when and where—she'll be walking in the gardens—and I'll deliver it a couple of days before."

T. admitted that this was thinking worthy, if nothing else, of a grown-up, and Father Lamy duly made the long rather nervous walk up the lawn to the house, where he gave the note to one of Wilson's daughters who, noting his cassock, said, "I never knew Mrs. Cleveland was Catholic."

Father Lamy assured her that Mrs. Cleveland was merely a friend, stopping nearby. Then he returned to T.'s lab, sweating from nerves.

"I wonder if that air in the future is good for us to breathe . . ."

"You're just nervous. Let's get Squaw. . . ."

"Who?"

"I mean Frankie. That's Mrs. Cleveland's nickname . . ."

Father Lamy was not only awed but deeply disapproving of the liaison of the soon-to-be-fourteen-year-old and the permanently twenty-two-year-old first lady. T. often wondered what would happen if he stayed within the Smithsonian's time frame. Would he age as if he was outside? He seemed to be aging normally—one golden hair had sprouted beside his left nipple and he assumed that the same thing was happening to his clone at St. Albans. If so, in eight years, he and Squaw would be the same age. Would she then drop him as no longer chicken? On the other hand, if he were some sort of exhibit he would always be the same age, like Squaw. He thought—against his conscious will—of the grown-up boy in the Military Exhibit. "Get me out of here!" But where did that boy think he was? Wounded and dying someplace awful—or just a cheery exhibit like Tom, like Squaw, like Grover?

They were in T.'s lab, where Father Lamy was fueling the special generator with a zeolite compound, when an old woman entered; she was dressed in black with all sorts of odds and ends hanging from the large person of what proved to be the widow Cleveland as of 1910.

Squaw was quite aware of the shock her appearance had caused. "It took me forever to go through the files to find out how I'll look at forty-six with all this gray hair which, if I ever have the chance to be that age in the Institution, I'll dye moonglow blond."

"Is this gray hair really yours?" T. was not into age.

"No, Veal, darling, this is gray powder. I've made myself up to look the way Mr. Wilson expects me to look. The other Frankie reminds me that we saw a fair amount of him during the eight years he was president of Princeton. After all, we were practically neighbors."

"And you're a widow."

Squaw frowned. "I asked Grover just how much history is going to change if Wilson doesn't get elected and he said, everything everywhere will change in the most dramatic way. And I said, is this a good idea? And he said, to stay out of one big war and stop a second one with these new weapons is worth anything, and I said, yes, but suppose something *worse* happens? And he said, one good deed is enough for anybody and anyway maybe somebody else will come along even later than now and help us all out. Or maybe not, I felt like saying but didn't."

T. was already very much aware of the endless permutations of what they were doing. One of his uncles had made a fortune in the First World War. Did this mean that without the war he'd not have had the money to buy the K Street house and T. might not have been able to go to St. Albans? Or, and this thought terrified T., suppose some attractive man killed in the First World War had lived instead and T.'s mother had gone and married him instead of his father, which meant there would be no T.

"This could be a really big mistake," T. said, more to himself than to Squaw or to Father Lamy who was now at the control panel, ready to go.

"Whatever that is not in accord with God's will must be accursed," proclaimed Father Lamy.

"We don't know God's will." Since T. had found no trace of God in the cosmos, he did not take seriously Father Lamy's occasional outbursts.

"I am sure," said the majestic widow of President Grover Cleveland, "that T.'s powers are God-given and to stop a slaughter in 1914 and perhaps the end of the world thirty years later is to follow God's will."

"Or the devil's." Father Lamy, in his state of jitters, had gone very white in the face. To make sure that the priest, in a fit of religious ecstasy, did not interfere with the controls, T. put them on a timer that only he knew how to set and reset. He also made the generator Father Lamy–proof.

Father Lamy had now produced a rosary. "First, pray with me. For I am the way and the life . . ."

The timer switched on dimensions one and two. Squaw was delighted at the beauty of the Lyme garden.

"I wonder if I ever got to go there in real life."

"*We'll* never know," said T., noticing with mild alarm that Father Lamy was on his knees, babbling in Latin.

Then dimension three switched on and warm honeysuckle air engulfed them. Squaw sighed. "This is one of the things I miss in our institutional life, flowers . . ."

Dimension four. Father Lamy covered his face with his hands, and repeated, "I am the way . . ."

"No," said T., very strong. "I am the way now . . ."

Then T. led Mrs. Grover Cleveland into Sunday morning, June 25, 1910.

6

I THINK I'VE been here before." Squaw looked up at the many-gabled gray-shingled house, visible in back of the willow tree.

"Then if you were here before, you probably know what we're going to do next."

She frowned. "Don't make my head ache. Anyway, back in my own time, I'm only twenty-two so I haven't got this far yet except as a . . . a presentiment." She was quietly proud of the word.

They were now standing next to the willow tree, nothing but green all around them. In the midmorning green distance, a gardener was pushing a lawn mower below the verandah where two lean strong-jawed young women were talking intently. "Wilson's daughters. Very plain, as I recall."

T. wondered what sort of lives they were going to lead without a president for father. The endless ramifications of what he was going to do would be so wide-ranging that . . . T. suddenly felt a bit uneasy. Suppose . . . ?

But he was saved from morbid introspection by the appearance of Woodrow Wilson; he was approaching them not from the house but from the shadowy part of the rose garden where, presumably, only T. and Squaw could see the vague outline of the door to the New Mexico laboratory.

"Mrs. Cleveland!" Wilson smiled. He seemed, to T., to have just about as many—and rather larger—teeth as the two presidents Roosevelt combined.

Then T. was aware of an entirely new Squaw. She was now very much the maturely gracious former First Lady of the Land. "Dear Mr. Wilson." She gave him her hand, which he took, looking as if he might kiss it while she looked like the queen of Sheba, ready for homage.

"Mrs. Wilson's not here. But she does want me to say how sorry she was not to have been able to attend President Cleveland's funeral and she only hopes . . ."

"The flowers—and the accompanying note—so sensitive—more than made up for any absence." Squaw laid it on. But, as she did, T. wondered just how the twenty-two-year-old Frankie could recall something that had not yet happened to her. Could it be that when she stepped into 1910 she acquired a "memory" of things subsequent? T. was aware that Wilson was now looking at him curiously.

Squaw was smooth. "My nephew. Master Veal. One of the Santa Fe Veals."

"Of course. Of course. Santa Fe." Wilson shook hands with T.; already a politician, Wilson affected an intimacy with every Veal that ever was. "Now, Mrs. Cleveland . . ."

"Yes," said Squaw with a bright smile. *"Now."*

"You said you had something of great urgency to tell me." He indicated a wooden bench back of the willow. Squaw motioned for T. to stay where he was as Wilson escorted her to the bench.

T. sat cross-legged on the grass. Downwind of the bench, he could hear a good deal of the conversation. At first it came in mysterious bursts, snatches.

"Bermuda . . ."

". . . lifelong friend of the family . . ."

". . . grieves me to say . . ."

"Blackmail!"

In the course of the exchange, Wilson's face had flushed a dark red and the thin lips shut tight over the great teeth. With his huge chin and shut mouth, he looked to T. like one of those mysterious Easter Island statues in the *National Geographic.*

"Blackmail." Wilson repeated the word.

"I know." Squaw looked at him compassionately. "I did everything—*everything*—to try and dissuade your adversaries from unearthing all this. Let the dead past bury its dead, I said more than once . . ."

"If that's the case, Mrs. Cleveland, why are *you* here if not to act on their behalf and get me to reject a nomination that the good people of New Jersey wish to bestow upon me?"

"Mr. Wilson." There was now an unexpected edge to Squaw's voice. "I am here to avert a great scandal. We hardly know each other but I have the greatest admiration for you and for poor Mrs. Wilson. I am also a good Democrat and I recall how when Grover and I heard you speak when you were sworn in as president of Princeton, Grover said, 'That could be our next Democratic president.' Well, you still can be but you must see to it that this story is—somehow—laid to rest between now and 1912."

"I shall tell the press, if challenged, what Mr. Cleveland himself said: 'Publish and be damned.' " Wilson removed his pince-nez and began to polish it with a handkerchief; his hands were trembling.

"That was the duke of Wellington who said that." Squaw smiled. "But neither he nor Grover had a lady standing by with a lawyer, ready to sue."

"I cannot believe that . . . the lady in question would. Upon what ground?"

Squaw removed some papers from her reticule; gave them to Wilson. "You will see that, according to her deposition . . ."

The brick-red face slowly turned sallow. Sweat beaded the receding hairline. "None of this is true, Mrs. Cleveland."

"I have no way of knowing. Nor do I care. All that I know is that should you run for governor of New Jersey this year, those lies or truths or half-truths or whatever they are will be on the front page of every newspaper in the land. This would not please the voters of New Jersey nor, in Grover's view, the blue-nosed trustees of Princeton."

"I can explain . . ."

"Please, Mr. Wilson. Don't. I am certain of your . . . uh, innocence. But once such a story is out . . ."

Squaw stared at Wilson who replaced his pince-nez and surveyed the rose garden. Finally, he said, "What assurance, Mrs. Cleveland, do I have that this will not be used anyway?"

"Your own good character. Also, you'll now have ample time to . . . deal with the lady. But you don't have sufficient time in the next few weeks, much less days. As you know, I am still active with the party's leadership and although you were, far and away, our first choice for governor—and *beyond*—we are now—reluctantly, in my case—backing the mayor of Trenton . . ."

"The blackmailer!" Wilson looked as if he might be having a small stroke. According to Grover, who had researched him closely, Wilson had been prone to minor strokes all his life.

"No, it is not he. This information came to me from the gentleman who asked me to come see you, the Speaker of the House."

"Champ Clark! So that's it. He wants the 1912 nomination for himself."

"As you do, quite naturally, for yourself, should you first challenge and then defeat Mayor Katzenbach for governor of New Jersey this year."

"Mr. Wilson!" The voice was that of a young man; he was standing at the top of the lawn, jacket over one arm, mopping sweat from his face. Wilson looked up, expression oddly vacant. Stroke?

Then he pulled himself together: "Mr. Inglis. Come down here."

"It should be simple now." Squaw rose, majestically. "Tell him to go back to Trenton, back to our friend Mr. Harvey— who agrees with me, by the way—and tell him that you prefer not to run for governor this year. Meanwhile, as a progressive and a reformer in the Cleveland tradition, you'll gladly support Mayor Frank S. Katzenbach. Come, Veal. Let's take a stroll through that lovely rose garden on the way to our motorcar. Good morning, Mr. Wilson." Squaw had carefully timed her departure to just a moment before the arrival of Inglis.

Before Inglis could shake the stunned Wilson's hand, Squaw and T. were halfway to their point of exit.

"That was super!" T. couldn't wait to get Squaw out of her old-lady costume and into bed.

Then, pushing to one side an arbor of red rambling roses, they stepped out of the lush green Connecticut morning and into the sagebrush-smelling shadowy laboratory.

Father Lamy looked awestruck when T. gave him the bull's-eye gesture with thumb and forefinger.

"I'm going to freshen up." Squaw vanished into what passed in 1886 for a bathroom.

"It worked!" Father Lamy shook his head. "I never believed it possible."

"Well, we got through O.K. But whether it really worked or not . . ." As T. switched off the generator, he wondered whom to get in touch with. Dr. Smithson, if he really existed, was not available from T.'s side. Except for Eleanor Roosevelt's direct telephone line to herself in the White House, none of the presidents or first ladies could communicate with anyone on the outside. There was always Stanley, of course, but if everything had changed he would have changed, too.

While Father Lamy replaced the radioactive fuel in its lead container, T. got through to Bentsen, who seemed oddly harried.

"Well, T. how did it go?"

"I think I . . . well, I hope I did everything right." For some reason T. found himself not wanting to volunteer anything to this . . . not entirely trustworthy Bentsen. "How are the first ladies?"

"How are the what?"

"The first ladies exhibit. Any changes in the . . . uh, lineup?"

"Should there be? I'm afraid those dummies in those awful dresses are just about the last thing on my mind today."

Squaw joined T.; she was now her youthful self. "So what's the big deal?" she asked Bentsen.

"Well, while the two of you were vacationing in the Land of Enchantment Exhibit, this is what happened last night."

Bentsen held up the front page of *The New York Times* for June 25, 1940.

JAPANESE BOMB PEARL HARBOR was the headline. Squaw gasped. T. did his best to read as rapidly as he could from the monitor. PRESIDENT TO ASK FOR DECLARATION OF WAR. Apparently, half the Pacific fleet had been sunk.

"What about the Germans?" T. asked.

The newspaper was replaced on the screen by Bentsen's face. "The Germans?" He sounded mystified. "What about the Germans?"

"Well, they have this alliance, don't they? With Japan . . ."

Bentsen had opened the newspaper to an inside page. "Well, let's see. The Europeans are all shocked—blah, blah, blah—and, naturally, they are all on our side, or so they say. Prime Minister Chamberlain is promising every assistance, short of war. The French, too. While . . ." Bentsen's eyes skipped down the page. "The Germans—since you're so interested—have promised us every assistance—short of war, naturally. Chancellor von Papen says . . ."

T. shut the screen off.

"Poor Veal," said Squaw.

"There's no Hitler and still there's a war." T. thought again of the dummy—himself—beside the door to the Military Exhibit. The dummy, he was grimly certain, was still there.

"But," said Squaw, who could often, he now realized, read his mind, "Bentsen's still in his lab. They're still working on the nuclear bomb."

"Are they?" T. was beginning to grasp the enormity of what he had done. "If there's no Hitler, Albert Einstein is still back in Europe and so is Fermi." T. turned to Father Lamy. "Can you determine if we're still on the same string of light—you know, history like we've known it so far—or have we skipped over to another string?"

Father Lamy produced his luminous strings on the screen. Then he focused the machine on one that had a slight curve to it. He zeroed in on the curve, raced backward and forward in time; north and south and east and west, encompassing space, until he picked up the Trylon and Perisphere of the World's Fair in New York.

"I'm pretty sure we're on the same string we've always been on. Somewhat altered, of course, by what you've just done which we'll never know, of course because we now have nothing to compare it to. Like what *might* have happened if Wilson had got to be president has never happened as far as we're concerned now."

T. was feeling definitely unwell. "So I've erased everything that was or was about to be from 1910 on."

"On our string, yes." Father Lamy had managed to get a close shot of what proved to be the Japanese air force blowing up the American fleet at Pearl Harbor. "Look at that!"

T. switched off the machine. "Listen! If I wanted to go back *before* I interfered . . ."

"You could go back to then, of course. But once you meet Mr. Wilson everything ever after is changed. Of course, if you went back and then *didn't* meet him, it's possible . . ."

"What about another—parallel string of light?"

"Why not? But which one? They are infinite, those strings. You could spend a whole lifetime looking for the right one to enter or not to enter, as the case may be . . ."

"But, look . . ."

"Veal, it's done." Squaw was suddenly in charge. "Don't panic. After all, you're still you, just the way you are—or were, and so is Dr. Bentsen . . ."

"But I've erased everything that was supposed to happen after June 25, 1910 . . ."

"Forever—on this string." Father Lamy raised his head high and smiled at the glory of God in His heaven as revealed in science. "This means that you could always go back again and *not* meet Mr. Wilson or meet him and have the same discussion— By the way—at the risk of sounding prurient, what did happen between him and the lady in Bermuda?"

But T. and Squaw had already withdrawn to the bedroom. They had never made love so wildly before. Squaw had always been playful older sister. Now she was perfectly fitted mate. At the end she touched his chest with wonder. "Look," she said, "hair."

T. looked; was surprised. "Must be that Connecticut air," he said. "I'm not chicken anymore," he said contentedly. He reentered her. "I'm hawk now."

———————

By the time T. and Squaw got back from the Old Western American Exhibit, it was night and the laboratories were shut.

"Come home with me. Grover will know everything." Squaw led T. into the Assembly of First Ladies, where what was, by day, a medium-sized exhibition hall now looked like a long street, covered with asphalt at Mrs. Roosevelt's far end and cobblestones at Lady Washington's end. Gas streetlamps, starting in front of Mrs. Madison's house, changed to electrical ones at Mrs. Harrison's house, next door to Squaw's. In the distance, down the line, T. could see several small figures, men and women in eighteenth-century dress converging on Lady Washington's "manse," as they called it.

"The Virginians!" Mrs. Cleveland sighed. "When we first got here we all paid and returned calls but it really just never works out. Oil and water. We have absolutely nothing in common with those folks from the last century even though Grover claims to admire them so much—some of them, anyway, like Mr. Jefferson, until he decided to enthrall us one evening with his fiddle! How I pitied the poor cat who'd given up his gut for that violin string."

"What about the twentieth century?" T. tried to look up the line to where he knew the Wilson residence was—or had been—but no one was to be seen anywhere at all in that section of the street except for Mrs. Roosevelt, whose tall figure resembled the Statue of Liberty in the distance. She was depositing a stack of mail in a modern postal box.

"That woman never stops working." Squaw waved at her successor, who waved cheerfully back.

Grover was in his usual chair, with books on the table at his side, and on the floor at his feet.

"So?" Squaw kissed the top of his head. "What's happening?"

Grover chuckled. "Well, you've come to the right person. But I must tell you it was touch and go for a while there if I was going to be able to remember the way things were before Master Veal intervened." He turned to Veal, seated now in a chair opposite him with a box of chocolates on his lap, thoughtfully provided by Squaw, who affected to worry about the nourishment of her "growing boy."

"Then everything *did* change?" T. had found nougat, his favorite.

"No one can ever know how much has changed. But I don't want to go through that sensation again, ever. It was just like dying all over again. Yet I guess that for those who didn't know what was happening it must've happened like . . ." Grover snapped his pudgy fingers. "Old memory was replaced by new memory. But as I was expecting the shift, it was most unpleasant. I saw stars . . ."

"Strings?" T. was curious.

"No. Stars. Thought I was going to faint. Then I came back to . . . well, normal. That is, I remembered everything about your mission and so, for me, nothing was changed. But then I took a stroll up the line. Past the Harrisons. Past me in my second term. Past the McKinleys. The Teddy Roosevelts. The Tafts and then . . ."

Grover got slowly to his feet. "I think we should go and meet Mr. Wilson's replacement . . ."

"I'll bet it's Teddy Roosevelt again, with his Bull Moose Party." Squaw put the box of chocolates away.

"No, not Teddy, though God knows he did his best to wreck his own party along with Taft."

As they strolled up the line, so like a Georgetown street on a summer evening, Grover bowed to Mrs. Harrison, who was spying from her front bay window. She quickly vanished.

"Awful creature." Squaw averted her gaze.

"Not as bad as in life. Sort of half and half. But then we're in-betweens, all of us here, except for Master Veal. Good evening, Mr. Roosevelt."

Theodore Roosevelt, in shirtsleeves, was standing on the brick steps to his front door, rifle in hand. "Mr. Cleveland." He clicked his teeth oddly. T. felt guilty that he knew practically nothing about him other than he was in some way responsible for the Panama Canal and everyone catching yellow fever from mosquitoes. "Thought I heard a prowler."

"No prowlers, TR, at the Smithsonian."

"Oh, yes. I forgot." Roosevelt frowned. Pressed his brow. "Had the oddest dream just now. Nodded off in my chair.

Dreamed that—what's his name? You know? President of Princeton."

"Wilson."

"Wilson, yes. Dreamed *he* got elected president. Beat both Taft and me. Then I woke up. Thank the Lord. Well . . ." He turned to go inside; paused. "You going to the end of the line to see my niece Eleanor?"

"No, not quite to the end."

"Terrible thing, those Japs. I warned against them years ago. But no one listens, ever, do they? Anyway, I built up The Great White Fleet."

"Which now they've sunk . . ." T. thought Grover sounded rather too chipper.

"Not all of it. We'll beat them, never fear. Though it's a tragedy that that lightweight cousin of mine's president and not me."

"You must tell him what to do, Mr. President." Squaw was radiant in the violet evening light. "Hold a convocation."

"I've already asked for one. Time of peril. I got Eleanor to ring Franklin just now. But she couldn't get through. She'll try tomorrow. He must get England and Germany on our side. As allies. As *natural* allies. To preserve the white race so that we can pursue our destiny to the setting sun if need be!" TR's high voice went falsetto and broke; then he aimed his rifle at the ceiling—sky—and fired. "Bald eagle! Damn! I missed." He bowed to the Clevelands. "Mr. President. Madam." He marched into his house and slammed the door.

"Was there really a bald eagle in here?" T. was curious.

"How would he know?" Squaw laughed. "He's blind as a bat."

"Curious how all the conservationists are forever shooting and stuffing wildlife." Grover was more amused than censorious. Then he stopped in front of a redbrick house with a fanlight over the door, much like all the others on the line.

He lifted the brass door knocker and let it fall. As they waited, Mrs. Roosevelt reappeared on the front steps of her house at the very end of the line. There was, T. noted, nothing but darkness past her: the future?

"Dear Mr. Cleveland, I think we must hold a convocation to discuss what has happened. Franklin will need all the advice that he can get. I have a call in to him now. So if you could rally the others . . ."

"Ancestral voices?" Grover was amiable. "Well, I'll make the supreme sacrifice and go down the line and talk to General Washington. I suppose it'll take me a day to explain to him what this is all about. He's probably never heard of Japan or anything west of all that Ohio River real estate he bought."

"You'll explain, beautifully, I know. We must rally round, unorganized dummies though we are. I must see if the Ladies' Garment Workers Union will take us in. We need—what is the phrase? Political clout." Eleanor disappeared into her house as a florid stout man opened the door for the Clevelands and T.

"Mr. Cleveland! What an honor. Come in. Come in. I was just having what is known nowadays as a nightcap." He smelled of whisky. Then Grover introduced T. to the late President William Jennings Bryan, who led them into the parlor where there was a smell of cooking from the back of the house.

"I ceased to be temperance upon arrival here as did Mrs. Bryan—she's making chicken and rice with red-eye gravy. You're welcome to stay for supper—and I agreed that since we're here, sort of on holiday, it's really too late to worry about our health or the voters or even our morals as the great book of life itself is closed for us."

"You have done your part, Great Commoner. More than your part. *You kept the faith.*" Grover struck a grandiose note that T. quite liked.

Bryan poured whisky for Grover and Coca-Cola for Squaw and T. "I *think* that this patented drink no longer contains the essence of the coca leaf as it originally did. What a row we had with Congress over the Coca-Cola syrup formula! The entire Georgia delegation threatened to walk out. Everybody must've been a drug fiend back then. But we made them change the formula."

"Settling in?" Grover gave Bryan a curious look. T. realized, then, that the Bryans had only arrived in the last twenty-four hours, abruptly replacing the Wilsons. Now T. would never get a chance to see the second Mrs. Wilson, unless he left the Smithsonian and paid her a call in—was it S Street where she was currently living? But then if Wilson had never become president, she probably would never have married him and so . . .

"Settled in?" Bryan looked surprised. "Why, we've been here ever since I checked out and rendered my bill to my Maker. What year are we in now?"

"Nineteen thirty-nine." T. was now the expert in these matters, since the exhibit celebrities tended to have little sense of time outside their own completed spans while employees like Bentsen had completely adjusted to the new history and totally forgotten the old—the shift had been a bit like going to daylight saving time in the night.

"Fifteen years ago, I was called. Praise the Lord!" Bryan raised his arms like a revivalist.

Grover and Squaw exchanged a knowing look. As far as Bryan was concerned, he had been duly elected president (on his fourth try) and now he was an historical personage on display with his peers.

"We were just chatting with TR . . ." Grover began.

Bryan nodded. "Yes. I heard a rifle go off and so assumed he was busy slaughtering our feathered friends in the street again."

"Luckily, he missed." Grover was serene; and mischievous. "He did say he had had an awful dream that Woodrow Wilson had been elected in 1912."

"Woodrow who?" Bryan added whisky to his water.

"The president of Princeton."

"Oh, yes, yes. I met him once. When I was vice president . . ."

"*Vice* president?" Squaw was startled: she prided herself on being able to name all the presidents and vice presidents—at least until T.'s intervention. Grover looked even more mysterious and amused. Later, after supper, he explained to Squaw and T. how the Speaker of the House of Representatives, Champ Clark of Missouri, had been elected president in a three-way race with Taft and Roosevelt. Clark's running mate was Bryan, who took second place on the ticket in the hope that, at long last, lightning would strike, which at really long last it did.

On a visit to New York City, President Clark died of a stroke in the arms, it was said, of the dashing actress Ethel Barrymore, wife to the half-British war correspondent, Winston Churchill. President Bryan then, "single-handedly," his own phrase, kept the United States out of the European war, which petered out in a stalemate shortly after the Kaiser became a Christian Scientist. Bryan, meanwhile, had been elected in his own right in 1916 on the irresistible platform "He kept us out of war." Once peace was assured, the United States and Russia, now the two great world powers, proceeded to work in close concert to help rebuild the ruined economies of Britain, France, and Germany.

"Now tell me what happened last night, at—where was it?" Bryan lit a great cigar.

"Pearl Harbor," said T., not certain that Grover knew where it was either. "In Hawaii."

"Always preferred Miami Beach myself," said Bryan. "Anyway, if the Czar had done as I told him and put Russia on the silver standard—ten not sixteen to one was my advice—there would have been no communist-atheistical revolution in Russia and no Japan throwing its weight around today, which they would never have dared do when Czar Nick and I were running things. You know Miami Beach, don't you, Grover?"

"Well, it was just a sandbar back in my day before—what's his name, Saddler?"

Bryan frowned. "No, begins with an 'F' . . ."

"Flagler," said T. who knew his geography because Mr. Pratt did not teach it.

Bryan beamed, his thin mouth wide like a catfish. "That's it, sonny. Bright boy. Well, the wife and I found this wonderful bungalow on the beach where I was looking forward to retirement but then I had my stroke just before Harding got elected and . . ." He sighed. " 'Thus, the best laid plans o' mice and men gang aft a-gley,' as the poet says."

From the next room, a woman's voice: "Com'n git it!"

Despite his girth, Bryan sprang to his feet—like Tarzan of the apes, thought T. "Mother's got enough for all." Bryan led them into the next room. As they passed through the parlor, Squaw whispered to T., "You should've seen this place when the Wilsons were here, like a college reading room. Now it's real nice and down home."

T. gazed with awe at the rooms, literally redone overnight with the arrival of the Bryans, who had come from who knew what predummy limbo to take up stately residence, presumably forever, on the line.

———◦———

The next day T. returned to his lab next to Bentsen's. The assistants appeared to be busy but, actually, everyone was reading newspapers while, in the background, the radio was never switched off. President Roosevelt was now on his way to the

Capitol to ask Congress for war. Apparently, the losses at Pearl Harbor were greater than the administration was willing to admit, while there were rumors that in the next few hours Los Angeles was due for an air raid.

"And there's no defense of any kind." Bentsen and T. were now in T.'s former lab. As they talked, T. tried to figure out what he had been working on before the time shift. For all intents and purposes he was a different person from what he had been before; and with a memory of only the pre-Lyme world. He was also, he noticed with some amazement, much larger than he had been before the visit to Lyme, while the golden peach fuzz on his cheeks was now wiry and Bentsen had said, pointedly, that he would lend him a razor. None of his clothes fit. What had happened?

As Bentsen discussed, in his jittery way, the perils that faced the United States, T. was working his way through the memory banks of his various computers.

"They've already started an invasion of the Philippine Islands and it's obvious that they are headed for the oil fields in Java and Sumatra . . ."

T. could summon up very little interest in what the Japanese were doing at the far end of the Pacific. But he was amazed that (pre-Lyme) everyone had been so mesmerized by Hitler that the simultaneous crisis in Asia had gone practically unnoticed—at least before T.'s intervention.

While Bentsen droned on, T. was beginning to reconstruct his own work since his arrival at the Castle in the post-Lyme world. The theory for a fission bomb had been worked out; there would be no chain reaction. So far so good—at least so far as he was able to remember what had been accomplished. The atomic center at Los Alamos was further along than it had been before. This meant that the Japanese had been threatening the United States before he took his trip to the past—or was it the other way around?

"Ever since 1937 when they sunk our gunboat, the *Panay,* in Chinese waters"—Bentsen tried and failed, thanks to trembling fingers, to light his pipe—"they've been preparing for this attack. And what's more, the administration knew what was coming. General Lindbergh even went public with his fears when he dedicated the Earhart air base at Howland Atoll in the Pacific. But the president and Congress weren't listening."

T. was not listening to Bentsen either. He was beginning to find some very strange things indeed in his memory bank.

Someone—T. himself?—had been doing highly advanced work on space-time. Indeed the approach to any crossroad was now simplicity itself. Zeolite provided velocity while a new scanning device could comprehend and isolate in an instant the desired point of entry. The future was still less accessible than old light, but much of it was within easy range. Even so, T. quickly scanned the immediate years ahead in the Washington, D.C., area. As he suspected, everything was in flux. A new building would start to go up; then be replaced by an even newer one, a brand-new highway would abruptly turn into a park. Everything fluid; random; potential. Like life itself.

Lindy ambled into T.'s lab. He alone seemed at ease and unperturbed. He wore the uniform of an army major general, with silver wings. Bentsen sprang to civilian attention. "Congratulations, General."

"For what?" asked T.

"I'm the new chief of the Army Air Force."

"We all feel a lot more secure," said Bentsen, who did not look as if he felt even halfway secure.

"Oh, we're secure enough. For now. They can't deliver a bomb to our mainland . . ."

"What about this coming raid on Los Angeles?" Bentsen, in a last attempt to light his pipe, lit the cuff of his smock.

"They had one aircraft carrier, west of Catalina. Now sunk. Well, T., it looks like we're going to be needing your work sooner than we figured . . ."

"You predicted this, almost two years ago." Bentsen had put his burning sleeve into an empty drawer where lack of oxygen put out the flame. The homely practicalities of a scientific mind always impressed T.

"Well, so I did. Though I can't say the president was all that grateful for my advice. But self-defense comes first. Even for an old-time pacifist like me." Lindy motioned to Bentsen. "Would you excuse us please?" Bentsen left.

"The problem is this, T. . . ." Lindy began.

"How do we deliver the bomb?" T. had worked that out from Lindy's reference to the so-called raid on Los Angeles which had turned out to be one small bomb that landed in a parking lot in the San Fernando valley.

"So you tell me, genius kid."

As always, T. was flattered to be treated not only as an equal but as an expert by the Lone Eagle himself.

"Aircraft carrier?" T. knew the answer to that one.

"Have to build new ones first. Because with Pearl knocked out . . ."

"Six months?"

Lindy shook his head glumly. "A year at the least. Meanwhile, they have a thousand miles of island bases between us and them and a first-rate air force. We're going to have to island-hop all the way across the Pacific Ocean, or so naval intelligence tells me."

"There isn't that much time." T. thought of himself.

"Two, three years unless we can come up with something spectacular."

"A long time." T. heard his own voice as if he were someone else. Then a bell went off in his head. "Time. That's the key."

"Time always is, in a way. That's why they hit us first, of course. We'd already quarantined them. We cut off their access to fuel oil so they figured they had nothing to lose by knocking out our fleet and heading south for the Dutch oil fields. Once they get them, there's nothing much we can do except . . ." Lindy sighed. "Go nuclear, only . . . How do we deliver?"

"Time-space is one way of delivering."

Lindy was attentive. "So when, in time? And where, in space?"

"I don't know the answer to either but that's how we'll get them. In time."

"Well, you've been working on nothing but space-time. Success?"

"A bit." T. grinned. He was not about to tell even the sympathetic Lindy how he had eliminated two world wars in Europe while stupidly ignoring the Japanese in the Pacific and on the mainland of China. Worse, he had even got a perfect grade in the *Time* magazine "Current Events" test that Mr. Sofield gave his class each year. He should have known better. Instead, he had simply figured that with no Hitler and no European war, there would have been no Axis pact between Japan and Germany and so with peace in Europe—the civil war in Belgium was pretty dull stuff—he had quite overlooked far-off Asia. Well, T. could not be expected to memorize all the history that was going on at any given minute.

Mr. Lincoln's face filled T.'s monitor. "Tonight, ladies and gentlemen, in the Assembly of First Ladies, there will be a convocation of all the presidents—and their ladies, of course—as well as a special midnight visit from Mr. Franklin Delano Roosevelt on whose—how shall I put it—watch, this terrible catastrophe has taken place. He comes to seek our counsel. Therefore, we shall, as in times past, rally round the flag. I shall also take advantage of this unique opportunity to reveal our latest acquisitions of yellow glazed earthenware, presented to the Institution by the ever-generous du Pont family of Wilmington, Delaware."

T. switched off the curator of pots. The image of Mr. Lincoln was immediately replaced by a highly magnified letter written in the now familiar purple ink.

"My dear young man, do not despair. You accomplished brilliantly what you intended to do and saved millions of twentieth-century lives—not to mention beautiful buildings and works of art which, unlike us, are truly irreplaceable. You could not foresee more than the one war at a time and so do not blame yourself for the present embarrassment to American self-esteem brought on, if I may be critical of my host nation, by a most unbecoming racial arrogance. I know you think it time we meet but I prefer that you work your own way through this particular game of Parcheesi. You hold the key to the lock already. Meanwhile, one hint: it is in the land of ice and snow and the Aurora Borealis where glory awaits you. Also, Stanley Sofield has news for you. I remain your most obedient servant. James Smithson, as penned this historic day from beneath the basketball court."

T. promptly rang Stanley, who was between classes and sounded hungover. "If only Landon had been elected in thirty-six none of this would be happening."

"Stanley, how old am I?"

"Are you all right?"

"The Smithsonian is running me ragged."

"All play and no work I'll bet." Stanley sighed. "Well, it's right here on your card. You were born in 1923. And next June you'll be graduating from here, at seventeen. You still haven't come back to us, have you?"

"No. I've been too busy."

"Don't stay away too long. Time's passing."

"Listen, Stanley. Something's off. Way off. I used to be born in 1925. But for some reason, with no First World War, I'm born two years earlier . . ."

There was an ominous moan from Stanley. "I can't—repeat cannot—deal with this. You'd better get back here and rejoin your other self before it's too late. That place is doing you no good." A bell rang in the background. Stanley hung up.

It took T. several hours to reconstruct what he had been doing since the now—in every way?—altered Good Friday. The doodle theorem on the algebra exam still had to do with the limiting of chain reaction. Dr. Oppenheimer had been called in and the program to create a "safe" nuclear bomb was proceeding at a leisurely pace. No one, apparently, had feared a nuclear attack from the Japanese or, indeed, an attack of any kind. President Roosevelt, however, had been faced in 1938 with a recurrence of the Depression and so he had asked Congress for a military buildup with an emphasis, thanks to Dr. Oppenheimer, on what was vaguely termed "unconventional weapons." Within a year of the buildup, there was full employment and Japan was being targeted as the official enemy for a future war. Lindy, a loyal friend of military aviation, was now a loyal friend of the president.

As T. went through the memory banks, he looked in vain for his second and most important doodle, the one dealing with time-space. What had happened to his notes? He knew that most of his work had been with time-space and that there had been a number of breakthroughs based on extrapolations from the Minkowski square. He could now set his space-time coordinates in a fraction of the time it had originally taken him to get to Lyme, Connecticut; he would also, he realized, need only a fraction of the power. He—or someone—had been doing an astonishing amount of work in the now—for him—lost year at the Castle.

T. threw a single switch and walked into Father Lamy's New Mexican lab.

"I thought you'd be dropping by." The priest acted as if they had just seen each other, which was probably the case. "What's the latest?"

T. gave him the war news. Father Lamy played with his rosary. "Is this Armageddon at last?"

"I doubt it. According to army intelligence, they know how to make a nuclear bomb but they haven't got very far along, five years maybe . . ."

"We'll need at least three. Then how to deliver?"

"Lindy will think of something. I just saw him. He wants me to keep on the . . . uh . . . well, the way we've been going . . . You know? with space-time."

Father Lamy adjusted his blue-glass picture window. What had been opaque was now transparent. A huge world-of-the-future World's Fair sort of building now occupied the middle distance. T. did his best not to appear astonished: after all, the post-Lyme T. must have watched "the factory" as it was being built on this string of light.

"There was a very moving dedication yesterday. Top secret, of course. But even so, Vice President Garner was here and all the military brass. That German architect, too. He's a world-class genius, no doubt of it."

T. was not interested in German architects. "You know we're top priority now," he said. "I mean they got their nuclear fission stuff all lined up and now they'll need us to . . ." T. trailed off. This was getting rough. How to find out what he was supposed to know?

"More trips to Lyme, Connecticut, to see . . ." Father Lamy chuckled. "Who *was* that chap you and Mrs. Cleveland talked to?"

So far so good. Father Lamy had forgotten all about Woodrow Wilson. "Oh, just a mathematician. From Princeton. Listen."

"Yes?"

"Well . . ."

"I'm listening."

"Just when would you say we first started in, I mean on our own out here. With . . ." T. was aware that Father Lamy was looking at him oddly.

"Are you all right?" the priest finally asked.

"Oh, sure. It's this war thing and Lindy wanting me to— you know . . ."

"I don't know. But if you want to retrace your steps, you better take a look at your secret tape . . ."

"Secret tape? What's that?"

"If you'd ever let me know what was on it, it wouldn't be secret, would it? You've locked everything up. In your lab— I suppose."

Obviously Father Lamy had been snooping.

"O.K." T. started for the door.

Outside in the dusty roadway, a large German Mercedes was parked. Two men sat side by side in the front seat, staring raptly at the new building with its cylindrical towers, each topped by a stylized American eagle. Farther up the road was a barbed-wire fence and a guardhouse with armed soldiers. At the factory, military men as well as civilians were going in and out of the building. Everyone looked appropriately grim: Pearl Harbor. Only the two Germans in the car seemed entirely at ease and content.

"Let me introduce you," said Father Lamy to T. "This is the Cher Maître and his assistant."

Politely the two men got out of the car and shook hands with T. The younger man, the assistant, spoke perfect English. "We already know about the work of this wunderkind."

"How?" T. was supposed to be the best-kept secret (after Dr. Smithson?) of the Institution.

"Through our dear friend Dr. Einstein." The great architect spoke clear if guttural English. He had a sort of halo of golden hair about his head and piercing gray-blue eyes. He looked like a saint in an old picture book, which was, no doubt, his intention. Not for nothing had T. studied from the gallery that marvelous zoo, the U.S. Senate, where ninety-six members each had his own unique act, ranging from angelic to amusingly diabolic.

"We've been hoping Dr. Einstein would come help us out, now the war's started."

"Cher Maître begged him." The young assistant looked sad.

Cher Maître nodded. "But he's such a pacifist—like me, of course. But I told him, look, Albert, when our civilization is threatened by the yellow hordes of Attila and Genghis and Tamerlane"—the voice became that of an archangel—"you must, I tell him, come to America's aid, as I have done with *this*!" He indicated the complex of buildings.

"Cher Maître's masterpiece," said the assistant, voice hushed. T. tried not to look too obvious as he stared at the security tag in the architect's lapel. The man was so famous Father Lamy had not even bothered to mention his name. On the tag, there was a color head shot of the archangel above his name, *S. Grubert.* A French not a German name if Stanley Sofield's expertise at keeping exactly one chapter ahead of his French class was to be relied on.

T. excused himself and left the Germans to worship Maître Grubert's masterpiece.

It took T. some time to figure out his own "masterpiece," if such a thing existed. Everything had been refiled according to a system whose code it took him the better part of an hour to break. Finally, he had more or less mastered his own handiwork.

There was a series of scanning shots of various crossroads in time, with incomprehensible notes. There were also odd lapses. The record of how he had got to Lyme, Connecticut, was not to be found. Instead, he had apparently been scanning the Japanese both at home and in their attempted conquest of China. There were several tapes where, accompanied by Lindy in a Stinson plane, they flew over various Japanese bases on various Pacific islands. One island in particular gave T. the creeps. Unfortunately, the name on the tape was in Japanese—had he learned Japanese in his post-Lyme year? A battle was in progress. An American fleet was offshore. Japanese troops were either underground or on guard in cement forts. A huge mountain, like a dinosaur, rose at one end of the island. More Japanese writing. A shot of Lindy, looking grim. Then a mathematical notation. T. switched off the set.

It did not take him long to work out what he had accomplished during his time in the *un*–Woodrow Wilson world. He had identified the arrow of time and fixed it in a number of directions, using the C., P., and T. formulas. C. meant exchanging particles for antiparticles. P. meant the mirror reversal of images so that what was on the left-hand side in one world was on the right-hand side in its exact opposite. T.—himself—represented the ability to reverse the direction of the motion of all particles—to go to what is past; to what is future. To go from disorder to order and back again in order to reorder.

After a number of breakthroughs, T. was assigned the task of gauging the effectiveness of the Japanese military. A pile of Japanese dictionaries and code banks showed that he had penetrated the language, but whatever it was in his brain that continued to comprehend and recall the pre-Lyme world now kept him from becoming who he had been—and what he had done—in the un-Wilson world that he had created one summer morning, with Squaw, in Connecticut. For the moment, he regarded it as urgent that he continue to know exactly what he had done—the extent of the disorder that he had created or, perhaps, deliberately ordered.

T. was surprised to find that one tape was locked off from the others. Lindy had emphasized the importance of total security, which had seemed pointless when he was working at Los Alamos in 1886 but now, of course, 1940 had occupied the mesa. The cantina down the road from Father Lamy's mission church had been replaced by a bar and grill, while the dirt road to Santa Fe was paved. All this had happened in post-Lyme time.

But, T. wondered, could T.—the quantum T.—go back to before? He set the coordinates—how simple it was now—and there was the old dusty road, the lean dogs, the cantina with Tom, Yank, and Reb entering it while Father Lamy stood in the roadway staring at the desert where . . . T. shifted time again and the German masterpiece was now in view though the Mercedes and the French archangel were gone. Only Father Lamy was still there. Dr. Oppenheimer must have given him a special time clearance; certainly, he deserved it.

Idly, T. punched out his new birth date on the screen: as he half suspected, that was the code for opening the secret tape.

There was Mr. Lincoln in his dusty office. T. was seated in the leather chair beside the curator's desk. "Although the physical sciences are a closed book to me, I do follow, as best I can, what's going on here in the Castle and in the laboratories along the mall not to mention your private activities out in the territories."

T. made polite sounds. Lincoln's desk was covered with pots, many of them of Pueblo Indian manufacture. "I am occasionally briefed—in a general way—on your work in what is known as time-space or space-time or whatever. I also know that you regularly visit the year 1886."

"Not exactly, sir. It's the Smithsonian 1886, not the real thing, actually. It's only an exhibit."

"Well." Mr. Lincoln smiled. "I guess it will do until the real thing goes away. You've also been able to enter other doors to the past and you have interfered with election results." T. could not tell from the expression on Lincoln's tape whether or not the Lyme, Connecticut, visit had taken place. If it had, how would this dummy have known about it?

"Let's say, sir, that I can pay a call on people in the past. In the future too, sort of, but I—we—no one can *do* anything on these trips. You know? *Because that would alter events.*"

Mr. Lincoln favored T. with a wink. "Bull-shit," he said amiably. "Or as the farmer said to the lawyer, never bull-shit a bull-shitter. I happen to know that you've met Mr. Baird, a one-time secretary of our Institution, and I know that he told you how he got me out of Ford's Theater that night with what proved to be a very mild concussion. I am now pretty much the man I was as of early evening Good Friday, 1865. It's taken time, of course, and I'd never have got myself back, you might say, if it hadn't been for these." There, like an ominous dark tower on the desk, were stacked the six volumes of Carl Sandburg's biography of Lincoln. "Had Mr. Sandburg—how I long to meet that bard!—not published the last four volumes last year or whenever 1939 was—or is—I would never have got to know myself again, never reacquired the memory that was lost from what felt no worse than your average bang on the head. But now I am truly Abraham Lincoln again, ready to begin my second term and change the unhappy years that the South was obliged to endure under my successors."

As T. watched himself listening to Lincoln, he was amazed at how well he was keeping his cool. "But, sir, assuming you are yourself again—uh, mentally—you are still, technically speaking, a dummy."

Lincoln nodded amiably. "You're quite right as to my current physical condition, but get me back into Ford's Theater earlier that night, and I am flesh and blood again, and history will take up where it was so savagely broken off even as lilacs in the dooryards of the republic bloomed. My boy, *you* can get me back to the theater and to my place in time so that government for some of the people for some of the time will not perish from some of the earth. I would appreciate it if you would not blab all this to Frankie Cleveland. Meanwhile, in this delicate matter, Dr. Bentsen will act as our assistant."

Lincoln rose to his awesome full height. "I must go now to prepare for the convocation. We are short eleven folding chairs."

In a state of perfect confusion, T. switched off the monitor.

One thing was certain. This monster must not be allowed out of the Castle. Wooden stake though the dummy's chest? Silver bullet? A lighted match? Sandburg's Lincoln must be stopped.

7

A T S U N D O W N T. reported for duty on the line just as the first of the two Cleveland houses materialized. The usually rather empty street was now full of presidents, coming and going. Ladies were conferring on what to wear while husbands were meeting along the sidewalk to discuss the convocation—and the crisis that had initiated it. At the start of the line, opposite the Washingtons' house, there was a sort of wooded village square not unlike a miniature Lafayette Park. Already in place were a number of folding chairs, a small stage, and numerous American flags from different periods of the republic.

Squaw opened the door; she was in her inaugural finery. "Grover's with Frank in the other house," she said. "I've never seen everyone so upset." She frowned. "My God, you've grown!"

"You like me, Mrs. Chicken Hawk?"

"Well, I'm still twenty-two. And older than you. But even so . . ."

T. looked at himself in a mirror. Yes, he was at least two inches taller than before Lyme. He also definitely needed a shave. He also noticed that instead of smelling like new bread he now smelled more like a western pony. Mr. Lincoln's blind secretary had bought him a new suit from Woodward & Lothrop's. Shoes and shirts, too. The Institution paid but T. was obliged to fill out a dozen forms, certifying his need for proper clothes in order to fulfill his scientific duties.

Squaw explained to him about convocations: apparently, there was always one before each war or military action. "Mr. Polk called the first one. He also opened the Smithsonian after we finally got Mr. Smithson's money out of England, all in gold and silver coins, they say. Anyway, Mr. Polk was very war-minded and started the war with Mexico so that we could get our hands on California and the West Coast."

"Poor Tom."

"Yes. Poor Tom. Then there was a terrible row at the 1861 convocation. Civil War doesn't bring out the best in our statesmen. Luckily, Grover and I hadn't arrived by then. But the biggest row was about twenty years ago when the government decided to carve those four heads on that cliff in the Black Hills. You know? South Dakota. The four greatest presidents is what Congress wanted. So a convocation was called by whoever was the living president at the time—I think he's one of the ones we've replaced—and it was decided to hold a secret ballot with only former presidents voting. Well, it took them a month! I've never seen such dirty politics in my life. No Southerner wanted Lincoln, so there goes the other end of the line. TR was considered a joke by everyone except himself. General Washington, of course, was everyone's first choice but he declined, most graciously, on the ground that the actual first president at the start of the Revolution was John Hancock. Oh, it was a mess. At one point, there was a compromise and Chester A. Arthur, General Garfield, Theodore Roosevelt, and Martha Washington were chosen unanimously."

"Martha Washington?"

"The general insisted. He didn't quite say so in so many words, but without her money he'd never have amounted to much . . ."

"So what stopped those four . . ."

President Cleveland and the older Mrs. Cleveland entered the parlor. "The good sense of Congress, finally," said Frank. "Though we still don't know how Teddy got his face up there in the end. Some sort of payoff, I suppose."

"He's ruthless," Grover observed mildly.

"You've gained weight," said Squaw, adjusting Grover's waistcoat. They were all dressed as they had been for Inauguration Day. T. enjoyed seeing the two Mrs. Clevelands together. They were like twins except that the older version had a few gray hairs and a small worried line between her brows. Squaw had assured T. that Frank had no idea of the nature of their relationship. "She's very prim. Funny, isn't it? Since we're the same person really but at different times."

Then the Pullman car chimes sounded.

"It's time," said Grover. "I must say I'm glad I'm not in Franklin's shoes."

Through the window that looked out on the line, presidential couples—and Mrs. Roosevelt by herself—made their way to the Washington manse. Grover stared with amusement at the passing parade. "I don't know how long I'm going to remember the way things were but I'm certainly enjoying all the changes that you two made in our lineup."

Squaw, who was sticking out her tongue at Mrs. Harrison's back, turned, in surprise, to Grover. "We just made two changes. Wilson's first term went to Champ Clark and there he is. Though what on earth Ethel Barrymore saw in him I'll never know."

"Why, Frank, it's always the office," said Grover, playfully, "never the man."

"You know what I mean. And then we produced, T. and I, President William Jennings Bryan for Wilson's second term and that was that."

"That," said Grover, "was *not* that. Harding was elected, as he was before your meddling—*inspired* meddling, of course— and then came Coolidge, who didn't run again . . ."

"And Herbert Hoover and that attractive wife got elected . . ." Squaw was waving at the Bryans, who waved back.

"No, dear." Her older self set her straight. "Mr. Hoover never ran. He was only famous because he fed all those starving Europeans after the Great War, which, thanks to you two, never took place and so there wasn't all that much starvation around. Anyway, Mr. Coolidge, who had said he wasn't going to run, changed his mind . . ."

"And so," said Grover, "Calvin Coolidge had to face Franklin Delano Roosevelt in 1928 and got himself thoroughly beaten because the voters couldn't be sure whether they were voting for TR or his cousin, FDR, so they just voted Roosevelt to be on the safe side."

Squaw put on her hat, a mass of bright ribbons. "How could Franklin Roosevelt get elected in 1928 and then re-elected in 1932 and then again in 1936?"

"I know, dear. It's astonishing. He's the first president to have three terms and now, with this war of his, he'll get a fourth term come November. General Washington refuses to discuss him. The general thought two terms more than enough for anyone, not to mention the poor country."

Grover opened the front door and the two versions of his wife preceded him into the street. T. paused a moment. "If I hadn't . . ." He stopped.

"Intervened." Grover smiled amiably. "What would have happened? Well, as I recall—*still* recall I'm happy to say—Roosevelt wouldn't have been elected until 1932. So he would now be running for a third instead of a fourth term, thanks to the war in Europe you stopped. But now, thanks to the war in Asia you may or may not have let happen . . ."

"Well, I suppose that I could always go back . . ."

"My boy." Grover was suddenly stern. "The first law of politics is, when in doubt, do absolutely nothing."

"Quantum physics is different."

"Then you stick with that. Meanwhile, you've changed quite enough history for one young life. Now let us join the ladies."

———•———

The Cleveland party was last to arrive in the small park opposite the Washington manse. The presidents and their sometimes duplicated wives were already seated in a semicircle beneath a towering chestnut oak that appeared to be actually growing out of the floor. On the platform, General Washington, wearing a brown silk suit with a much-ruffled shirt, sat in a throne at the center of the stage while Lady Washington sat directly below him in the audience.

This was the first up-close glimpse that T. had had of the original eighteenth-century presidents and he was struck not only by how small they all were, except Washington and Jefferson, but how pittèd with scars their faces were. They looked like the Catholic boys from Gonzaga High School, famous throughout the district for their raging acne.

On a trestle table below the platform there were several dozen yellow glazed pots and a sign that said BEQUEST OF THE PIERRE DU PONT DE NEMOURS FAMILY.

Mr. Lincoln ambled into view. He was regarded somewhat ambivalently by the occupants of the line. Some realized just who he was, an addled as well as martyred president, while others simply thought of him as just another redundant Smithsonian chief. The dividing line between the two schools of thought was Buchanan, Lincoln's immediate predecessor. Those presidents from the beginning to Lincoln detested the Civil War and everyone connected with it while those who had come after regarded Mr. Lincoln as the recreator of the old ramshackle republic. Although his relentless advocacy of the ceramics collection set everyone's teeth on edge, he himself was regarded as peculiarly tragic the farther up the line you went; yet he was neither one of the historical conclave nor even a serious member of the Institution's hierarchy. "He's crashed," as Squaw remarked, "between two stools."

T. whispered to Squaw, "Where's Mrs. Lincoln?"

"She never goes out. She doesn't acknowledge that the dummy up there is her husband. And I must say, in her place, neither would I."

Mr. Lincoln gazed thoughtfully at his predecessors and successors. T. wondered just how much he understood of his situation. Probably not too much until he had immersed himself in the rich sorghum of Carl Sandburg's prose. Now he was giving an impression of a great president that didn't sound quite right to T. who, admittedly, knew nothing at all about such things, but he did observe that the other presidents looked embarrassed and uncomfortable when Mr. Lincoln, standing next to the seated Washington, said, "I wish to welcome you to this convocation, tragic as the day must be for each man who has once, no matter how briefly, held the awesome rank of Commander in Chief in war—as Mr. Roosevelt does now—as well as first magistrate in peace. Tragic, too, for humble families named Bixby all up and down the land whose sons will soon be at risk to preserve hearth and home and give, perhaps, their all, or a part of their all as the du Pont family has so generously done with their choice collection of pottery, on view, as you can see . . ."

A small dark-eyed man got to his feet. "If I may interrupt this fascinating discourse . . ."

"That's President Polk," Squaw whispered in T.'s ear. "The Mexican War was all his doing. And the original Mr. Lincoln hated him."

"Of course you may." Mr. Lincoln was genial. "After all, you are the official Founding Father of this Institution, as

General Washington is the Founding Father of the original republic."

Washington gazed blankly at Mr. Lincoln. T. wondered if the Father of His Country was deaf, or simply disapproving.

"I do have a certain proprietary feeling about our common abode," said Polk, "and the fact that it gives us, no matter how inadequate, a second chance to brood upon the affairs of the nation that each of us was so proud to have served.

"In the few moments that we have before President Roosevelt takes time off from the land of the living to confer with us, his ancestral voices, I should like to get the sense of this group on the subject of the war now begun in the Pacific Ocean, amongst islands few of us had even heard of in our time, busy subduing, as we were, this great continent."

Mr. Lincoln had now left the stage and was rearranging the pots on the trestle table, while Polk had gone up onto the stage, where he bowed stiffly to the seated Washington, who inclined his head regally.

"The question that I think we should now entertain is a simple one," said Polk. "Essentially, this hemisphere is controlled by us, a matter of some celebration for the Spanish-speaking peasantry to the south and to the motley unfree bands of British and French colonists to our north in Canada." There was a murmuring throughout the audience. Several faces looked very grim at the mention of Canada. One was that of General Washington. The Canadian Pratt's one interesting piece of historical information was that George Washington had tried and failed to conquer Canada.

"They all want us to take over Canada," whispered Squaw. "Only Grover was ever sensible on the subject."

T. was also sensible. A million new citizens like Mr. Pratt seemed far too many.

Polk ignored the mutterings. "It's not necessary, Conscript Fathers, if I may address you in the Roman style, to place one's flag over every capital in the world to establish one's rule, as I demonstrated with Mexico when I annexed only the best parts and allowed the rest to continue as they were— so many grateful clients of our indulgent supremacy. But now we are faced with the prospect of an Asian empire. The British have their Indian empire, though they are far too small an island and much too far away to govern so vast and populous a territory for much longer, any more than the Dutch can maintain their control of Java and Sumatra, threatened, even as I speak, by the adjacent Japanese empire. The question that we eminences from another time must presently address is shall we—this extraordinary, even exceptional nation, now the very first of the white nations—reach out and take the prize? And by the prize I mean not just the Pacific Ocean with its galaxy of islands, including those where dwell the bloodthirsty perfidious Japanese, but China, too, and all Asia. In short, Conscript Fathers, has the time not come for us to take all the world into our arms and allow mankind to enjoy those freedoms, those liberties that we enjoy, placing us in the uniquely blessed position of offering to every man in every land the means, as you so famously put it, Mr. Jefferson, to pursue each in his own way his own happiness . . ."

Polk paused and gazed down at Jefferson, who sat slouched between Lady Washington and the tiny James Madison. Jefferson was a tall, gangling, rawboned carroty-haired figure whose eyes, when not shut as they had been, tended to dart this way and that as if he feared—what? Ambush? T. quite liked his looks but regarded any man who was more proud of having started up the University of Virginia—of all places— than of being the president as someone who had a screw seriously loose.

Since all eyes were now on Jefferson, he slowly got to his feet, the top of his head on the same level as Washington's throne. The voice was weak and, to T.'s ear, just like the English actor Ronald Colman in *Lost Horizon*. But then all the founders sounded English to him as well as to Squaw, who had once pointed out that that, after all, was what they were to begin with. "I have contended always, fellow magistrates, following the classic authorities from Plato to de Montesquieu, that although a republic is by far the best place to pursue happiness, no republic, once it becomes an empire and holds sway over other races and systems of government, can endure. For the annexation of Louisiana I have been taxed by political enemies, often themselves of monarchical disposition." The eyes began to dart about—in search of enemies? A very nervous man, T. decided. "Though not my one-time rival, now friend, Mr. Adams." Jefferson glanced to his right, where sat the absolutely round John Adams, who smiled a yellow-toothed smile at his former enemy.

"I think now, as I survey from this peculiar perch, the republic which I so hurriedly doubled—nay, tripled in size—that in the process we ceased to be a potential Athens, a school for all the earth in how best to pursue happiness, and how, in due course, even to *overtake* happiness. That was the course I had intended to set for us. But, when I bought from the French most of our continent, this grotesque enlargement of our original territory did not make us, I now confess, any the happier. Then Mr. Polk's well-intentioned war with Mexico revealed us as no longer a virtuous republic but as an imperial European sort of power, bloodily transplanted to a new hemisphere and bringing with us, we now see, ancient poisons for which there are no antidotes in the Pharmacy of Time. We are Rome, indeed, Conscript Fathers. And the die has been well and truly cast. And our Athens is long dead. Now the Pacific Ocean lies before us. Mr. Polk speaks, if he will forgive me, as someone infected with a malady for which only a cleansing, a terminating epidemic in some future time, can be thought of as deadly cure, or sharp cessation."

The park was now still. Jefferson stared a moment at the ground. Then he looked up in the direction of the park's far railing through which a tall man and a tall woman were approaching.

"My fellow ghosts," murmured Jefferson. "Pray rise and greet His Excellency, the current president of the United States, and his wife, Mrs. Franklin Delano Roosevelt."

Everyone stood and Eleanor Roosevelt, the Smithsonian Eleanor, moved briskly into the park to greet her husband and older self.

T. whispered to Squaw, "I thought he couldn't walk. Doesn't he have polio or something? You know? All that March of Dimes stuff." In every movie house, sooner or later during the intermission, ushers would come round with tin cans to collect dimes for the resort in Warm Springs, Georgia, that Roosevelt had created for his fellow polio victims.

It was Grover who answered him. "Whatever you did to the past, you kept him from catching polio and becoming a cripple. God knows what he's going to be like without all that suffering, which Eleanor says—or used to say, anyway—was the making of him."

Frank was grim. "He's going to be another TR."

"Bully!" said Theodore Roosevelt, fortunately not to Frank Cleveland but to his once-despised fifth cousin. TR was also, confusingly, Eleanor's uncle. "I must greet the boy."

TR hurried toward President and Mrs. Roosevelt, who received him—she, at least—warmly. T. noticed that General Washington had also risen, out of deference to the office if not the man.

T. had seen FDR in a thousand newsreels and driving about Washington on state occasions, always seated: the total paralysis of his legs had been generally kept secret from the people at large. But now, in T.'s post-Lyme world, he was tall, portly, vigorous, red-faced, with a thrusting, somewhat brutal aristocratic charm.

With the two Mrs. Roosevelts, he made his way down the line, shaking hands with each of the presidents and his wife or wives.

When the Roosevelts came face-to-face with the Clevelands, T. duly noted that the president was not much taller than his own new six feet one inches, but the great sleek head with the thin gray hair brushed straight back made him seem a giant, out of proportion to most of the others, particularly Lincoln, whose head was small in relation to his body, or General Washington, whose powdered wig made him seem more statue than man.

"Mr. Cleveland! The first president I ever met . . ."

"And I hear you still go around telling everyone that I said that I prayed that *you'd* never be president."

FDR laughed loudly. "I only say 'prayed' when I tell the story to Republicans. I say 'hoped' when I talk to the faithful. Mrs. Cleveland!" He shook each Mrs. Cleveland by the hand. Obviously Eleanor had warned him about the odd marital arrangements of a president with two noncontinuous administrations. "I saw you, Mrs. Cleveland, a few months ago when I was down in Princeton. I must say you look very handsome in your old age. But now I see what you had to work with." This went down very well with Frank as well as Squaw, who said T. was a relation working in the physicists' lab.

Then TR drew his cousin away from the lineup and began to squeak at him, right fist striking repeatedly his open left hand. All FDR could do was nod and say, "Quite right, Uncle T. Quite right."

The two Mrs. Roosevelts sat next to the Bryans, as FDR bounded up the steps to the stage, where he bowed low as he shook Washington's hand. The general motioned for him to take his place on the throne. But FDR re-ensconced Washington in his proper place, and remained standing.

"I wish," said FDR, "that all my dreams were as pleasant as this one, particularly nowadays. And I only hope that when I wake I'll be able to remember everything that was said and how all of you, so familiar to me as inspiring images, looked in real life or, perhaps, I should say real dream . . ."

"Not bad," murmured Grover. "They say all his speeches are written for him."

"Well, this one couldn't be," said Squaw.

"Unless he has a ghostwriter," was T.'s contribution, which made huge Grover heave with silent laughter.

"We have been, as you all must know, attacked, without warning, by the empire of Japan. I have just asked the Congress for a declaration of war, which they duly gave me and so . . ." FDR turned toward Lincoln, who was now seated in the front row, next to Champ Clark.

"The war came," Lincoln quoted his own great chilling line.

"The war came. Yes. Now we shall prosecute it to the fullest. There will be no mercy on our side, only justice. I shall require an unconditional surrender on the part of the Japanese and, of course, we shall occupy their home islands indefinitely as we try to undo the cruel damage that they have done their neighbor China, which is now, fragmented though it be, our grateful ally. Meanwhile, we are experiencing reverses. Our Philippines, England's Hong Kong and Singapore, Holland's Java and Sumatra may yet fall to the yellow hordes . . ."

"Lay it on," muttered Grover, mysteriously amused.

"But, in time, this great arsenal of democracy will turn back the tide and we shall offer those freedoms that we cherish not only to the Chinese but to the former colonies of England and France, Holland and Portugal."

There was considerable stir in the audience as Polk rose to question FDR. "Sir, we are as one with you in the defense of our country and its hemisphere and its island possessions in the Pacific, so absently obtained for us by later administrations."

"Absently!" The asthmatic TR let go a great burst of air containing the three sharply enunciated syllables. "Mr. Polk, President McKinley, whom I had the honor to serve as undersecretary of the navy . . ." That plump worthy smiled vaguely into space. He had curious dark-rimmed eyes and Squaw said that he was supposed to be a morphine addict, with an epileptic wife who was now sleeping peacefully beside him as the turbulent history of the republic entered its potentially most stormy phase.

TR was now on his feet. "If ever empire was more carefully thought out than our Caribbean and Pacific conquests, I have yet to hear of it."

"Now Uncle T." The second President Roosevelt beamed down upon the first. "We all know of your splendid achievements. At least we later arrivals on the scene know. Look how I got your splendid head up there on Mount Rushmore."

"If I may continue." Polk was politely single tracked. He bowed to TR, who sat down with a crash. "I chose my words carelessly because in my day to show any relish for conquest was considered bad form, even *European*. Is that not so, Mr. Lincoln?"

"That is so, sir."

"But now we are in a new century with complex weapons and machinery and the possibility that our manifest destiny, as someone after me put it, is at hand. So, Mr. President, do you see Asia, as much of it as we can absorb, as a permanent part of our—let us call it by its proper name—empire?"

The never-used word caused even Jefferson to sit up straight. FDR himself looked suddenly pale and uncertain.

"Our position, Mr. Polk, has been clear from the beginning." T. could see that he was stalling for time, trying to think of something to say to justify that ever-expanding Military Exhibit on the Mall. "We want only peace in the world, open boundaries, no tariffs—sorry, Uncle T. . . ."

"I didn't like tariffs either." TR was unexpected. "But I was a Republican. We *never* have the leeway you Democrats have."

The end of the line laughed while the beginning was bemused. "To be a good neighbor to all has been my goal, and I believe the goal of you gentlemen who preceded me. I think we are as one in that sentiment."

Then a very clear, even youthful, British voice sounded and resounded in the park. George Washington had risen to his full height. As he gazed down upon his thirty-first or, post-Lyme, thirty-second successor, he spoke. "I have, of course, followed as closely as I can in this limbo of ours, the adventures of the republic that we set in motion at Philadelphia in what was a highly different world. Although I never expressed an opinion at that time, privately I thought of our handiwork as not only fragile but, at best, temporary and that the mob which Mr. Adams so feared or the would-be tyrant that Mr. Jefferson so feared would, one or the other, more soon that late, sweep away our peculiar vessel, our improvised ship of state. None of us foresaw that, as an idea, we would mean so much to tyrannized Europeans who would then come as immigrants to our not so comfortable new land where, at least, there was space for all. The only peril that I did foresee (and warned of upon leaving office) was the danger of abandoning the great, the endless work at hand here to conspire with—and against—foreign powers, and to imitate them militarily. In short, to become ourselves conquerors. But, my warning was never heeded. 'From the halls of Montezuma to the shores of Tripoli' is now a rousing military song. So unlike our own, perhaps immodest, 'The whole world turned upside down.' Mr. Polk you are most eloquent when you speak of your war against Mexico, conducted as you yourself have conceded to acquire California and the Pacific coast, while you, Mr. Theodore Roosevelt, have just now expressed great pride in your conquest of the Philippine Islands, and their reluctant inhabitants who suffered great casualties when they tried to rid their islands of what they had been assured, mistakenly, would be their saviors—their *good* neighbors—but proved to be their conquerors.

"Now Mr. Franklin Delano Roosevelt, you have come to us to . . . report." Washington's tight-lipped smile did not quite hide his stained wooden teeth. "We were attacked at dawn by weapons undreamed of in my day, by an alien people who live three thousand miles from our western continental shore, the shore that Mr. Polk so generously obtained for us to add to Mr. Jefferson's great purchase of what are now a dozen new states. My question, sir, if I may be so bold as to question so great a sovereign of so many people in so many lands as you, why?"

FDR looked at Washington blankly. Then: "Why . . . what?"

"Why, sir, did the Japanese attack the United States of America?"

"Because, General Washington, they mean to make all of Asia and all of the Pacific theirs, and we alone, the sole democracy with the greatest military potential, stand in their way." There was a definite edge to the president's voice.

"And so to save Asians from Asians, the white race, as I perhaps wrongly persist in regarding us, must do battle with an island people far, far away in every sense."

"General Washington." Roosevelt's face was flushed and Grover murmured to Squaw, "High blood pressure. We'll be getting him soon."

"We did not bomb *their* fleet by stealth in Yokohama Harbor. They bombed ours, several thousand miles away."

"At the risk, sir, of monotony, might I repeat my question. Why?"

"At the risk, General, of equal monotony, they mean for the Pacific Ocean to be theirs, for the colonial possessions of the Europeans to be theirs, including the vast oil fields of Java . . ."

"If they be so minded, what business is it of ours, faraway, in our safe hemisphere . . . ?"

"Safe? Our fleet has been sunk at Pearl Harbor."

"A harbor located on a distant Pacific island. Sir, let me phrase my question more precisely. What did your administration do to provoke this attack?"

"Provoke? We . . . *provoke?*" T. had never thought it possible that the mellifluous Roosevelt could ever stammer. But now he was stumbling over his words.

"*Panay.* U.S. gunboat. Sunk. In cold blood. Every provocation came . . . comes from them. For humanitarian reasons we have done our best to help China during its long war with the Japanese invaders." The president was now getting his second wind. "In order to weaken the Japanese military, we banned the sale of gasoline and scrap iron to them last July."

"Then, sir, you have made our country the arbiter of war and peace everywhere in the world."

"There are times, General Washington, when a nation must act for the good of others. Nor are we alone. Presently, England, France, Holland, and Portugal will join us in our war to bring democracy to that great part of the world which has turned to us for help. I mean, of course, China."

Again the thin Washington smile. "I did not think you meant Japan. So your European allies—each an Asiatic colonial empire—wish to fight to regain or hold on to their possessions. But I thought, sir, that you were anticolonial. Now you object to the Japanese supplanting, let us say, the French on the mainland of Asia."

"There will, of course, be new arrangements in that part of the world once the war is won. Meanwhile, we simply stand for the self-determination of all people everywhere."

"Do your Dutch allies know that you intend to set free their Indonesian colonies?"

"History, General Washington, moves to its own beat and tempo. We move with it or we are left behind."

"There are rats in Norway which I have read of." Jefferson spoke, slouched in his chair. "As an amateur naturalist, I enjoy contemplating their habits, of which the most dramatic is a sudden rush, on the part of all of them, at some signal as yet undetectable to us, toward the sea, where they proceed en masse to swim ever farther and farther out until all are drowned. Presumably enough are left, somehow, to start a new race. So much, Mr. Roosevelt, for the tempo of your history. You have provoked the Japanese into attacking us, and now we are all to rush behind you into the sea—the sea, in this case, being those new weapons that have been developed, many of them right here at this Institution. Should they ever be used against us there may be no more rats left in our Norway to—pursue their own happiness."

TR was on his feet again. "Franklin, Mr. President, I should say."

"Yes, Uncle T." FDR was again his masterful self.

"I assume that once the war is won you will detach the European colonies from their current owners and give them their freedom, as I gave the Philippines theirs, after a time, of course, to learn the ways of civilization."

FDR nodded. "Your analogy with the Philippines is the right one. We shall remain as long as necessary in Java and Indonesia and so on until those primitive peoples are able to go it alone."

Grover Cleveland was now on his feet. "I should note that the Philippine Islands, after close to half a century, are still the property of the U.S. Do you plan to allow as long a time for the French to stay in French Indochina or the British in Singapore?"

A radiant smile from FDR. "I certainly hope so. The current problem for us is that neither the Philippines nor Puerto Rico *want* to be free of us. But I shall be firm." Cleveland sat down, quietly chuckling.

FDR turned to Washington, "Yes, the empire—a word we are right not to use—will be global if all goes well for us. But it won't be one of force or intimidation. Rather it will be based on certain freedoms of the sort we enjoy as well as on a global prosperity that we shall be able to promote on the largest scale."

"Like your Depression?" Calvin Coolidge, a thin dour figure, known when he was alive for his long silences, was now, on the line, considered something of a chatterbox. FDR looked very grim; his dislike of Coolidge was famous. "And going off the gold standard. And killing all those little pigs . . ."

"I'm sure, Calvin, these great men are not interested in such domestic details . . ."

"Oh, we are. We are!" said Grover. "I had a Depression on my hands. Couldn't fix it any more than you could. Now, of course, this war of yours will certainly put an end to your Depression, but, if I may ask the one question of poignant interest to every president in this room, how are you going to pay for the war?"

"I'm glad you asked me that, Grover." FDR was now in friendly, even chatty mood. "From General Washington's problems getting money—or anything—out of the Continental Congress right down to Calvin's boom and bust, the problem of federal revenues is recurrent." T. himself had never given a moment's thought to taxes and federal income, but the great men in the room were all alert and definitely interested.

"As you might guess, we have seen this war coming for almost a decade. During that time we have alerted the great corporations to the need for swift expansion and, presently, we shall produce more airplanes and tanks and weapons than the Western world has ever seen before. In the process unemployment will come to an end."

"Who pays?" It was Coolidge again.

"The corporations to begin with. I am levying a ninety percent tax on excess profits." There was an angry murmur from most of the line.

"Socialism," said Coolidge. "Confiscation!"

"Don't worry, Calvin. The corporations will get the money back—with interest—in government orders for more and more arms. Then there is the personal income tax. Never exactly popular. Mr. Lincoln got away with it in an emergency. But later the Supreme Court said it was unconstitutional. Of course, we got it back again, but, as of last year, only ten percent of the workforce paid income tax, some four million returns. Drop in the bucket, my friends. Well, now, to finance the war, *everyone* will be paying. The newly hired workers at excellent salaries—will be paying tax for the first time. Every single one of them."

"How're you gonna make them?" Coolidge was sharp.

"No problem. We have devised something called the withholding tax. We take the money out of their paychecks *before* they get them."

There was an astonished murmur. President Taft, a very fat man who had also been Chief Justice of the United States, said, "That *is* confiscation, sir. Without due process of law. No court will uphold you."

"The courts I'm appointing will take a different view. If not . . . well, we'll have everybody at work and everybody prosperous and the whole world ahead of us to do, as Mr. Harding would say, business in."

There was a round of applause. General Grant, a stubby grizzled man, stood up. "I propose that we support unanimously the president in his resistance to the Japanese attack."

Washington called for a show of hands. There were several abstentions but not one negative vote. "We are with you, sir. How long will it take for our restored forces to be in a position to attack the islands?"

FDR frowned. "We *should* be ready in a year's time—to make the long, long journey from island to island . . ."

"A very long journey," said Washington, "even with your modern ships and flying machines."

"Too long in my view." FDR sounded almost candid, unlike his usual comforting family doctor self. "But should certain new weapons prove feasible, we could end the war in a few days of terrible destruction if we can find the right base from which to strike. Fortunately—this is top secret by the way—I have a private agreement with my great friend Leon who will let us, when the time comes, use his territory for a northern strike."

"And who"—Washington was dry—"is your great friend Mr. Leon?"

"President Leon Trotsky, of the Soviet Union."

"Good God!" Coolidge's voice broke with emotion.

FDR was demure, even pious. "Yes, I pray that God will be good to us Americans. Certainly the friendship of the Soviet president, overwhelmingly reelected last year, was definitely a God-given event for us."

FDR gave the frosty Washington a warm handclap. "Lovely to see you, George."

T. noticed that Washington blinked his eyes on the "George" but otherwise showed no emotion. The presidents from the start of the line looked shocked at the liberty Roosevelt had taken but by now he was bidding them good-by as, accompanied by both Eleanors, he headed toward the exit.

Squaw gave T. a shove. "Ask him about you."

"What about me?"

"If there will be a draft of all the boys, like the Civil War. Go on."

Reluctantly, T. followed the Roosevelts to the end of the line. "What a nightmare! *Literally* a nightmare." FDR's genial smile and serene manner had given way to a scowl. "The things you get me into, Eleanor. I swear this lot is worse than the worst of your do-gooders." He was addressing the Smithsonian Eleanor.

"Well, dear, there was no backing out. This was a summons from your predecessors and you had no choice but to comply."

"I'm getting the most terrible headache. Did someone drug me so that I'd have this awful dream?"

"Of course not!" The White House Eleanor was firm. "But you did drink a third martini before . . ."

"Sir. Mr. President?" T. was at FDR's side. Immediately the famous smile was switched on just for him.

"Yes, my boy. Are you a president that I've forgotten all about?"

"Oh, no, sir . . ."

The Smithsonian Eleanor graciously made the introduction, adding, "Master Veal is considered to be one of the foremost quantum physicists in the world."

"Well, I'm sure they're keeping you busy these days."

"Yes, sir. If I may ask you a question . . ."

"Shoot! Plainly this is one of those dreams where anything goes."

"Are you going to draft an army? From everybody?"

Roosevelt frowned. "Well, I see no alternative. The Japs have several million men under arms. That means we have to catch up fast and so . . ." He trailed uncomfortably off.

"I suppose," said the Smithsonian Eleanor, "he recalls your speech, how you will never send an American boy abroad to fight."

"Yes," said T. "That's exactly what I was thinking of."

"That was then." The president was very grave. "This is now. Who would ever have . . . well, dreamed that they would attack us when they did? A date that really will live in infamy, if I may quote myself."

"But you said just now that you've been preparing for this war for the last ten years."

"For the *possibility*, yes. There is not room for two great powers in the Pacific . . ." He rubbed his eyes. "Or in Asia if it comes to that . . . I'm starting to wake up."

"Good-by, dear," said the Smithsonian Eleanor, as her White House self led the drowsy president through a row of trees and out of sight.

"That means I'm going to be drafted . . ."

Mrs. Roosevelt was reassuring. "You're only—what? sixteen. Who knows what will happen in the next year or so? Besides, Dr. Oppenheimer is bound to get you an exemption. We need you here."

Back on the line, T. joined the Clevelands, who were chatting on the sidewalk with several other up-the-liners. As usual, Theodore Roosevelt had the most to say. "I don't think Franklin quite grasps how much there is to be gained by this war. It is well known, historically, that whoever controls Shansi Province in northern China will be the master of the earth. Japan wants it. Russia wants it. But *we* are going to get it now."

"It sounds like attractive real estate," said Grover mildly. "But we're also going to need a fleet first and a land army. And boats to get the boys all the way to China." He shook his head in wonder. "It seems like only yesterday I defeated a few dozen Apaches and now we're taking on a billion or so Asiatics."

Before TR could rewind, Grover and company had moved on.

As they passed the Lincoln house, curtains as always drawn, a tall old lady in black, with white hair piled high beneath a wide-brimmed hat, stopped Squaw and said, "Friday at five, dear Mrs. Cleveland. We shall have two tables of whist and a dessert luncheon with Baked Alaska, made by Mr. Jefferson's cook."

"Of course I'll be there, Mrs. Buchanan."

"I don't suppose we can tempt Mr. Cleveland and the other Mrs. Cleveland."

"It is a kind thought," said Grover, "but I am hopeless with cards."

"But thank you anyway, Mrs. Buchanan," said Frank.

The old lady smiled and let herself into the door to the house next to the Lincolns.

"I thought President Buchanan never married."

"He didn't," said Squaw, giggling. "*That* was President Buchanan. He always dresses in what he calls his widow weeds and expects to be addressed as Mrs. Buchanan."

"Gosh," said T., wondering how he could get the word back to St. Albans.

"Hopeless president," said Grover, "and an excellent argument for not giving women the vote."

"Nonsense," said Frank. "Besides, he's not a woman, as far as we know . . ."

"How can he be when he's so plainly a lady." Squaw was precise in her Buffalo, New York, way.

"And I can think of a great many women right here on the line who would've been better presidents than their husbands." Frank looked very grim.

"Who?" asked Grover.

"Eleanor Roosevelt to start with." T. could tell Frank was serious.

Grover shook his head. "Women are far too straightforward. Can you imagine Eleanor making a political party half Tammany Hall and half Ku Klux Klan? Such duplicity is man's proper work. Nurture your children, mother."

T. left the Clevelands arguing in the street.

8

───◇───

BY EARLY AUTUMN, the American fleet was operational and the newspapers were filled with reports of battles on Pacific islands with outlandish names.

T. spent most of this time in the labs of the Smithsonian. Los Alamos was too crowded. Meanwhile the German government had persuaded Einstein to pay a call, and Dr. Oppenheimer was chosen to show him about. Disappointingly, he spoke only German, using as an interpreter Cher Maître's young aide, Albert.

"You are very young," the great man said to T.

"I know," said T. But he had aged swiftly since the time shift. He was also growing a respectable mustache.

"But then I'm very old." Einstein was amused. He was surprisingly tall, otherwise he looked like his pictures, with fright-wig hair on end. He was not in a good mood. "I don't like this war," he said to T., as T. showed him how to project onto the monitor the space-time equations that he had been assembling.

"We don't like it all that much either." Like most Americans, T. resented the fact that Einstein was not coming to the aid of the United States because he was a pacifist. It was rumored that Chancellor von Papen had threatened him with a reduction in staff at the University of Berlin if he did not at least visit Washington. So he had come.

"I never thought that our play with numbers should ever cease to be play and become murderous," he observed at large.

"So you made clear," said Dr. Oppenheimer, "when you refused to sign our letter to the president proposing an all-out effort to build a nuclear-fission bomb."

"The—how you say?" He muttered in German to Albert, who translated for him. "The genie is out of the bottle now. I don't think you realize what you've done—what you are doing—to future generations."

"We have taken every precaution and thanks to this young man's efforts . . ."

"Among others!" Bentsen gazed fawningly on Dr. Oppenheimer.

"There will be no chain reaction. We have total control over fission."

"What about the debris?" Dr. Oppenheimer and Bentsen looked puzzled. Einstein and Albert spoke quickly to each other in German. Finally, Albert said, "There is—after any explosion of anything—leftover material of an organic nature. Dr. Einstein points out that in the case of plutonium there will be a long life of irradiated particles injurious to the health and well-being of living organisms."

"There is minimal risk only." T. wondered why Dr. Oppenheimer was sounding so positive. Certainly no one had the slightest idea what would happen next year when the first bomb would be set off in New Mexico. T. had tried to simulate what would happen but he had never had enough data to work from. In any case, a presidential order was not to be questioned. Yet Lindy, alone, had been as disturbed as T. by what he called fallout. "I'll tell FDR it's bad for the sinuses. He's a martyr, he says, to sinus." But no one else dared warn FDR.

Einstein was now involved with T.'s formulas. Suddenly he said to the others, in English, "Could you leave me alone with the boy? You too, Albert."

Reluctantly Dr. Oppenheimer and the others left T.'s lab. Einstein was now peering at an equation involving mass and its countervailing use to overtake light, a reverse of the usual application of relativity's theory.

"Ingenious." Einstein sat down on a stool opposite the monitor. "Does this . . . check out, as you say?" He spoke English easily now.

"The equations do."

"So I see. So I suspected. Tell me." The old man was staring hard at T. "When I first saw your . . . your . . ."

"Doodle?"

"Well, that sounds like a word which means what it sounds like, an improvisation . . ."

"At random, sir."

"Nothing is random. Not that I can *prove* that—just yet. But I was told last year that you were a child of thirteen and now I see that you are a young man of—what, sixteen, seve teen? What has happened to you?" The question was put in Einstein's usually amiable if quizzical manner.

T. was sufficiently astonished to tell the truth. "I intervened, sir, *in time.*"

"You? A boy? Altered . . . ?"

"Yes, me, a boy. What, sir, do you recall about last June 24?"

Einstein laughed. "I can't recall where I put my briefcase this morning."

"June 25 was the day the Japanese attacked us . . ."

"Yes. Yes. I certainly recall that and I thought your ever-smiling president put them up to it. That is, he gave them no choice. Not that I mean to criticize. I try to stay out of politics—without success. My life keeps getting split between equations and politics and of the two only equations are for eternity if they are the right ones, of course." He frowned, nodded. "I had dreams that night, strange dreams."

"A different sort of world?"

"Well, yes. An absurd world. You know of my architect friend, Grubert?"

"Yes, sir. I met him in Los Alamos."

"In my dream, he was totally different. No halo of dyed gold hair. No genius of any kind except . . . He had gone into politics. He was—very popular. And a hopeless bore. He'd also changed his name. Now what was it?" Einstein shut his eyes; concentrated.

"Hitler," said T. "Adolf Hitler."

"Yes, that was the name. Why replace the ancient Hebrew, Shekel Grubert, with dull Hitler? A fantastic sort of dream."

T. told Einstein everything about Lyme, Connecticut. The great man listened, without expression. When T. had finished there was silence except for the radio in the next room. A notorious American army officer with an actory voice had gone over to the Japanese; he was now broadcasting from Manila. "This is *Lieutenant* Colonel Douglas MacArthur from Imperial Japanese Headquarters in the Philippines. His gracious majesty, the emperor Hirohito, has asked for the surrender of the remains of the American fleet now at anchor off the impregnable island of Guam . . ." There was laughter in the next room and the radio was switched off. Just as Einstein switched off T.'s monitor.

"You have done a monstrous thing. I have said that God does not play dice with the universe; now, due to this— diabolic intervention, *you* play dice with the universe. Or at least with our time-space."

T. was not prepared for censure. He responded, he thought, amiably. "I don't think our human history has a whole lot to do with your eternal equations."

"How do you know? Think of what discoveries might have been made if you hadn't meddled."

"How do *you* know? I've saved millions of lives in two European wars. Think of how many discoveries might be made by those who would otherwise be dead."

"There's still the Japanese war . . ."

"I cannot—could not—did not—allow for everything."

"Yet you played God . . ."

"As I was intended to do." T. startled himself with his own answer. "I lost over two years of my life in the process, of no consequence to anyone else but all-important to me, as I automatically skipped two years and who knows how many ideas I might have had that I won't have now because, overnight, I traded in a boy's body for a man's body with mind, presumably, to match."

"Men's brains are often as good as boys'." The old man was sarcastic. "But to be honest, I can't say that I've advanced much beyond my twenty-sixth year—and I was young for my age. The unified field theory still eludes me."

"That's only because it isn't there."

Einstein sighed. "You are a quantum mechanic, of course."

"So were you. And I'm also a relativist. So much so I can't apply a single law of creation to all phenomenas. I also don't want to. But you do."

"That's science."

"That is religion, sir."

The old man shut his eyes. Then: "We cannot see what we are not given the means to see. In the end . . ." He opened his eyes and stared intently at T. "We are stuck with that simple, rather dull Englishman and his theory of natural selection."

T. had already come to the same conclusion. "Darwin. Yes, sir. To survive we must know more about where we are or if, indeed, there is any*where* for us to be located in and able to describe."

The old man smiled. "Perhaps your—precocity is the next step toward our finding out. I seem to have completed my work, much against my will, if I may say so."

T. nodded. "I know what you mean, sir, but something's going wrong with me, too. Before the shift in time, things were so clear to me that all I had to do was press a button in my head and the equations came. Now my head's a bit cloudy. Too much testosterone? I think I'm turning into everybody else. I'm a breeder who can't think anymore."

Einstein laughed. "That's the price we pay for being human. Once there is Eros, there is Thanatos."

On his own, T. had worked out the Greek for the human condition: once love—sex—began, death set up shop. "I know," he said. "Better to be an amoeba and immortal. Just dividing from time to time."

"Ah, but does that eternal amoeba see the beauty of an equation or even play Mozart badly? I started to fade at twenty-six and you're doing it—let's hope you're not—at sixteen. Natural selection is speeding up, at our expense. Well, I have a second career. Soon the Jews will have their own country, Israel, and the Zionists have asked me to be the president. I told them that although I've always been a Zionist, I am far too stupid about politics to be a president."

"If there is anything I've come to know, sir, being around here, it's presidents. You couldn't be any dumber than this lot."

"You console me!" Then Einstein frowned. "Now, mischievous boy, let's see what we can do to tidy up what you've done to space-time."

As it turned out, there was nothing anyone could do about what had been altered, since only Squaw, Grover, and T. had any memory of what history had been like pre-Lyme and the first two, as T. tactlessly put it to Squaw, "Are just dummies from an earlier time."

"What about Einstein?" Squaw and T. were on the bed in his bedroom after some very athletic sex in which he had lifted her high in the air and then slowly lowered her upon his no longer boyish sex, he standing as she tightened her legs about his chest.

"My God, you're strong!" she had observed.

"Think I'm too old for you now?"

"Well, no. Not quite. But seventeen is my limit. Except for those young-looking Indians and Eskimos." On the last word each had experienced an orgasm.

"Oh yeah, Eskimos!"

T. gasped as they fell back onto the bed with a crash. Then he was absorbed by pleasure. Sex was now entirely different for him. Before it had been fun but slightly apart from him. Now all of him was a pounding sort of machine, the brain switched off until she mentioned Einstein again. Brain cleared.

"Einstein's no use to us," he said. "Fact, he got so carried away by my equations that he forgot everything about that dream of his, where his closest buddy, Shekel Grubert, had been Adolf Hitler first time around. But before he forgot, he said I'm our species' best adaptation to altered circumstances, just like he was the one before me."

"Aren't we vain!" Squaw's smooth, white, blue-veined left breast was resting lightly on T.'s rosy nipple, aureoled now in golden hair. "Just how hairy are you going to get?"

"No idea. Want me to shave my chest?"

"Was your father hairy?"

T. frowned. "Don't recollect him anymore, which means he was dead when I was little, and so he couldn't have been on the . . . *Hindenburg*? that zeppelin that went down, which I'm sure has—had—a new name back then . . ."

"If it even existed. We've certainly left a lot of loose ends dangling."

"Well, nobody's ever going to know. Now, about the Eskimos . . ."

"Hairless. Like the Indians. Like the thirteen-year-old you."

"Squaw, you've got to—you know?—mature. Grow up. You're a woman. I'm a man. Want to take a bath together?"

"They smell a bit high, the Eskimos. It's the whale blubber they rub all over themselves. Helps keep them warm, they say. Why?"

"Why." T. shut his eyes. Visualized Dr. Smithson's note. "There's a shortcut for us. To win the war. It's up in the Arctic somewhere. You got an atlas?"

"Grover's got one—an old one—naturally. So we take a trip to the Arctic and beat the Japanese, you and I?"

"No. The American air force goes there. Establishes a secret base and . . . Bang."

Squaw retrieved her breast from T.'s nipple. "I can't say I'm all that enthusiastic about the bang part."

"We're stuck with it. I thought after Lyme we wouldn't have to use the bomb for a long time, if ever. But—"

They lay side by side, caressing each other. T. had been worried that his new body would not appeal to her but, instead, as they came closer to each other in age and physical maturity, she was more womanly—or what he took to be womanly from his study of the movies—and less tomboy. For the first time, he wondered about her relationship with Grover. For the first time, he was almost jealous, just like an adult in the movies.

But "father and daughter" she had always explained the relationship and, later: "He only sleeps with Frank." Would the three of them make a good couple? He daydreamed, knowing perfectly well that once his work was done he would be thirteen again and go back to Stanley Sofield's class, replacing his clone—except he would still be sixteen inside and he truly needed Squaw a lot more than he'd ever need St. Albans or baseball practice. Since he was due to graduate next June, in ten months' time, he would . . . Time. Time? Space. What if . . . ? Lights still went on in his head. They were just not as bright.

"What are you thinking about?" Squaw was seated on the edge of the bed, putting up her hair.

"Could you, uh, *live* outside of here?"

Squaw laughed. "You idiot! Of course not. I'm a dummy for eight hours a day, at least when I'm on exhibit. Though when I want to moonlight, Frank's very good about spelling me. She puts my dress on a real dummy and covers for me. Then, don't forget I am still alive out there. A very old lady, living in Princeton. A widow for the second time and not about to take up with a chicken—or a recent chicken."

"But you—the old lady—you're bound to die and then if you're the only you out there . . ."

"I'm still just a dummy, as you so tactfully put it. I'm only flesh and blood off duty here."

"So what do we do when I have to go?"

Squaw turned her back on him. She had the palest skin he'd ever seen. A mole on her shoulder blade moved up and down.

"Oh, shit! You're crying." T. pulled her close to him and then they both cried.

———•—•———

Grover had placed the open atlas on the big table in his study. "The Arctic is deceptive. Of course, I speak only from hearsay. For a base—a military base—you will need rock or tundra under the ice or, preferably, a place with no ice at all. The problem is not mistaking what seems to be terra firma but then turns out to be a glacier."

T. sat next to the president while Squaw and Frank chatted in the next room. Grover then made a page of notes with lines of latitude and longitude in the area of Far Eastern Siberia. "The best position to strike at the Japanese—from the air—will be—this should thrill TR!—from northeast of his precious Shansi Province. So let us hope FDR's dear friend Leon"—Grover gave a good imitation of the Rooseveltian voice—"will let us use the Siberian Arctic for a base." Grover gave T. his notes.

"Now, Master Veal, how do you intend to get there?"

"The Eskimo exhibit." Squaw came into the study. "It's a special one. Like the Old Western American one."

"What about the distances?" Grover was intrigued.

"I'll take a sighting. You know off the sun or the stars or both. Then once we know where we are . . ."

"Suppose it's Alaska?"

"Well, I'm sure Lindy can get someone to fly us to . . ." T. held up Grover's notes. ". . . wherever this is."

"Siberia," said Grover, solemnly. "Another country. Another continent. Another century."

"I'll let you wear my heavy coat," said Frank to her younger self.

"I've been there before—to the exhibit, that is—it's about like Buffalo in February."

"That's too cold for me," said Frank.

"Frankly, I think the current president's actually a bit on the optimistic side. Russia letting us blow up Japan from her territory doesn't sound right. Of course, 'dear Leon' could be a fool."

Squaw and T., bundled in heavy coats and scarves despite the warm September evening, hurried along the red Parcheesi corridor that led to the Arctic Exhibit, which occupied an entire ground floor.

Wax guards stood on duty in front of locked mahogany doors. "Here we are." Squaw produced a key, and let them into the exhibit. "This one's always locked because of the cold."

But there was no cold when they stepped onto a sheet of artificial ice. The sky was a deep dark electrical blue; the fake ice purest white. In the distance, a blue-black sea with white floating icebergs like some huge dessert. Several plaster Eskimos, in furs, were fishing through a hole in the ice. Close by them was an igloo, a dome of ice with a chimney.

"I thought it was going to be cold."

"Wait till they come to life." Squaw looked at the pendant watch about her neck. "We're a couple of minutes early."

"But the guards . . . ?"

"Went off duty early."

Suddenly a blast of literally freezing air struck them. The hairs in T.'s nostrils promptly froze. The fishermen began to move about. Smoke started to come out of the chimney. In the distance ice floes moved slowly over the blue-black sea under a blue-black sky.

"Out of this world!" T. was delighted. "Only"—he looked up at the sky—"there's no sun."

"It shows up." Squaw was vague. A young Eskimo came out of the igloo; he beamed at the sight of Squaw.

"Great to have you back!"

"Wonderful to be here, Omoo. I've missed the . . . brisk weather. This is my friend, Master Veal."

The young Eskimo was so close to T. that he could smell the whale blubber. For a moment he was afraid that Omoo wanted to rub noses with him, but instead they shook hands. "Come on in," said Omoo, "and get out of those hot clothes."

"They undress for strangers," said Squaw. "It's a form of hospitality. They like to share their families with their guests."

At the entrance to the igloo, two plumply pretty girls with Mongolian features smiled yellow-toothed smiles at T. who was, he knew, blushing.

"My sisters will show you velly good time as the Nips say. They play Sea-lion, Lost-whale, and—this is the Arctic, after all—*Sleeve-job.* You never had nothing thrillwise till you get complete Arctic sleeve-job."

"I'm afraid," said T., spooked at the thought of what went on inside the icy dome, "we better hang out here. You see, I've got to get my bearings."

T. produced his sextant and notebook. "Locate our longitude and latitude."

"One hundred sixty longitude," said Omoo, "fifty degrees latitude. I can't be more exact because I have my orders."

T. was studying the map that he had copied out of Grover's atlas. "This is Siberia, I'd say."

"Hole in one," said Omoo. "Yes. We also play a lot of golf up here. On the ice. You see, this British fishing boat ran aground years ago and they had to stay here so long that we taught them how to hunt seal and they taught us golf. Want to go a few rounds?"

"No, thanks," said T. "But tell me, have you got any sort of level land around here? Under the snow and the ice, that is?"

"Something suitable for an airplane base? Yes. Over there." Omoo pointed to an area next to the blue-black sea. Then he clapped his hands; a dog team, pulling a sleigh, came into view. "Hop in," he said. "The Red Army's already checked this one out." To the dogs: "Mush!" They mushed over the terrain.

T. was amazed, but Squaw simply shrugged and said, "Well, if Hyannis Hyena Joe Kennedy could get to my Indians why shouldn't the Russians get to their very own Eskimos?"

Omoo proved to be chatty; he was also, T. could tell, wild about Squaw, who flirted with him, occasionally muttering what T. took to be an endearment in the local language. How many times had they met? Why should he care? Time shift effect checking in again?

"Actually, I'm with the KGB looking after the education of my people, and reporting to Moscow by shortwave. I wanted to go to the States for college but now I'm stuck in this ridiculous exhibit so I can't ever see the rest of the United States, but I can travel in the neighborhood. That's how I spent two years at Shansi U.—way down south in North China."

T. recalled Theodore Roosevelt's hymn to the riches of Shansi Province.

"What's so special about Shansi?"

"Largest and finest coalfields in the world. Enough fuel to last the human race centuries."

"Only now we have oil . . ."

"But nowhere near enough whales to make the oil we need . . ."

"I meant," T. began.

"Omoo is making a joke, aren't you?" Squaw was benign.

Omoo laughed uproariously. T. noticed that his teeth, young as he was, had been worn down to stumps—blubber chewing?

"According to Moscow news, Nips just took the Java oil fields."

They were now traveling over a diamond-bright, smooth field of ice that reflected what midnight sun there was. Off to their right was the dark sea, which kept shifting about uneasily as if afraid that, any minute, it might freeze solid.

Omoo shouted at the dogs, who stopped on command, heads wreathed in vaporous breath. "Here is perfect landing field."

"How far are we from Tokyo?"

"By sled a hundred moons in halcyon weather . . ."

"In miles?"

"As eagle fly a thousand miles."

Omoo walked them across the brittle ice to the slow-tided sea. Then, with an ivory cane, he punched the surface of the ice. Gray granitelike stone was only a few inches beneath the snow covering. "There is your landing field."

"That's great, Omoo. Now, I know you have your orders to report everything to Moscow, but try not to tell too much about our—trip here. We're just tourists, you know."

"O.K. Anyway, the Japanese have broken our Russian code. They always do. Very superior people, the Nips."

"I hope"—T. was stern—"you don't have any divided loyalty. That you're not one of those hyphenate Eskimos you read about in the *Evening Star,* secretly working for the enemy."

"No, sir. I am one hundred percent white man's burden. We all are up here, you can bet your last ukulele."

"I shall report that to President Trotsky." Squaw was now First Lady of the Land. "You will be promoted."

At that felicitous moment, the Aurora Borealis struck. The northern sky looked like an opening night at Hollywood's Grauman's Chinese Theater. White rays of light filled the sky like so many searchlights, purest white against the black. Then a blaze of color. Every shade of rainbow enveloped them. Also, colors not usually visible to the human eye began to register. T. felt as if he was drunk, and Squaw held him tight while their Eskimo host did a barbarous dance to the Aurora Borealis.

"Welcome!" he cried. "To Kamchatka in the spring." Then, with a superb tenor voice, he began to sing "Spring Will Be a Little Late This Year," his voice echoing and re-echoing through the multicolored night as the dogs, muzzles on high, howled their melodious counterpoint.

"Magical," whispered Squaw.

Then, as the lights faded, they got into the sleigh and mushed over the ice and snow. Omoo whispered into T.'s ear, "Want to have big sex party, big orgy in that igloo up ahead?"

"Well," said T., mildly tempted in spite of the blubber, "how many folks will there be at the orgy?"

"If you bring Frankie, that'll make three."

T. said they would take a rain check.

Back at the entrance to the exhibit, the fishermen at the ice hole looked as if they were already plaster, which, Omoo explained, they were. "It got so nerve-wracking, this constant switching back and forth from flesh and blood to plaster of Paris that we decided that these three at least would be permanently on exhibit. By the way, they are anatomically correct. Want to see?"

T. was about to take another rain check, just as dogs and Omoo froze into their exhibit selves. Electric lights replaced natural lights. The mahogany doors opened. A dozen schoolchildren were admitted with their teacher.

One of the guards said, "Now here comes the Aurora Borealis."

He threw a switch and there, against the crudely painted sky, was a garish version of the real thing.

As T. and Squaw started to leave the exhibit, Squaw pointed to a sign by the door. "Why, here's where we were. Latitude and longitude and everything."

And so it was all duly noted. T. felt a bit silly as he copied out the figures in his notebook. "Anyway, we've been up in Kamchatka. Which is in Russia."

"So Omoo told us."

"But I thought these were American exhibits."

"Not all. You should get a look at Ancient Egypt. The jewels, the costumes, the perfumes: I could stay back there a month of Sundays."

Humming "Spring Will Be a Little Late This Year" they Parcheesied their way back to T.'s lab in the Castle.

It took T. several hours to get military clearance so that he could penetrate Lindy's office in a new building on the Mall.

Finally, he was admitted to the Army Air Force floor, which he couldn't help thinking of as the Up-to-Date Military Exhibit. There was a long row of offices and map and radio rooms as well as a large canteen where dozens of officers were constantly eating cheeseburgers and French fries. The war was not going too well.

Lindy was standing in front of a map of the Northern Hemisphere as T. entered. He wore no jacket or tie or insignia except for a pair of wings. The radio was on and T. heard the now-familiar voice. "This is *Lieutenant* Colonel Douglas MacArthur. My prediction of Wednesday last has come to pass. The invincible forces of He Who Sits upon the Chrysanthemum Throne have occupied, at small cost, the Dutch slave colony of Java . . ."

"Turn that off," said Lindy.

T. did as he was told. "Why is this guy working for the Japs?"

"Crazy. He was passed over for promotion so many times he went to work for the enemy. He was a West Pointer, too. Well?"

Lindy sprawled on a leather sofa in front of the map while T. showed him the section of Kamchatka that he had visited. Lindy was intrigued by the KGB Eskimo, Omoo. "They've really got that country of theirs organized. Now let's hope he's not a Japanese agent."

"Does the field sound O.K.? For a base?"

Lindy was now at the map, checking distances. "It's a bit far, but if we're undetected, that's the end of them."

"The bomb?"

"Exploded day before yesterday near Los Alamos."

"No chain reaction?"

Lindy grinned. "None. You were right. I think Oppenheimer was a bit disappointed that the whole solar system didn't explode."

"Fallout?"

Lindy frowned. "They're still checking. I expect they'll find a lot. Anyway, we're committed. Now how do we set up this base, six thousand miles away from here?"

"Actually, it's more like six thousand feet."

"Through the exhibit?"

"Why not? Get them to shut it down so everything's, you know, for real and then get your men and material onto Kamchatka."

Lindy chuckled and looked very boyish. This was the sort of stunt he liked. "We'll have to take down a lot of walls to make room for the new B-29s. Biggest plane ever built. Fact, I'll have to use the whole Mall as a parking lot, and what do we tell the public?"

"Defense of the Capitol." T. had thought that one out. "The president can do a fireside chat."

"Well, he can get anybody to believe just about anything." Lindy was almost admiring. Despite the time shift, he still didn't like politicians in general and FDR in particular.

"O.K., boy. We're going to do some Arctic flying. I want to see what you've come up with."

"Spirit of St. Louis?"

"Suppose we crash? That's the end of a great tourist attraction." Lindy was on the phone. "General Lindbergh speaking. Get me a Lockheed Electra out on the Mall opposite the Smithsonian American History Building. . . . Yes, I know there's no landing strip, but malls were invented before airports. Shut down all traffic. And get me a couple of dozen men . . ." Lindy groaned at the obtuseness on the other end of the line. "To help me get the plane into the museum. Why else? ASAP!" He hung up. "They're awfully slow, these regular army guys."

"Well, it's not standard procedure."

"That's what they said when I took my trip across the big pond."

Lindy pulled down a map of the Pacific. "I know you've been worried about some relative of yours. Some kid. Well, the island-hopping's already started." Lindy pointed to a small island called Guam. "We've got this far. Lots of resistance. They fight like devils, the Japs. It's going to take years to get to Tokyo, going this route and even then . . . Hope your relative's O.K."

"Thanks for telling me."

Led by the Chief Engineer himself, and to the amazement of bystanders in and out of the Smithsonian, the Lockheed Electra was got, somehow, into the building and through the mahogany doors.

The Chief Engineer switched off the exhibit lights. The terrible cold began. "Boy, this is really the real thing." Lindy was delighted.

"Welcome, Lone Eagle!" Omoo approached them from the direction of the sea while the permanent plaster fishermen continued to fish.

Omoo gave Lindy a smart salute. "Wind's from the north, as you might expect."

Lindy asked the excited Omoo aboard; then, with T. in the copilot's seat, they took off into the north wind. Omoo showed them the sights. Ice. Snow. Black water. The prospective air base proved to be large enough to accommodate the super runways needed for the B-29, a plane so large that the air force was going to have to remove one side of the museum just to get it to the Kamchatka exhibit.

"This is it." Lindy made the O.K. sign with thumb and forefinger. Then he switched on his radio, and gave a series of rapid call numbers. Then: "Lindbergh to president. Urgent!"

Within a week the Mall had been shut off to the public. What looked to be a giant airplane hangar now covered the entire area. No one from the Castle, or anywhere else, could see who—or what—was coming and going. From Seventh to Fourteenth streets there was nothing but a great corridor as army trucks, covered with tarpaulins, entered from Seventh Street and exited, empty, at Fourteenth. One part of the wall of the American History Museum had been removed so that the complex machinery for base building could also be admitted to Kamchatka, where Lieutenant Colonel Omoo, U.S. Army Air Force, was in charge of Eskimo labor. By presidential decree, no reference was made to the mysterious business at hand. When *Life* magazine managed to get a photographer inside the covered Mall, he was arrested along with the publisher, Henry Luce, who was sent to Leavenworth prison for the duration. Later, the president airily noted, "I'm personally fond of Harry but he *is* a Republican."

T. now had other things on his mind. Specifically, himself. One afternoon when the Castle labs were relatively quiet, he punched out Graduation Day, 1941. Now less than a year away.

Carefully, he scanned the sunny scene. Saw himself, as always. Saw the dark girl, not unlike Squaw. He and his other self had the same taste in girls. Saw Stanley in the shadow of the chapel tower, holding his flask and animatedly talking to a young man whose back was to T. Then Dr. Lucas passed by and the young man waved at him. Dr. Lucas gave his stately smile; stopped; looked back, startled, but the young man was now facing away from him. In fact, he was looking straight into the monitor. It was T. himself. "Come on in," he said to T. in the lab.

So at last contact had been made, a bit late in the day, thought T. as he set his coordinates and stepped not only into the future but, literally, into himself.

Stanley noticed nothing. He was still talking to the same Smithsonian T. who had now penetrated the same time and space as himself on an earlier visit. He had often wondered why he had never found himself at the graduation on previous scannings. The answer was simple. He had not yet—future "yet"—arrived until now. In the distance, the St. Albans T. was talking to the boy in the wheelchair.

"Well, *you* had better talk to him." Stanley was winding up what must have been a pretty long speech, "because he doesn't listen to me, or anyone."

"I will." But T. felt suddenly nervous at the thought of talking to this entirely strange version of himself.

"You're duplicates!" Stanley blinked his eyes, as if he were seeing double; then drank from his flask, which always tended to bring the world into rosy focus for him.

"I never did come back." T. was beginning to feel guilty.

"I suspected you didn't. I'd drop an occasional hint—you know?—mention the Smithsonian but he was always—well, not you. We did stop him from growing that mustache of yours."

"You don't like it?"

"You'll be old enough in time. Why hurry the process?"

"I'm not so sure of that." A picture of the dummy in the Military Exhibit forced itself onto the inner screen of memory. "Listen. Can you get him to come over here? If people see the two of us . . ."

Stanley nodded. After steadying himself against the side of the chapel, he walked, with solemn, sober stride, out into the sunny day while T. remained in the green shade of the tower.

T. never thought of himself as particularly handsome, but if he were not already deep into women—or woman—this lean blond youth was very much what, two or three years earlier, he might have had fun with after dark in the dormitory.

"Hi," said the graduate T. Similar hand shook similar hand though the baseball hero's hand was calloused and T.'s was not.

"Hi," said T.

Then the other T. surprised him. "What took you so long in coming back to see me?"

"You remember?"

"Well, I'm not all that dumb. There I was in the room right next to yours in the Castle. Then Stanley came in a taxi and brought me back here where I've been expecting you ever since. But now I guess it's too late. I mean I've graduated. So you won't be taking my place, the way it was supposed to happen."

T. sat on a bench deeper in the shadows. The other T. joined him. They were hardly visible to their classmates and families in the sun. Invisible to the St. Albans T. was the door through which T. had entered from his lab, now masked by a great bush of mock orange.

"What are we, anyway?" The other T. was studying him, carefully.

"Well, we're the same person. At different times. I'm still sixteen at the Castle and you're seventeen here."

The St. Albans T. felt T.'s mustache. "That's sure me. They won't let me grow one here but then what's the point? I'm going into the Marine Corps next month where they shave off all your hair."

"That's why I'm here."

"You want to go in with me?" The other T. grinned—happily?

"No. I don't. And I don't want you to go."

"What's it to you?"

"You're me, too."

"But you're you, safe at the Castle, passing math exams all day long or whatever it is you do. Stanley says you're a genius. But I'm not. So we're not the same."

"What's the grand unified theory?"

The other T. frowned and shut his eyes. "Strong nuclear force gets weaker at high energies. Electromagnetic forces get stronger at high energies. At very high energy, these forces could *all* have the same strength and would be just different aspects of a single force—like you and me and those other boys in the Castle." The other T. laughed delightedly. "I don't understand a word of what I just said."

"That means you're right up there with Einstein. He hasn't got it either."

"But you and I are the same person in the way we're put together . . ."

"Brain, too, I think. You don't know what I know but sitting next to me, you just absorbed some of it." The boy in the wheelchair was being pushed past them by the other T.'s girlfriend.

"What happened to Rick?" T. was now beginning to know some of the things that his St. Albans self knew.

"He got his at Pearl Harbor. He was captain of the baseball team when we first came here. Then he was a navy pilot. Plane never got off the ground."

"You know, you don't need to go."

The other T. frowned; adjusted his white duck trousers. "*Need?* Well, maybe not. But I got to go."

"But they won't use you for anything except cannon fodder . . ."

"Well. If that's what they really need . . ."

"What I'm trying to say is we've got these new weapons. Japan's going to be knocked out of the war in a year or two, so whatever you do between now and then is pointless."

The other T.'s eyes, very green-blue even in the shadows, lit up. "So that's why they got that Mall at the Smithsonian all covered up."

Plainly, the other T.'s brain was linking up with T.'s. There must be some law of proximity—symbiosis—mysteriously at work. For an awful moment, T. feared that he and the other T., like two drops of mercury, would come together and be a single whole. Then who would save the one and only T. from the Military Exhibit?

In the distance, Stanley was charming parents.

"Are the three aunts here?" asked T.

"What three aunts?" The other T. looked at him oddly.

"Ours. In K Street. Where I lived. Where you live."

The other T. shook his head.

"Something's gone wrong. Or right. I live, like always, with Mother and my stepfather. Like you did. Out on Woodley Road. Near the Shoreham." The other T. indicated a handsome middle-aged couple talking to Mr. True. "There they are."

"You were never in the lower-school dorm?"

"Oh, sure. Twice. When they spent those two winters in Chile."

"And . . . our father. Did he die in that zeppelin crash?"

"Wow!" The other T.'s face was bright with amusement. "So that's what *you* remember?"

"Well, what really happened?"

"He left Mom when I—we—were about eight years old and she married this construction engineer. He's a swell guy. Does a lot of work in Latin America. Now his company's helping out in the Pacific, building bases. Come on over and meet . . ." But the other T. broke off. "No, better not."

T. made his last pitch. "If I tell you you're going to get yourself killed in the marines will that stop you from enlisting?"

The other T. grinned. "Maybe you're as wrong about that as you are about me living with three aunts in K Street."

"No. I'm right."

The other T. shrugged. "So I wait a year and get drafted into the army and get killed anyway."

T. stared with morbid interest at his other self. The thought of so much handsome flesh dismantled in a bloody flash was unbearable. His eyes felt hot and dry as he looked into the smiling face.

Once again, the other T. read his mind. He put his arm—the pitcher's arm—around T.'s shoulders and pulled him close for an instant. "Don't worry, buddy. We'll get through somehow. Dr. Smithson says we will. I got to go."

It was not until T. was back in his lab that what the other T. had said began to reverberate: "Dr. Smithson says we will." The other T.'s must have met him during their basketball games and this particular memory had survived the time shift, unless, and T. started to feel uneasy, Dr. Smithson was projecting a message onto his own brain which the other T. had duly received. It was time, T. decided, that he and Dr. Smithson met. But how to make an appointment? And where, indeed, to find him?

T. punched out the plan of the great Parcheesi board on which the Institution rested. Then, as he scanned the basketball court, the screen went dark.

Next: the familiar, feathery handwriting, in purple ink.

"You did your very best, as did I. But your other self is, at heart, a romantic and a patriot, and those emotions have quite filled up that part of his soul which, in you, is filled with quantum physics and not too much else: in this you resemble Dr. Einstein who is, by his own admission, generally indifferent to human relationships as are you, with the obvious exception of a certain lady whose name delicacy forbids my mentioning. Of the two natures, the romantic knows the greatest joy and is drawn to the greatest suffering, as your other self already suspects and will know more of in time. Dulce et decorum . . . But we are not at the end, nor is he. Actually there is nothing sweeter in this life than for a man to know and save himself.

"We shall meet in due course. But for now you must continue your great work, enmeshed as we all are in the myriad gold strings of

time which now begin to converge upon a spectacular great crossroad. I am, with every faith in your constancy of spirit, your most ardent admirer, James Smithson, as from beneath the basketball court at the point where the Parcheesi board signifies HOME."

The entire wall to the Kamchatka exhibit had been removed as had most of the museum wall that faced the Mall. Beneath the Mall's camouflaged ceiling, known to the army as "The Corridor," B-29s and other equipment were being towed into what had been the exhibit. Several hundred army engineers were in charge of this twenty-four-hour project, all conducted by artificial light that made for a somewhat hellish effect since it was never clear whether it was day or night outside the Smithsonian.

T. was obliged to identify himself at a series of checkpoints before he was allowed to step into what had been an Arctic-style exhibit but was now the near-Arctic itself. Where once there had been a single igloo with three Eskimos fishing beside it, there was a rutted icy road along which army trucks proceeded toward the interior of Kamchatka and the new air base.

A jeep stopped in front of T. A soldier jumped out and saluted smartly. "Colonel, I'm your driver. Order of the Commanding General."

T. enjoyed his temporary rank, which required him to wear a silver eagle on his shirt collar. He also wore a heavy parka and thick gloves.

The countryside was now unrecognizable from the pristine wilderness that T. had earlier visited with Squaw. The Chief Engineer had made many bitter complaints about the destruction of the exhibit until Bentsen told him that without this base the war was lost and the banner of the rising sun of

Nippon would be flying over the Castle. Then Bentsen told the Chief that he would provide him with a new site for an exhibit when . . .

When what? T. wondered as they drove along several miles of icy roads lined with Quonset huts—barracks, offices—and then numerous airplane hangars carefully frosted with white fiberglass so that, from above, the base would look like the field of desolate snow that it had been a few months before.

T. was deposited in front of a large hangar. Over a side door was the discreet sign: HQCG.

The CG himself greeted T. in the anteroom where clerks typed and mimeographed and a photograph of the Commander in Chief, President Roosevelt, gazed impersonally down on them from a plywood wall that he shared with a map of the Northern Hemisphere, whose southernmost tip was Tokyo.

Wearing coveralls and no army insignia, Lindy looked more like a mechanic than the Commanding General.

"Welcome to the North Pole." He led T. into his office, which was full of maps and mysterious pieces of machinery.

"How near are we?" T. sat on a sofa while Lindy put his feet up on a desk whose only decoration was a silver model of the B-29, the largest plane that T. had ever seen. When he first saw one being rolled into the museum, it looked like a metal skyscraper lying on its side.

"Close."

"Before Christmas?"

"Could be. So far the Japs know we're up here but not why."

"How did they find out?"

"Well, there's no way we could keep a base this big a secret for very long. But we busted their code long ago and so we know that they plan to take us out as soon as we're ready for invasion, which at the rate the navy and the marines are is-land-hopping their way across the Pacific won't be for another two years. The Japs have plenty of time, or so they think."

"Do they know about . . . ?" The reason for the base was never mentioned aloud, not even in ever-changing code.

Lindy shook his head. "We would have had a visit from them already if they knew. Lucky for us, their land army's mostly in China and their fleet's in the mid-Pacific. So where's that plan of yours?"

On a monitor T. typed out his coded variation to the already green-lighted Operation Knockout. Lindy decoded rapidly; frowned, then erased the various ciphers and hieroglyphs.

"It suits me," he said at last. "But I don't think we can sell it to the president."

"Why not?"

"Oh . . ." Lindy pulled down a map of the Pacific. The various American bases were marked in blue; the Japanese in red. "This is why." He put his finger on Pearl Harbor. "Revenge."

"Their total surrender ought to be pretty revengeful."

"I don't think he sees it that way. That's why the press is playing up all those Jap atrocities . . ."

"They aren't real?"

"Of course they're real. But for your plan to work the public's got to cool down first. Meanwhile . . ."

Lindy indicated several island clusters between Guam and the main island of Japan. "We're going to have to occupy each one of these if we're ever going to invade their mainland . . ."

"But we're not going to invade. They are going to surrender after . . . you know what."

"They might," said Lindy, staring hard at the murderous dots on the map, each representing a Japanese military base, well dug in, and waiting. "And then again, they might not."

"So if they don't, you can always go to the . . . original plan . . ."

Lindy was suddenly alert; cocked his head. Then T. heard the sound of planes overhead. A screen lit up back of Lindy's desk. RED ALERT.

An excited aide appeared in the doorway. "They're coming at us from the north . . ."

His next words were not audible as a bomb hit nearby. T. was momentarily deafened by the sound like two trains colliding at full speed. The room shook. A monitor overturned.

Lindy ran into the adjoining operations room, giving rapid orders. A screen revealed the Japanese bombers overhead. Then, as if from nowhere, American fighter planes appeared on the radar screen. Shadow duels. Fiery falls.

Further explosions rocked the base. But no bomb fell close to headquarters. In a few minutes it was all over. The Japanese bombers were returning north while American fighter planes pursued them off the screen and, presumably, into the Aurora Borealis itself.

Later, T. accompanied Lindy around the base. Little serious damage had been done. The B-29s were still hidden away in their underground hangars. Big Boy, as the atomic bomb was called, was safely under wraps in what had been the American Historical Handicrafts Exhibit, conveniently located just down the hall from the Arctic exhibit.

The midnight sun cast a white glare over everything as they watched the fighter planes return.

Lindy maintained constant radio communication with their commander and, through the static, T. could hear, "We scored three hits, sir. No casualties for us. They changed course at longitude . . ."

Apparently, they had gone west into Russian airspace and were, even now, en route to Japan.

Back at headquarters, Lindy held a staff meeting. Since T. was not invited to take part, he explored the headquarters, which smelled of coal smoke from old-fashioned iron Franklin stoves. T. thought that they might have worked out a better heating system, but then the entire base had been hastily built by, among others . . .

"You do look just like him." There was the other T.'s stepfather, Darryl Redpath, standing in a doorway, the Chief Engineer of the Smithsonian at his side.

"I spotted you at the graduation and he said you were a cousin. On his father's side."

"Well, sort of," said T.

The Chief Engineer motioned for him to come into what proved to be the office of Lieutenant Colonel Omoo, commandant of the base. "Welcome!" Omoo had taken marvelously well to army life. He now wore a spick-and-span full-dress army uniform and no longer even slightly resembled his premilitary blubber-smeared self.

On the radio the first chords of Beethoven's Fifth Symphony sounded, then: "This is *Lieutenant* Colonel Douglas MacArthur. Sad news today for many an American mother sitting 'neath her gold star as her boy was sent to slaughter in the Pacific . . ."

"Turn that off," said Redpath.

"No," said Omoo. "We want to hear what he says about us."

After a description of a failed marine assault on one of the Marshall Islands, MacArthur reported, "A successful strike against a supposedly secret American base on the Russian island of Kamchatka has just been carried out. We sustained no casualties while most of the enemy's base was destroyed. The base itself was of no strategic importance but the *political* consequences are grave. Nay, full of somber portent for the treacherous Russians who allowed your American leaders to establish an anti-Japanese base on Russian soil. Needless to say, He Who Sits upon the Chrysanthemum Throne now frowns toward the north, and President Trotsky in his Kremlin shivers at our emperor's displeasure."

Omoo switched off the radio.

The Chief Engineer looked nervous. "I hope General Lindbergh can keep the Japs away from here as long as possible, because one bomb five miles off target and we get hit."

"We—who?" Redpath looked puzzled.

"We, the Smithsonian. Specifically, the American History Museum where this exhibit is."

"This is Kamchatka . . ." Redpath began.

"But five miles to the east is the Smithsonian."

"How," asked Redpath, "can we be at the same time in Kamchatka and in the District of Columbia?"

The Chief Engineer sighed; looked at T. for help. T. gave none. "Top secret," the Chief Engineer was inspired to say, and left the room.

"We're dealing with a recent concept," said T., and he rattled off a series of formulas until Redpath asked him to stop.

"I just heard from my stepson." Redpath took a letter from his pocket. "It was written on Guam. He mentions you. He didn't dare send it through the censors so he gave this to a friend who was being shipped back to the States, who mailed it to us."

T. read: "This place is a real hell. We sleep on the ground with these long brown snakes who like to crawl into our sacks to keep warm. Nights are cold. Scuttlebutt is the marines are taking pretty awful losses in these island hops. One regiment had hundred percent losses in a single day. A record. Japs are dug in in tunnels underground and so we can't bomb them out or anything except just land on the beach and let them shoot us until we pile up so high we smother them. Well, you both warned me but I didn't listen. But then I didn't think that our real enemies were going to be the marine officers and the navy brass. They don't care how many of us get killed since they're the ones who get the medals at the end of the day. No, I don't want you to get me out of the marines. A lot of guys are using pull not to get killed, which is sensible. But I'll take my chances if only I was given better odds by the big strategists. Now you remember seeing that boy at the graduation, the cousin on my father's side who looks like me? Well, he's at the Smithsonian, working in the Castle, and he has the same name as me so he won't be hard to find. Tell him to help me out. He'll know what to do." The rest of the letter was about the other T.'s girlfriend. T. gave the letter back to Redpath.

"So what can you do?"

"I'm not sure." T. felt a sudden chill: someone had just stepped on his grave, as the Negroes said. "Give me his military address. I'll try to track him down."

Redpath wrote out the other T.'s rank, company, battalion, regiment, brigade, division. T. suggested they go into G-2, the intelligence room where busy clerks recorded hour by hour the progress of the war by putting thumbtacks into a large map of the central Pacific.

T. asked one of the clerks to locate for him the other T.'s unit. It was apparently still en route to the islands closest to Japan. "We can't say where, even if we knew, which we don't. But the big fight will be happening here." He pointed to Okinawa.

T. whistled. "That's pretty close to Japan, isn't it?"

"I can get him transferred," Redpath muttered to T.

"Don't count on it. He's already on a transport ship. He'd never live it down if you got him off now."

"At least he'd have a chance to *live* it down."

"If you'd only done this before . . ."

"We didn't know . . ." Redpath talked but T. had stopped listening. His own "before" was sounding over and over again in his head. Why not go back to before? If Lincoln had been taken out of his time, why not the other T.?

9

BENTSEN HAD a message for T. from Squaw. "Come see us tonight at ten, on the line."

T. pocketed the note. "Any more word from Los Alamos?"

Bentsen shook his head. "Everybody's just standing by out there, waiting for Big Boy to go off." He paused expectantly but T. was not about to tell him about his own contingency plan, which, as far as he knew, had not been adopted.

"How are casualties?"

"We could hear"—Bentsen's voice overlapped T.'s—"the air raid all the way over here. They say the whole American History Museum shook."

T. was puzzled. "I don't get the physics . . ."

"The base is at the same time we are so . . ."

"But in different space. Four thousand miles away."

"The same principle that got *us* there can get their bombs here *if* they hit the entryway, which they almost did. Thank God they haven't a clue that we . . ."

The radio went on, automatically, for the News at Noon. "This is *Lieutenant* Colonel Douglas MacArthur. The Incarnation of the Sun, the emperor, has discovered the existence of a new weapon, developed by the white race to use against the master race of Asia. Now, from the Chrysanthemum Throne, the Mikado warns . . ."

After a good deal of bombast, a much-concerned Bentsen turned off the radio. "So much for our top secret."

T. was not disturbed.

"They don't know what the weapon is and even if they suspect, they can't know what our plan is because a half hour ago Lindy didn't know. Now explain to me just *how* Mr. Baird got Lincoln into a later space and time."

Bentsen told T. what he knew, which was not very much. A stable two-way linkup between past and future—like the one between two precise places and times, Otowi, N. Mex., 1896, and Lyme, Conn., 1910—was possible with a constant and sufficient energy source. But a random removal of one human being from one place and time to an as-yet-unhappened future time and place had occurred only once, at Ford's Theater—mainly by accident. This meant that T. would have to work out another "accident" if the other T. was to be saved from—where was he, anyway?

By ten o'clock, T. had managed to find the other T. aboard a transport to the west of the Marshall Islands. He was a private in the Third Division, Marine Corps. But no scanner could locate him in those crowded ships.

———◆———

Grover Cleveland was wearing a frock coat and what hair he had was glued to his scalp by bay rum. "Master Veal! Come in. Come in. There's someone here who wants to meet you."

Grover led T. into the parlor, where Squaw was entertaining Thomas Jefferson, who rose to his full height when he saw T.

"Young sir," the voice was low but distinct. The handclasp somewhat ghostly, without pressure.

"We're having tea but I've got Coca-Cola for you." Both Clevelands seemed unusually lively. As Squaw brought T. his Coke, Grover said, proudly, "This is the first trip that Mr. Jefferson has ever made so far up the line."

"True," said Jefferson, sitting beneath a photograph of Geronimo in chains. "It's not that I lack amiability or curiosity, but I do feel a bit out of my depth so far from my own time."

"Admit," said Grover, jovially, "that you don't dare pass Andrew Jackson's house for fear he'll pop out at you."

Jefferson's smile was faint. "Well, sir, he is a noisy man, and not one I am comfortable with. But I do have visitors from your end of the line, like Mr. Theodore Roosevelt—also very loud—but he does keep up on the latest scientific developments. And of course he is a first-class taxidermist, no small gift." He turned to T. "I am told that you come from the war in the Pacific."

"Well, sir, from the very north Pacific. The Arctic."

"How I envy those people who can now see what, for us, was just the far edges to inaccurate maps, with that ever-maddening phrase, Terra Incognita, written in the margins. Dear sir, madam, might I speak with this young man of science alone for a moment?"

The Clevelands were all smiles as they withdrew. T. was getting distinctly uneasy: what did the great Jefferson want with him? Were the Founding Fathers about to intervene? One president seemed more than enough for the approaching crossroads.

"Long, long ago—in 1789 to be precise—I was American minister in Paris where, along with my political duties, I was much interested in the sciences and sought out the company of the learned, and we exchanged notes of every kind. One young man that I met, not much older than you are now, was an Englishman named James Smithson. We were both interested in a substance called Ulmin, from the bark of the elm tree, whose medicinal qualities form the basis, I believe, of what was much later to be known as aspirin." Jefferson smiled; darted a glance at T.; then quickly looked away.

"We were very much in advance of our time. But when it came to a common dislike of monarchy, we were at the right time and place and because of Mr. Smithson's reverence for the democratic ideas upon which this republic rested he left us, as you know, his fortune to create this institution." Another quick hazel-eyed glance. Jefferson could not, T. realized, look anyone in the eye for long. Shyness? Shiftiness?

"Mr. Smithson and I continue to meet here, as fellow scientists—or amateurs, I suppose, is the word. He keeps up-to-date and keeps me—*warned* of new discoveries." Again the slight smile. "He has now addressed himself to your problem."

"The alternative to using Big Boy to blow up Tokyo?"

Jefferson frowned. "He has *not* kept me up-to-date on that matter. Military secrets are not my forte. I seem constitutionally unable to keep any secret, or so my friends used to say, while my enemies . . ." He frowned; sighed; shook his head—to empty it of enemies? "No. The problem that we have discussed is the one that concerns you personally. Your other self, as it were, now at fatal risk in the Pacific."

"I'm surprised," said T., "that Mr. Smithson would bother with anything so unimportant."

"Whatever concerns you, young sir, concerns us all. You are precious to the human race, as Dr. Einstein duly noted."

T. flushed with embarrassment. It was now his turn to look away.

"Mr. Smithson's notes on just how Secretary Baird got Mr. Lincoln out of his time and space were burned in the fire. Secretary Baird himself has been more than obliging but he thinks chance played a large part in that—well, let us be precise—*disastrous* undertaking. It is not my habit to speak ill of any president or, indeed, I hope of anyone, with the possible exception of my first vice president. But in the case of Mr. Lincoln I hold him largely responsible for the great slaughter

of the war between those states that had every right—each—
to go its own way either to create a more perfect union or to
the freedom of disunion. So I cannot say I feel much sympa-
thy for the poor crazed figure who dwells among us. But I
digress. In contemplating the case of Mr. Lincoln, Mr.
Smithson has devised a way for you to save your endangered
self from certain death on a volcanic island with a barbarous
name."

"How?"

Thomas Jefferson told him how and in what proved to be
horrifying detail.

"I can't," said T., voice breaking.

"Do what you will. I do not advise. I am mere messenger.
As I was in 1776."

"There has to be another way."

"I am instructed to assure you that there is absolutely no
alternative way." Jefferson rose. Extended his hand. "I am
sorry."

———————

The next morning, as requested, T. reported to the American
History Museum's infirmary where he underwent a series of
disagreeable tests. Bentsen had been sardonic. "I think maybe
they want to clone you. Just in case."

But T. had already been cloned, or whatever process had
been used to create the other T's. Out of his rib? Was someone now playing God in the basement, beneath the Parcheesi
board's end?

When T. returned to his room, he found the Chief Engineer busy at work. The Chief had—with whose help?—set
up the power generator, while beneath the window that
looked out toward Pennsylvania Avenue he had devised a
port of entry into what was now being described as the
bloodiest battle since the Civil War.

"I've got us to D day plus nine," said the Chief Engineer, an amiable man plainly disturbed by what they were about to do. "There's quite a slaughter going on." He indicated the shadowy door-size rectangle that now blocked out the window.

"What time is it there?" T.'s throat was dry. He was dressed exactly like the other T.—marine combat fatigues as well as a thick navy sweater and dog tags so that he would, in due course, be identified.

The Chief Engineer checked his watch. "Four minutes to midnight, February twenty-eighth. Sun set at six forty-five. It's cold, very cold out there. Funny how we think of the Pacific as all tropical palm trees and white beaches, but not where you're going, not down there."

T. unfolded a small map of the area. The point where he would arrive was marked with an X. It was not far from a small hill, marked 362-A. The other T. was now in a foxhole atop a hill to the southeast. Just down the hill was a sort of field and back of that the Japanese were hidden in a series of underground caves.

"It's all guesswork," said the Chief Engineer. "About the Japanese, I mean. We know they are there but we don't know how many. Your friend's with seven other scouts. The Third Battalion of the Ninth Regiment is back of him. He's keeping an eye out for any movement. He's got a radio, or one of them has a radio, and they'll warn headquarters if there's any . . . movement."

"This is the night when there will be a lot of movement." T. took a deep breath. "O.K. Power."

The Chief switched on the generator. The room was filled with a deep humming sound. T. then set the coordinates for time and space. The fact that, except for the sun's position, Smithsonian time was precisely the same as that of the Pacific cut the amount of energy needed by half. All that T. could do now was hope that what he was about to enter was the right place at the right time.

Before him there was a rectangle of dark night with a fraction of what looked to be moon—or a flare—at its center.

"Is there a moon?"

"Forgot to check." The Chief was apologetic.

Then T. stepped carefully onto the volcanic soil of the island of Iwo Jima. Icy sulphurous-smelling air filled his lungs: then he was promptly deafened by a volley of rifle fire from the hill to his left.

Eyes accustomed to the dim light—more from huge stars than what looked to be a partial moon—he saw the other T., standing, back toward him. T. had studied this moment a dozen times on the scanner. He knew that an instant before his arrival, the other T. had stepped out of a foxhole that he was sharing with another scout. Now the other T. turned and saw him. This part had not been rehearsed.

"Password!" the other T. whispered urgently.

"It's me." T. took a step forward only to find a rifle aimed at him.

"Password! Damn it. Or I'll shoot."

"Smithsonian Institution. It's me. I've come to get you out of here." Then T. knew—how?—the password. "Franklin Delano Roosevelt."

"You?" The two were now face-to-face. They were at last the same age, nineteen—presumably to the minute. Only the other T.'s face was streaked with volcanic ash and, despite the coldness of the night, sweat.

"I've found a way to—well, remember how I got to see you at your graduation?"

"Tricks?"

"Quantum physics."

"How?"

T. pointed to the oblong blur that only his eye could tell was the bedroom which he'd come from.

"What's that?"

"You'll see. Come on."

The other T. pulled back. He was shaking now. "I can't. Can't desert." He wiped his face with the sleeve of his navy sweater. He coughed as soundlessly as possible. "I think I got pneumonia. I'm freezing to death."

"Here." T. rubbed the other T.'s arms. It was like touching, smelling himself. The same grass-green eyes were now on exactly the same level. T. held on to the other T. until he stopped shaking.

"I saw that letter to your stepfather. From Guam. That's why I came . . ."

"You're too late, buddy. We're all going to get it now. Twenty thousand Japs out there, underground."

"Well, *you're* not going to get it. Come on." T. pulled the other T. toward the port of entry.

But at the very edge the other T. pulled back. "I can't . . ."

A sudden fit of coughing gave T. his chance. With all his strength and weight, he half shoved and half threw his other self through the entryway into life.

"So long . . . buddy," he said, as the other T. sprawled on his belly in the shadowy bedroom that promptly vanished as the Chief switched off the power at the other end.

This is death, thought T., stepping further into the nightmare. Acrid smell of cordite now mingled with the fumes from powdery lava in which only dry twisted bonelike branches of scrub trees grew. He sat on the edge of the other T.'s foxhole, and slid down into what must have been a natural sort of trench—very like a grave, he noted grimly.

"Where you been?" It was the other T.'s partner.

"Felt sick." T. was in no heroic mood nor was his companion.

"See any movement?"

T. shook his head; then all of him shook. Fear. Regret. Anger. Why had he agreed to this crazy exchange?

Far-off, the sound of bombardment. From U.S. battleships? No, he decided when he saw flashes of light high above the island. From Mount Suribachi, a dragonlike silhouette up ahead where American troops had recently set the flag, inspiring the Japanese in their warrens to open fire.

Well, no matter what happened, the other T. was safe; he'd survive; marry and have children. Everyone had agreed that if T. was in himself a Darwinian step forward, then the other T. was also one, potentially. He could be trained in case Smithson's intricate plan should fail.

There was a great explosion from the field below. Powdery dust shifted into the foxhole, half covering them. Then pale white incandescent flares filled the night sky, making a hellish day all round them. Below their foxhole was a cratered field with chunks of lava rock and concrete and dunes of volcanic ash like coffee grounds and wisps of sulphurous steam escaping, presumably, from hell beneath.

T.'s partner saw something behind him. "Hey!" was all he said, unpinning a hand grenade as a Japanese bayonet went into T.'s right shoulder blade. T. felt shock but no pain. He fell on his belly and aimed his rifle. The Jap was gone.

"Here they come!" T. and his partner lay flat, rifles aimed at the small figures that were now racing up the hill and shouting, in English, "Die stupid marine!"

From nearby foxholes, marines threw grenades, fired rifles. But nothing could stop the wave of shouting, shrieking Japanese as they hurled their grenades and fired their rifles and used their bayonets on those in the foxholes.

Two grenades landed in T.'s foxhole. One landed between the legs of his partner; simultaneously, one went off behind T. The world seemed to explode. But, an instant later, he was still alive. So was his partner, who put out his hand to drag T. from the foxhole just as a Jap leaped into it and threw his arms around T., who tried to break away as something hard and metallic ground into the small of his back. The mine attached to the Jap's belly killed both of them, filling T.'s head with light as all air left his lungs. Then he outdistanced light itself.

10

T OPENED HIS EYES. Quiet. Diffused light. He was on
his back. He could hear low voices nearby; could not
make out what they were saying. He had the sense that what
he was now experiencing he had already gone through before.

But when he tried to move, he could not. Was he in a hospital? He looked down at himself. He had no arms. He could
not see as far as his legs, yet there was no blood; no bandages
either. Then he realized he was lying on a floor, surrounded
by what looked to be camouflage sacks.

A tall blond boy looked down at him. Their eyes met. The
boy shivered. Shut his eyes for an instant. Recognition?

T. tried to get enough air into his lungs to say, "Where am
I?" But the traditional question got no answer. However, the
boy was now crouched down beside him staring into his face.
T. recognized the other T. as of years before.

"Get me out of here," said T.; and fainted. In the darkness,
he felt himself being picked up and—dismantled? Was that
possible? Yes. Last thought: he was the dummy that lay beside
the door to the Military Exhibit.

* * *

"He's practically as good as new." This was the first thing that
T. heard as he came to. He was in a hospital bed in a large
room filled with all sorts of intricate medical machinery. Be-

side his bed was his monitor from the lab. Beside the monitor stood two strange men in white smocks; they looked down at him with what seemed a proprietary air.

T. took a cautious look at his body, which was covered by a sheet. It looked complete.

"I'm Dr. Carrel," said the older of the two. "Welcome back to life. No, you don't need to ask where you are, since I shall tell you. In the Science Building of the Smithsonian. This is the top-secret ward for which only a half dozen of us have security clearance."

"So I *was* dead." T. raised his right arm; then he raised first one foot; then the other. All in order.

Dr. Carrel's assistant answered: "You were, to be blunt, a perfect mess. The grenade went through your back and out the front. You've now got Lindbergh's artificial heart inside you, and some other odds and ends. Luckily, we cloned you long ago. Remember? Well, before we let those boys go we grew all sorts of organs from their tissues, so we'd have enough to rebuild you from scratch, if we had to, which is pretty much what we did. Anyway, you're now as good as new except for some scar tissue which cosmetic surgery can probably get rid of."

T. remembered the dummy with the hole through its chest. He had thought it was another—if not *the* other—T., but it had been himself all along.

"What happened to . . ."

"You saved his life, as you meant to do. He's married now and playing professional baseball."

"Good." T. lifted the sheet to get a look at his naked body. Except for a red scar down the middle of his chest, he looked as he always had, only hairier, more muscular, older.

Dr. Carrel smiled. "It's not a boy's body anymore, as you can see. That's because it took us nearly two years to put you together again . . ."

"Two years!"

"Yes, two years." A familiar voice. It was Lindy at the door. He, too, was wearing a white smock. "Welcome back to life." He was now at T.'s bedside, shaking T.'s hand vigorously.

"Thanks. Where's your uniform?"

"The war's over. I've come back to work here. Like before, when we first met. Secretly, I've always been with the medical unit. Planes were just a hobby. Until the war started."

"What happened?"

"What happened to what?"

Dr. Carrel and his associate excused themselves.

"Remember? I've lost two years—again. What about the war?" T. wondered just how many years one could lose and still retain the requisite number of marbles with which to think.

"Oh, we won. They surrendered about six months after your visit to Iwo Jima."

"My plan? Or the president's?"

"A bit of both. First we followed your plan. Operation Fireworks. It was beautiful! Big Boy took the whole top off of Mount Fujiyama. There's now a beautiful crater lake where the peak used to be. The emperor wanted to quit right then and there but Admiral Tojo wanted one final battle. So we took out their entire fleet with Big Boy II. A general named Eisenhower is now in charge of Japan while President Truman has put most of Southeast Asia under Admiral Nimitz."

They were joined by Bentsen. "The hero returns."

"Pieces of him, anyway."

"The right pieces," said Lindy. "Your brain wasn't touched, so you're still you. We did get a look at it."

"At what?"

"Your brain. You've developed—or you're developing a third lobe."

T. said nothing. But he knew that that was bound to be the next step.

Bentsen was oddly skeptical. "How *is* your memory?"

"For what?" asked T., suddenly feeling a bit sick as he realized the enormity of what he had been put through deliberately by James Smithson, or whoever was acting in his name.

Bentsen switched on the monitor beside the bed. "For this," he said.

T. concentrated. Saw, alarmingly, what looked to be the same stars that he had seen when the mine burst through his back. Then the stars became yellow wriggling strings of light. This was odd. Usually, he got the numbers first and the visualization second.

T. began, slowly, to punch out Father Lamy's string theory of creation. As he did, the monitor filled with writhing serpents, aglow in time–space.

"Wow!" Lindy had never seen the strings before.

"Yes," said Bentsen, "but the application . . ."

"Isn't it clear? The possibilities for anything from amoeba to the human race are infinite. What you're seeing there, on the monitor, is a fraction of the possibilities. What's his name?—from Princeton—gets to be president on one string and I get to be dead at nineteen on the same one. So I got myself off the string." T. realized that he had made a breakthrough into what was a new dimension, undreamed of by anyone until . . . He switched the monitor off.

"We'll come to all that *in time*. Now let me out of here. I've work to do." T. sat up. "What day is it?"

"Sunday," said Lindy. "Easter Sunday."

"I see," said T.; and saw, clearly, what had once been invisible.

For old-time's sake, T. and Squaw made love in the cotton-woods of the Early Indian Exhibit. The Indians had greeted T. on their knees while the chief moaned, from his belly, praises to the Great White God who had come among them. No talk of veal stew or even of what was now mature beef.

"Oh, it's been awful!" Squaw held him tight. "These last two years, wondering if they could really put you together again."

"Was it that close?" They lay side by side, nude, in a shallow spring where salamanders darted in and out of watercress.

"They wouldn't tell *me,* of course. We're just the dummies after all."

"Am I?"

Squaw turned him away from her so that she could see his back. "The scar's like Tom's. Only there's more of it. I don't really know what you are. You *should* be in the Military Exhibit all day when the tourists come, just as I am with the First Ladies. But so far you're you full-time, aren't you?"

T. rolled over onto Squaw; a salamander slithered between their bellies. "So far. But Lindy said I'll soon be told . . ." But told what, he wondered, even as he spoke; then he pulled Squaw on top of him. "You still like me, now I'm not chicken?"

Squaw gave him her special half smile, the hazel eyes gleaming. "So what are you?"

"I'm hawk!" T. shouted; and entered his kingdom.

———•◦•———

An awed Bentsen placed the letter on T.'s console. Purple ink. Red wax seal. "Maybe you'll be able to penetrate the Secret of the Smithsonian."

"You mean *he* is alive after all these years?"

"Well, yes. We're more or less onto the dummies and their biology even though we are just employees and like everyone else. But with you, the medical staff seems to have done something exceptional. General Lindbergh thinks that you are now something entirely new under the sun."

Bentsen left T. to read the letter:

We were far from certain that you would survive. Yes, I was disingenuous when I first persuaded you to give up your own life in order to save your other entirely human self, due to die of a kamikaze mine wound. I understood the risk to you and yet I let you go because there was a possibility—one in ten—that we could reconstitute you as we have so many other lads lost in battle, for our ever-popular Military Exhibit. But the task proved to be a daunting one. Fortunately, the science of morphology has been advancing rapidly, as it always does during wartime, and my own experiments in the 1820s that resulted in what are known as the half-and-half dummies have undergone, in you, metamorphosis. You are now what is known, in these current times, as a state-of-the-art reconstruction, complete with unaltered mind—in your case, genius—that it was our supreme task and, perhaps, my—our—human destiny to nurture and to preserve.

I shudder now at the risk that I took in sending you to your "death" on that terrible island. I rejoice that you now have metamorphosed into something not known before in our race though I am sure that a journey through those luminous strings of yours will reveal other versions of you but we have not the time to move into yet another unknown history like the one that you plunged us all into thanks to your fateful visit to Lyme, Connecticut.

Now, dear young sir and the son of the Smithsonian, son and sun, we shall gladly receive you tomorrow at noon beneath the basketball court, at the Parcheesi board's end where I remain your most obedient servant in all things. James Smithson.

T. was even more nervous than he had been the first time that he had made his descent to the great Parcheesi board beneath Castle and Mall.

At a quarter to noon, he was the only person, as far as he could tell, using the intricate underground where the pavement glowed in the fluorescent light: square upon square painted in vivid primary colors, each with its admonition, warning, compliment, for the game player if not for T.

The main corridor—"The Home Path"—comprised an enormous square frame to what must have been numerous offices and laboratories and exhibits, each approached by its own mysteriously numbered door.

But for anyone who persevered to the end, which was, presumably, the starting point to the game, there was the basketball court, looking rather dusty and unused. On the floor, in large letters, the word HOME. Under it the word PARCHEESI and under that TRADEMARK REGISTERED IN U.S. PATENT OFFICE. SINCE 1874.

What next? T. wondered.

An English voice answered him. "Go to the end of the court. Back of the basket, as I believe the hoop is oddly called. You will find a staircase. Go up it and you will be back to where you started. Go down it and you will have arrived at what you Americans like to call a residence, *my* residence."

T. did as he was told. On the level beneath the court there was a small rectangular room with a crystal chandelier in which real candles burned, illuminating a mahogany door with a silver plate, JAS. SMITHSON, ESQ.

T. knocked. Jas. Smithson opened it.

T. had never tried to visualize the founder of the Institution. The one painting of him that he had seen could have been of anyone in an eighteenth-century wig. The reality was as small as James Madison. But instead of a wig he wore a blue velvet cap that covered what looked to be a bald head. Smithson wore an eighteenth-century costume, considerably frayed with time and use. He seemed to be in his sixties—gray-eyed, pale-faced, with peculiar dentures more or less at liberty to travel about in a wide mouth.

The handshake was firm but silky as old men's hands tended to be. "This is a joy for me, young sir. Do come in."

Smithson led the speechless T. into a drawing room that could, with a sign in place, qualify for "Late Eighteenth to Early Nineteenth Century English Drawing Room." The only unexpected touch were the glass cases scattered about the room, containing minerals, fossils, butterflies. Numerous important portraits looked down upon them.

"Brandy?" Without an answer from T., Smithson filled a crystal goblet from a decanter. "I made sure that you would be able to enjoy all the pleasures of the flesh. Unlike me. As a simulacrum I am not as far advanced as you. I am crude work. But still going after a hundred and twenty—or whatever it is—years. Please sit down."

T. drank half the brandy in a gulp. "That's powerful, sir." he said, throat burning.

"It should be. It's older than I. There's not much left." He smiled. "Of either of us."

T. studied Smithson carefully. He wore stockings that revealed the contours of short thin legs . . .

"Am I a dummy, you are wondering?"

T. blushed. "Oh no, sir . . ."

"Oh yes, sir! Are we not both scientists? So, to answer the question you did not ask, I am more of one than you but then so are all the others. You, sir, are something entirely new. You're still a man but restructured in certain essential ways and so should last indefinitely. I am powered only with primitive zeolite and am now beginning slowly to run down."

Was it the brandy or—fear? T. could not tell what the sudden rush of blood to his head meant. "If I can last indefinitely, then will I last forever?"

Smithson chuckled. "Are you immortal? Well, sir, nothing is immortal. Everything wears out. Including this planet. Including, let us pray for his sake, our poor Mr. Lincoln."

"But I shall have a long time to work."

"Yes. And that is why you are here now. Since the Institution began, I have cast my net as widely as I could, considering the restraints of having to remain close to my Parcheesi home base and a limited supply of zeolite. But thanks to my friend Mr. Sofield, you were produced. Exactly what I wanted. Exactly what the human race needed. I'll show you one day Dr. Einstein's private report on you, as the first empirical proof of Darwin's somewhat—to my skeptical mind—optimistic notion of evolution as applied to our species."

"Then would a son of mine, if I can still have children . . ."

"You already have a son." Smithson, as if in celebration, refilled T.'s glass.

"How?"

"You remember the tests you underwent before you encountered your destiny at Iwo Jima?"

T. nodded; he was beginning to feel the brandy, warming his system.

"We took, if you recall, quite a quantity of your sperm in the event that . . ."

"I was killed during my rendezvous with your destiny?"

"Well, yes. Happily, you survived as did that excellent youth, your other self—who is you, less the genius. But we did persuade him and the handsome Laura, his wife, to accept your sperm with our guarantee that the resultant issue would be a lifelong fully paid up member of the Smithsonian Institution. The child looks just like you—and his father, of course. In time, we shall put to rigorous tests Dr. Mendel's laws, vague as they are when it comes to seriously applied eugenics. Can you yourself have children? Yes, and I would encourage you to disseminate yourself as widely as possible. In a sense, *you* are the marker on this crossroad of time. One of your descendants, with a fully developed third lobe to the brain, is apt to be the next."

Smithson looked up at a portrait of a scowling Englishman, holding a coronet.

"That is my father—true father—I am illegitimate—Hugh, the duke of Northumberland. While my mother, there"—he pointed to the portrait of a sad woman wearing many jewels—"was a Hungerford and descended from many of our kings. So what did I inherit in character from either parent? Well, my fortune came from my mother and, thanks to that, I could be a scientist and create this institution. All to the good, of course, but hardly an advance worthy of Darwin's attention. From my father I inherited a passion for gambling. In my time—*life*time, that is—I lost a fortune at Arago. But I also had curious wins, so much so that I designed the foundation of the Smithsonian to resemble a game of chance, Parcheesi. Which it is. Which life is. Which makes you my biggest win."

They looked at each other with interest. Father and son? No, T. decided, amused at the thought. More Baron Frankenstein and his monster—played now by T. instead of by Boris Karloff in the movie.

"So," said T., "what is next? I stopped one war and made another war a bit less dangerous but, sooner or later . . ."

"The human race will kill itself. That goes without saying. The virus—us—will kill our host the earth, or at least make it uninhabitable for us."

"Then is any of this worth bothering with?" T. astonished himself. Was it so easy to become God? Or a god?

"We are limited," Smithson reminded him, a bit sharply. "We cannot constantly go back and change events to suit ourselves, as you did on your notorious trip to Lyme, Connecticut, which I only allowed in order to see if you could do it, knowing that if you were to succeed, you are indeed the next step forward . . ."

"To the end?" T. saw the void ahead.

"No endings, as far as I can tell, thanks to your original work. Only metamorphosis. All life changes into something else." Smithson switched on a monitor that was an exact copy, T. noted, of his own. The void was now filled with strings of light.

"In all this, you are, of course, my master." Smithson was not in the least ironic. "Thanks to your approach to what—for want of a better phrase—we shall call the fifth dimension, or the simultaneities of different time-space, I now understand what is known to us gamblers here as the Lincoln conundrum."

T. grinned. "You figured it out, finally?"

Smithson frowned. "Please, young sir, be a bit less patronizing. Without my zeolite . . . But I sound almost human, don't I? Envious, that is."

"We still don't know how Mr. Baird made such a mess at Ford's Theater . . ."

"No," said Smithson. "And we probably never shall." He adjusted the monitor. One string of light was now more vivid than the others. "Here we are. With a vast contradiction. In the tomb at—is it Springfield, Illinois? How I long to visit those exotic states that I shall never see, much less ever saw!"

T. now became teacher. "In a tomb at Springfield, we are told that the body of Lincoln lies. But here we have another Lincoln, the one whose skull the bullet struck but did not penetrate. Question. Are there multiple versions of ourselves instants apart? And did Baird get one and Springfield the last?" T. touched a light string back of "theirs." "Or did another Lincoln visit another Ford's Theater . . ."

Smithson was excited. "That's it. Since we cannot penetrate and retrieve from our own past, as opposed to reviewing its old light, we go not *back* but *across* to a world exactly like ours, with infinitesimal differences, until someone truly clumsy like Baird crossed into that world's past and extracted Lincoln as the bullet struck him, which means . . ."

"There is a fifth-dimensional version of our world in which Lincoln was kidnapped from a box at Ford's Theater and never seen again. In that world there is an empty tomb at Springfield. There are also identical worlds—time-spaces— entirely without us, the human race."

Smithson switched off the monitor. He was suddenly grave. "I wonder if you are the next step toward chaos?"

"I don't know what I am. But I *am* in this time, this space. If chaos is to be, why not? As you say, all is metamorphosis. Change. If I am its temporary agent, so be it."

"So be it." Smithson rose. "You are master here."

"Of course." T. smiled. "Until I change."

It was Grover Cleveland who proposed marriage—between T. and Frances Folsom Cleveland the First. "I believe in regularizing these things even though we no longer, thanks to the Smithsonian, have to worry about public opinion. I've also spoken to the Chief Mechanic, who says there is no reason you two young people cannot live right here, since Frank and I are perfectly happy in the other house up the line."

T. and Squaw were seated in Grover's library as he made his announcement, standing in front of the fireplace, pewter mug full of beer. "Grover!" Squaw embraced what would, presently, be her ex-husband.

Frank gave T. a sisterly kiss. "Welcome to the family."

"We'll hold the wedding in Santa Fe. After all, I'm still president there. We'll say Frances is Frank's younger sister."

So T. and Squaw were married at the La Fonda Hotel by the governor of the territory, and Grover, in his element, made a splendid speech promising the territory statehood immediately, muttering to T. as he sat down to thunderous applause, "In twenty years, if they're lucky."

Then T. asked Squaw, "When you told us, the boys and me, you had a wedding to go to when we were up in Otowi, was it this one?"

Squaw nodded. "I should have brought you, you could have been flower boy at our wedding."

———•—•———

T. looked out his office window at the Mall. Spring day. People everywhere. It was some sort of holiday—he had lost all track of time. Days, months, years, were passing him by at a great rate. But he did not age. He worked at his equations. He did notice that both Bentsen and Lindy were now gray haired. On the other hand, Squaw was as young as he. "So we're not *exactly* authentic," she had said to him one evening at Otowi, where they had acquired a pueblo-style house in the year 1886. "But whatever we are, it's probably better than nothing."

T. had agreed.

Now from T.'s window, he saw a man and a blond boy enter the main door just below his window. It was the other T. and his son? T.'s son?

T. found them—where else?—in the Military Exhibit. As the boy looked to be thirteen or so, the other T. was now thirteen years or so older than T. who was forever—whatever age he was. He couldn't recall. Had he been nineteen or twenty at Iwo Jima?

The other T. stopped in front of the marine exhibit from the Japanese war. T.'s old uniform was now worn by a proper dummy who, thanks to the Department of Morphology, was not T. He could never have endured the boredom of being, even part-time, an exhibit. Squaw had been mildly indignant when he told her this; as if he were obscurely criticizing her. "It's *very* restful. You should try it for a day."

T. introduced himself. The other T. introduced him to their son. "You don't change, do you? But I guess that's part of the contract." Several tourists came over to the other T. and asked for his autograph. He was now a lean handsome man in his midthirties with a ruddy weatherworn face.

"You're still playing baseball?" The other T. nodded. "But I'm starting to lose it. My arm. Age."

"What'll you do now?"

"Television. Sports commentator."

T. must have looked blank, for the other T. said, "You do have TV here, don't you?"

"Oh yes." The guards and the workers in the lab often watched, but since T. could not take part in any world outside the Smithsonian, he preferred not to know what he was missing.

T. showed them the first ladies exhibit, pausing in front of Squaw so that she could get a good look at his son.

"I never really thanked you." The other T. was awkward. "For giving up your life for me."

"I gave it up for me, too." T. tried to smile.

"You can't leave here, can you?"

T. nodded. "Part of the contract." Then T. took them to his office. The boy was wide-eyed at the various wonders encountered on the way. He was overwhelmed when he saw Lincoln seated at a corner window, gazing fondly upon the memorial to himself set in green-reflecting water, and crossed by the white obelisk to Washington.

"A lovely view," Lincoln said, rising.

T. introduced him to his "brother and nephew." Lincoln was polite but distracted. "I've left on your desk my latest plan for the reconstruction of the Southern states. Also, why it is *urgent* that I return *now* to finish my work. If you need me, I shall be in Ceramics Repair."

Then he was gone. The boy stared after him, mouth ajar. "Was that really . . . ?"

"No," said the other T. "It's a sort of dummy, isn't it?" He looked at T.

"That's right. Very lifelike, too." He turned to the boy. "Are you interested in math?"

"No. It's pretty dull. At least the way Mr. Sofield teaches it. He also says that that's what you said, too, when you were my age."

The other T. withdrew from his pocket a blue examination paper. "Stanley wanted you to see what the boy scribbled on this exam paper."

T. felt as if he might faint. Was the past overtaking him or was he overtaking the future?

But then, to his astonishment—and relief—he saw that the boy had written the same equation that he had written years earlier, as storm clouds gathered over Europe, to be dispelled by him.

T. quizzed his son. They were like and unlike. The equation had been a mistake. T. turned to the other T. "Let me know how he grows up."

"He's not you all over again, is he?"

"Lucky for him, no. We don't really understand just how—qualities are inherited." T. shivered. "Remember how cold it was that night?" T. was face-to-face with himself again. The first flares went off.

"I can't desert." The other T. was there, too.

For a moment, T. thought he would lose consciousness. "So long . . . buddy," he heard himself say from what seemed a long-lost world.

Then the world at hand steadied itself. "Officially," said T., "six thousand eight hundred and twenty-one of our men were killed during the invasion. But one got away. So the deaths are six thousand eight hundred and twenty, to be exact. You got away."

"And what about you?"

"I don't know," said T. "I'll never know. But I think, maybe, I'm still there and so the figure is still six thousand eight hundred and twenty-one. But then, as they say around here, this is how the human race evolves. Death and war, love and sex, space and time."

The other T. embraced him. "Thanks," he said. Then he and the boy were safely gone.

Problem, thought T. automatically. What was—if anything—the human race for? Surely, a third lobe could see what had always been impossible for . . . For an instant he was dizzy. Something *was* happening to him. He saw space, textured. He was breaking free of his old biology. He was . . .

There was a knock at the door. Then Lindy entered, accompanied by a peculiar-looking man with big ears, a thin mustache, a large Adam's apple. T. was his old self again.

"We've got a visitor from Hollywood," said Lindy, and introduced the man to T. who greeted him absently, his mind still on the very edge of itself.

"What can we do for you, sir?"

"Well, first, let me tell you how thrilled I am to be here, to meet General Lindbergh, and see all your shows. You're really . . ."

"State-of-the-art," T. said automatically. "We feel we owe the public a good show for their money."

"Just like I do. That's why I've asked General Lindbergh if we could copy the *Spirit of St. Louis* for this sort of amusement park we're making and he says if it's all right with the Smithsonian, it's all right with him . . ."

"I'll have to ask our lawyers." T. abandoned the fifth dimension for the first three that encased him.

Lindy was in high good humor. "Our Hollywood friend here has been hard at work on dummies that can talk. You know, historical types."

"Well," said T., "we've had some experience along those lines."

"I sure wish you'd help us out because no matter what we come up with, it either looks wrong or it sounds wrong or it is just plain wrong."

"What," asked T., unable to believe his incredible luck, "have you been working on?"

"An Abraham Lincoln."

T. and Lindy exchanged a look. "And what," asked T., "do you want this Lincoln to do?"

"Just move about a little. You know? A bit of facial expression. Open and shut eyes. That kind of thing. Move arms, legs, while he gives the Gettysburg Address."

"Is that all?"

"Is that all? It's too much for us."

"I think we can help you out," said T. "Go talk to the legal office. They'll draw up a bill of sale. And don't worry about the price. It will be reasonable. After all, we're here for the American public."

"Now it's got to be really authentic looking and sounding." The rodentian face of a Hollywood tycoon had replaced that of grinning oaf.

"Authentic—or your money back." T. was at his desk. He rang for the legal department; told them what he wanted. Then: "What's your name again, sir?"

"Disney. Walt Disney."

Lindy winked at T. "I'll escort Mr. Disney over to Legal. Then all we do is change the wiring in our Lincoln dummy and Mr. Disney's got quite an exhibit for . . . for what?"

"How do you like the name Disneyland?" Then Lindy and Walt Disney left T.'s office.

A random solution to a minor but annoying problem.

T. looked at his monitor, where the spidery purple handwriting was again to be seen: "Congratulations, oh Captain,

if I may quote Mr. Lincoln's second favorite poet after Sandburg. You are starting to move into the next of many as yet
undreamed of dimensions, secrets at last revealed."

T. punched out a question: "Are you the Secret of the
Smithsonian?"

The response on the screen was prompt. "No. You are.
Now."

"Before me?" T. typed.

The screen showed, in bright colors, a Parcheesi board.

"Just a game?" T. spoke to the monitor.

Smithson's voice answered him. "Just a game? Why 'just'?
You have gone from Good Friday to death to Easter and res-
urrection—one of the prevailing stories on this string of
light—and now our game shows that, at last, you are home or
HOME."

CPSIA information can be obtained at www.ICGtesting.com
Printed in the USA
LVOW13s1545050913

351163LV00002B/334/A